WILLOW DOWNS

Trilogy of Triumph

To Karen

Embrace Change

Linda

LINDA RAKOS

Willow Downs
Copyright © 2025 by Linda Rakos

tellwell 🖋

Tellwell Talent
www.tellwell.ca

ISBN
978-0-2288-6179-9 (Hardcover)
978-0-2288-6178-2 (Paperback)
978-0-2288-6180-5 (eBook)

PROLOGUE

Lola Grande and Valley View shared much more than a boundary fence. The lives of the Grayson family and the Calhoun family had intertwined many times over the years, so they had strong personal ties. It was those strong ties that helped them through the traumatic death of Trace Grayson that devastated both families. Life changed for everyone. The Grayson family had met the challenges the last year presented, and the black sorrow was behind them. Time had allowed them to heal. They had accepted life as it was. Trace was gone.

Life goes on and it only goes in one direction. The Graysons were ready to step into the future and embrace each day. They were now the future of Lola Grande for the generations to come. This was their home, their land, their legacy. They were Lola Grande.

Life changes just like seasons change from one to another. Seasons teach one to acknowledge change. Life teaches one to accept change. Life can be complicated with twists and turns that can change one's life in an instant. Fate is a powerful force. So is faith. God had given them the strength and courage they needed to move forward with renewed hope.

CHAPTER ONE

Tough times don't break us. That seemed to be the Grayson motto. The Grayson family had endured a challenging year and survived a major tragedy, the fire at Lola Grande that had taken Trace Grayson's life. The first few months were difficult for all of them, but they had no choice but to adapt. They struggled through the sudden changes one day at a time while learning to adjust to the changes within themselves and each other. Time allowed them to heal so they could embrace the changes, adjust, and move forward. There were still stressful times, but life had settled into a routine as it returned to normal. Everyone moved forward and accepted the changes in their lives.

It had been a difficult year, especially in the beginning. The Graysons were a proud family. Even though they wished they didn't need it, they had to accept outside help. When Rio Ortiz first arrived at Lola Grande, he was hired as a temporary employee to help out after the fire while living on site in his camper van. Lola Grayson, the family matriarch, was a strong, independent woman and everyone knew she was the boss. She could also be very intimidating. Though Lola Grayson's manner was polite but cool, it was much warmer than that of her daughter-in-law. Kit Grayson didn't want Rio Ortiz there. She wanted her old life back. She wanted her husband. She wanted her kids to still have their dad. Rio figured Kit was trouble the day he met her. He also knew she didn't like him, but she irritated and attracted him at the same time. She was feisty, spirited, and argumentative. For months it seemed like every encounter resulted in conflict. He had learned early that Kit and her mother-in-law, Lola, were stronger than they looked. Both women were stubbornly independent, outspoken, and honest. Rio soon learned the two women were demanding, and every once in a while one of them would catch him off guard. He knew better than to mess with either one of them.

Rio had no idea what he was getting into and there were days when he wondered why he stayed. The fact that they needed him was reason enough. His being there helped them get through what could have been an even harder time. The Graysons were dealing with an agonizing loss, and Rio was determined to do anything he could to help.

Rio's temporary employment became permanent, and he moved into the living quarters that had been added onto the horse facility during the rebuild. Rio had made an impact on all of their lives and continued to do so. In the beginning, Kit struggled with his presence and all the attention he was giving the kids, but she accepted it knowing the kids missed their dad. He was unlike anyone they had met. The kids were fascinated by him. The long-haired, tattooed man didn't depict the cowboys they were used to. Despite everything, Rio had earned Lola's respect and Kit's trust.

*****

Spring brings renewed life, Mother Nature brings beauty, and a new day brings hope. Kit understood why mornings had always been Trace's favorite time of day. He would often have a coffee outside waiting for the rest of the family to rise. The house was quiet as Kit grabbed a coffee on her way through the kitchen. The early glow in the eastern sky welcomed her as she sat in one of the wicker chairs and leaned back to admire the view. The delicious smell of her coffee could only be outdone by the fresh mountain air blowing in off the mountains. She never tired of the view as she slowly scanned the landscape. This morning it was positively stunning as the pale dawn light crept over the horizon. It had rained during the night. The leaves had been freshly washed, the dew sparkled on the lawn. Spring had brought everything back to life.

Everywhere Kit looked, Trace's presence was there. It always would be. Kit found it hard to believe it had been a year since he was gone but there were days if felt like a lifetime. Kit had accepted what happened and was getting on with her life, grateful it was back in balance. For a long time, one side weighed heavy with loss. In one day, Kit Grayson's life had been destroyed. When it happened, she had been consumed by bitterness, drowning in sorrow, and angry at life. She had worked her way out of her heavy depression, and acceptance allowed her to move forward. It also made life easier. Kit was learning to keep Trace in her life while at the same time letting him go. She had emerged from the darkness that had engulfed her. Now that her eyes were no longer clouded by despair, she could again appreciate the beauty of a new day.

Trace had been her life. She missed what they should have had. This wasn't how their story was supposed to end. They were going to live happily ever after as they spent their lives together. Instead, fate had stepped in and taken him from her. A future with Trace was never to be. Kit knew she would always treasure her years with Trace. Recalled memories no longer brought bitterness, just a sense of loss of something precious. A wave of sadness washed over her, and tears gathered. Kit missed the emotions Trace always evoked, the depth of their feelings for each other, the sole deep satisfaction of their love.

The Grayson family had met the challenges the last year presented and survived. The black sorrow was behind them and the world around them was again familiar to the sight. This was the start of a new journey down a familiar road. Kit was grateful to be back in the regular routine she silently described as her new normal. Trace was gone but his dreams for Lola Grande were still alive. It was a solemn day when Finn faced his mom and his grandmother with his plan of action. His words left no room for discussion, "Caballo Stables was Dad's mark on something that was to stand for generations. Dad had a reputation for being an excellent horse trainer. Lola Grande is also known for fine stock. We will continue on with the breeding. I'm a Grayson and I'm not afraid of hard work. I'm not too young to take over the business and you know I'm responsible." Finn had no intention of disappointing anyone. From the day his dad died, Finn continued to keep his dad's business operational. Caballo Stables hadn't lost any business due to the fire.

Caballo Stables started as Trace's dream, but that dream was passed down to his son. Finn had the same desire as his dad and was keeping his dad's dream alive. Trace wanted the Grayson name to mean something, but he started Caballo Stables because of his love for horses. He never let his meager upbringing hold him back. Instead, he focused on his future.

Trace had paid his dues and earned a reputation for training excellent cutting horses. He had passed his skills on to his son. Finn stepped into adulthood and filled his dad's shoes. This was his reality. Caballo Stables was his future, just like it was his dad's. Like his dad, he loved this life, and this was what he wanted to do. Finn was also an excellent trainer. Finn had already earned a sound reputation, so Caballo Stables maintained their credibility in the industry. Finn was training the horses while Rio took care of running Lola Grande and helping Finn when needed. They had adapted to life without Trace and with Rio living at Lola Grande. Having Rio on site made a difference. The changes were working out better than Kit expected.

Sadly, Finn carried a high level of responsibility at too young an age. He was still in high school when his dad died. His life had changed more than the younger ones. Not only had he taken over the role left by his father as a full-time horse trainer, horse breeder and businessman, he also felt he was now the head of the family.

The Grayson name meant something beyond their own area due to Trace Grayson's commitment and hard work. They had lost Diego, their renowned stud horse, in the fire, but the breeding program was continuing with Rebel. Phoenix, the last foal sired by Diego, had the same undeniable fine lineage in his veins. He would be raised as a stud horse, but they would wait another year. Caballo Stables would retain their reputation for having fine stud horses. Meanwhile, their own stock was growing. Coco had delivered a beautiful filly named Buttercup. Rebel would breed Coco again as soon as she was ready.

On top of everything, Kit had three children that needed her, now more than ever. It was time to stop dwelling on dreams that were gone and focus on her family. Finn would be graduating, Kenzie was already a teenager who had gradually adjusted to the death of her dad. Eight-year-old Benny was struggling. This weighed heavily on Kit who was dealing with her own struggles. It was hard being a single parent and Kit missed being able to turn to another parent for support. Kit would often ask Lola for advice, and it usually brought a sense of comfort. Hearing her family stir, Kit headed indoors. Kit still had responsibilities and obligations. She would be glad when school was over. It would make life a little easier, especially for Finn.

Lola Grayson remained the matriarch of Lola Grande and continued to live in the suite above the garage. Lola had also become a widow at a young age when her boys were still teenagers. She had left her native Mexico when she married Tom Grayson against her parent's wishes, thereby severing all ties with her family. Her new life became a transient lifestyle due to her husband being unable to keep a job for long. That changed when they arrived at Valley View and the sudden death of her husband shortly after. A chain of compelling events resulted in Lola and her sons putting down permanent roots as the owners of Lola Grande and establishing the future of the Grayson family. Lola continued to devote her life to Kit and her children, who she loved unconditionally despite the challenges they often presented. There were times tempers flared, and angry words were spoken, especially between Kit and Lola. They both had fiery tempers but given time they worked things out. That's what family did.

Most evenings cooled quickly, and tonight was no exception. Kit went outside to bring in more firewood. It would be a treat to sit by the fire and read the latest book by her favorite author. She was anxious to escape her life for a while. With the fire lit, Kit crossed the room and sat in the rocking chair. Tonight, her book couldn't hold her attention. Rocking gently back and forth, tucked away memories emerged as she drifted in thought, silently reliving parts of her past. Her grandmother had bought the chair when Kit's mother had discovered she was pregnant, but it was her grandmother who had spent hours rocking her precious granddaughter because her own mother continued to abandon her. This was the chair that had brought comfort to Kit during her own pregnancy, knowing there would be no father to welcome her baby because her husband Mike had died. She had spent hours rocking Benny, the little boy who had been the one that tied the Graysons and the Calhouns together. So much had changed. Kit accepted there would aways be changes and nobody knew what the future would bring.

Her life had been overshadowed by Trace's death and for too long her world was cloaked in darkness. The old Kit had slowly emerged as she worked her way out of her heavy depression. She once again began to appreciate the gift of today and all she had to be grateful for. Kit had picked up the shattered pieces of her heart and time had helped her put it back together. She would not keep it closed. Kit knew both Doc Parker and Rio Ortiz had feelings for her. Could she put her life with Trace behind her and move on? Was she willing to open herself up to love again? The thought was as scary as it was exciting. She would have to wait and see what the future held.

Kit's mind immediately turned to Rio. She really had been judgmental about him when he first arrived. Once she got to know him better, her outlook changed. She knew she had judged him unfairly. She had pegged him as a poor immigrant looking to take advantage of the system that allowed him to work in Canada or of his family who had migrated here. Or both. In time she discovered he was well-educated and well-traveled. There was a self-assurance about Rio. Like Trace, the look in his eyes was always direct and despite an aura of power he had a sensitive and caring side he tried to keep hidden.

Kit remembered the day Rio had arrived unexpectedly at Lola Grande. Deep in thought, she had rounded the corner of the barn and bumped into a solid wall of muscle, knocking the wind out of her. She was unable to hide the fact that his unexpected appearance had unnerved her. She was not happy to see a stranger on their land. Kit was aware of everything about him as she openly inspected him. He was tall and formidable, an imposing figure and there was a quality of roughness in his lean, hard features. The stranger was dark-skinned with eyes as black as coal. His face was weathered from sun and wind, light crease lines at the corners of his eyes. The dark stubble covering his strong jaw only emphasized the chiseled planes of his face. A small scar over his eyebrow added interest to his rakish features. The imperfection enhanced his masculine appeal. He was so blatantly macho, yet he was attractive in a savage way. When he turned away from her, she was shocked to see his hair was braided and hung down to his waist. Kit was more aware of him than she would have liked. Dormant feelings stirred as Kit continued to assess him. Her eyes slid appreciatively across the taut power of his chest and down his strong arms, taking in the corded muscles in his broad shoulders, and the aura of power was more than well-developed muscles. Rio was a remarkably disturbing man, and he continually annoyed her. Not in the same way as Trace, who could annoy and charm her at the same time. Rio never made an effort to charm her, but he kept igniting the desire she missed from Trace. There was a draw to him. The kids, Lola, even the dog liked Rio.

Because Kit and Rio had gotten off on the wrong foot, there was often underlying tension between the two of them. She knew she could have handled things better when Rio first arrived at Lola Grande. It had taken Kit time to see Rio for who he was instead of looking through her grief that had clouded her vision for a long time. She had been stuck in a negative space caused by the traumatic turn of events due to Trace's death. Life-changing events and she didn't know how to cope. She was depressed and feeling sorry for herself, and angry at everything and everyone. She was too angry to think clearly and kept lashing out at everyone, especially Rio. He was the perfect scapegoat. It wasn't fair, but she didn't care. She couldn't let her anger go because Trace's death was unjustified. It didn't have to happen.

Rio was so different than what she first thought. She finally dropped her guard to give him a chance since he was part of their lives. Things were now comfortable between them. His presence at Lola Grande had helped everyone get through what could have been an even harder time. He was a hard worker and he and Finn had formed a strong bond as well as a good working relationship. It took time for Kit to see Rio for who he really was instead of through her grief. She had to admit her preconceived ideas of Rio were unfair and unjustified. She really had judged him unfairly. Now that she knew him better her outlook had changed. In time, Kit discovered the nurturing side of him as he spent more time with her children. Kit had to admit Rio had proven himself day after day. He could do anything and did everything. He had put in long hours to get the inside of the rebuilt barn set up so Finn could donate his time to training. She had learned to respect his opinion even when it differed from hers. Given time she found him to be confident and sure of himself and had nothing to prove to others.

Things had become more comfortable between them, but he was still a very disturbing man. Despite the fact that Rio could confuse her, desire kept surfacing, especially when he looked at her a certain way. Guarding herself against it or not, Rio got to her. He bothered her like Trace used to. There were as many similarities to Trace as there were differences. Was that the draw or was it the man himself? Trace could always make her heart beat faster. For some reason, being around Rio brought back the old familiar ache of missing Trace.

Kit's train of thought shifted, and she smiled when her thoughts turned to Doc. Her dear friend was thoughtful, charming, and funny. He was a kind and decent man, and they shared the same strong values. They had so many things in common and they were comfortable with each other. Doc had a relaxed and easy manner. He had a caring nature and was always considerate. She knew he was someone she could always rely on. She liked his quietness and gentleness. Kit knew Doc would like to fill the role vacated by Trace. She hoped she wasn't the reason he never married. During her grieving stage, Doc had revealed his deep feelings for her and his gentle kiss on the cheek advanced to more. The only catch in her heart was due to the fact that she didn't have the same feelings for him. It was different when Rio kissed her. It was his kisses that ignited buried feelings. Kit wondered if that would change if she looked at Doc as more than the tender vet who had always been a family friend. She had never had romantic feelings for Doc, but could that change if she gave him a chance? Doc had always been overshadowed by Trace as he stood in the background of their lives. With Trace gone, could she see Doc in a different light? To do that she needed to discover who the real Dr. Jim Parker was. Would she discover a different person behind the guise of indifference he had always worn due to a loyal friendship?

Thinking about other men no longer felt like a betrayal. It was just confusing. Even though both men were confident, they were two totally different men. Doc was loyal and settled. He had an established practice and a secure future. Rio had no deep roots. He could disappear as suddenly as he had arrived. Here one minute and gone the next. For some reason that thought made her heart catch. The time spent thinking of Doc and Rio reminded her of the aching void in her life. She felt a combination of emotions as she vowed not to remain caught in the past. Life was filling the emptiness in her heart with happiness. Would there be another man in her future? For now, her questions remained unanswered. She would have to wait and see.

Recalled memories no longer brought bitterness, just a sense of loss of something precious. It wasn't fair that some had to die so young. Kit was able to look forward with a clear vision, not one that was clouded by her loss. Trace now joined a host of others who had passed. Even though she missed them, she chose to remember the happiness she had with them, rather than the emptiness left behind. It was time to stop dwelling on dreams that were gone and turn to those around her. If her past had taught Kit anything, it was that she was strong enough to endure the changes life presented. Change will happen and a person had to learn to embrace it and move forward. She knew she was blessed so she would meet each new day with grace and thanks. New memories would be made. She would live in the present and look forward to the future. It would continue to be full of surprises, good and bad. If that took on the form of a new love, Kit would welcome it. She had moved on when Mike died, and she found love with Trace. She would always love Mike and Trace. Both men had been a significant part of her life. She was grateful for all they had added to her life, but she would move on.

Time passed unnoticed. Sitting alone brought the stark reality of her solitary existence. Life could change quickly, and it wasn't always what you expected. Kit ached for something but wasn't sure if she was ready to commit. It would mean another big change in her life. She knew she cared for both men, so she had to give them a chance. She was still learning new things about both of them. She wasn't the only one who had changed in the last year. Kit knew Rio Ortiz and Doc Parker would both have an impact on her life moving forward. She felt pulled in two directions between two decent men. She didn't want to hurt either of them so continued to try to keep her feelings neutral. Nor did she want to give either of them false encouragement, but she needed to spend time with both men to see what her true feelings were. She would know who was right because she would want to build a life with him and have him be the father to her children. Change didn't have to be bad. Kit's eyes became blinded by tears as she slowly removed her wedding ring, the final act of acceptance.

CHAPTER TWO

K it allowed herself to remain in bed for a few more minutes even though she heard her kids begin to stir. Their lives had been rather chaotic for the last year, but they had survived. A few minutes later she tossed back the covers and got up. On her way to the shower, she stopped to gaze out her bedroom window. The mild winter had come and gone but spring could still bring unexpected storms. Kit loved spring but those weren't friendly clouds forming over the mountains. The forecast was for showers by late afternoon with heavier rain in the evening. At this time of the year the rain was welcomed by everyone.

Kit was on her way downstairs when Kenzie called her into her room. Kenzie was all sweetness and charm when she wanted something. "You look nice this morning, Mom. I like it when you wear your hair down. Mine takes so much work if I want it to look like yours. I don't know why people keep saying I'm lucky to have curly hair."

Kit was tall and willowy for a woman. She remained fit due to the physical work she did around the ranch. Usually, she pulled her luscious auburn hair up in a loose knot, but she was running late because she had remained in bed longer than she should have. Her face was free of make-up and she was casually dressed in jeans and sweat shirt. Kit tried to help where she could, because ranching, like parenting, was a job you do every day. Some days, parenting was the harder job. Kit had to smile to herself. She recognized Kenzie's attempt to practice the art of subtlety, but she was far from mastering it.

Kenzie was usually direct like her mother. Kit immediately wondered what was up. When Trace was alive she could always wrap her dad around her little finger but with him gone Kenzie still had to work on her skills to get her mom to do what she wanted. She gave her mom a pleading look, "I'd like to change my room. I've outgrown this childish decor."

Kit looked around and smiled. Kenzie was right. Her little girl had grown up so much over the last year. It was time to pack tangible childhood memories away to make room for positive changes. "Do you have anything in mind?"

Kenzie was surprised by her mom's response and opened her iPad to pull up a few items saved in "Favorites".

Kit was impressed and could see Kenzie had put a lot of time and effort into planning her new bedroom. "Let's talk later; it's time to get ready for school. I'm going down to start breakfast." She knocked on Benny's door as she passed by and got an abrupt, "I'm up."

Lola had joined them for breakfast for a change. She was still a striking woman with natural beauty who had aged well. As always, her hair was pulled back and knotted at the base of her neck. Having lived in rural Alberta for years, she had adapted to casual western clothing. Before they were even seated, Kenzie was telling Lola what they were planning. It remained the topic of conversation throughout breakfast.

Lola couldn't help but smile at the excitement in her granddaughter's voice, "It sounds like you are leaning toward a vintage look that will be a balance of sophistication and youthfulness."

"I guess I am, Lita." The grandchildren had always called her Lita which was short for grandmother in Spanish.

Kit interjected, "I have an idea. Before we do anything, let's go over to Valley View. I have some of my grandmother's furniture stored there. I didn't need it when I moved to Alberta because I lived with my grandparents until I married your dad. I know there's an old desk and chair that might work. Anything we find and you want can be refurnished and painted."

"Can we go tonight?"

"We'll go Sunday morning when we have more time, and I can give your grandpa a heads-up that we might need some man muscle to help load things into the truck. Besides, it's going to rain all day."

"Can I paint my room?" To Kenzie's surprise, her mom readily agreed. "And the ceiling? It will look really cool."

"I don't see why not. We can also look at wallpaper if you would like to do an accent wall. This will be a great project."

Lola turned to Benny who had been quiet throughout the whole meal. Hoping to draw him into conversation she asked, "What about you? Do you want to change your room too?"

"I've had enough changes in my life." These days Kit's little boy was often sullen and withdrawn. If it wasn't that, he would lash out in anger. Benny fled up the stairs without saying another word. Lola expected Benny to want to change his room like his sister, so she was surprised by his reaction. Benny's reaction bothered Kit.

After lunch, Kit went outside to prepare the flower beds for her annuals to be planted. The air was heavy, but she wanted to get it done before it rained. Kit was the one who tended to the flowers. Lola spent her time out in the garden behind the house. Everyone enjoyed the fruits of her labor. Fresh vegetables at meal time were always a treat and canned and frozen vegetables carried them through to the next growing season. The wind had increased, the sun hid behind the clouds, and the temperature had dropped considerably. When Kit was done she grabbed a coffee and went back outside. She had just sat down in her rocker when the bus pulled up to the drive. She watched Benny and Kenzie, thinking how much they had changed in the last year. Kenzie had seemed to bounce back from losing her dad, but she knew Benny continued to struggle. Her loveable Benny was gone, and she didn't know how to get him back. She missed the little boy who liked to cuddle and was carefree and happy. "How was school, Benny?" Kit frowned when her question only earned a glare as he walked past her without a word.

"Geez Mom, you better make a doctor's appointment for Benny. I think he's going deaf."

Kit wasn't amused. "Honestly, Kenzie, you could make more of an effort not to always bug your brother."

"Sorry," she said, even though she didn't feel sorry in the least.

Benny went inside but Kenzie sat down in the chair next to her mom. Together they watched the light show in the west.

"Do you have any idea what's bothering your brother?"

Kenzie shook her head. He was always the annoying younger brother, so she didn't see anything different about him.

The next crack of thunder was much louder. When it started to rain they headed indoors. They could be in for a real storm before the day was over. Kit started supper and to Kit's surprise Kenzie stayed to help, and they talked about the end of school and the upcoming graduation party to celebrate the end of junior high.

Lola usually had her evening meals with the family and more often than not Rio was invited to join them. Kenzie began setting the table, "Don't set a place for Rio." Rio had gone to the city and said he wouldn't be back until late. As soon as supper was done both kids headed up to their rooms, Kenzie to do homework and Benny to mope. After they were finished cleaning up Kit and Lola sat back down and had a second cup of coffee and chatted. Kit told her about Benny's rude behavior. "I'm not quite sure how to deal with Benny these days but I can't allow Trace's death to be an excuse to allow bad behavior." Kit hated confrontations. They were extremely upsetting, but parenting never stopped. There always seemed to be one challenge after another. Some days were more challenging than others.

"Give him time and be grateful that Finn and Kenzie have adjusted as well as they have. Benny will get there, too." Lola treated Kit as an equal in the running of the ranch, but Kit was the head of the household. She tried her best not to interfere, but she readily acted as a sounding board for the frustrated mother.

By the time Lola headed back to her place the rain was relentless but by midnight it was only a faint drizzle, and the wind had died down. Kit went up to bed and checked on the kids before heading to her room. It remained part of her nightly routine since the night Trace died.

It had been quite the storm and a moist, earthy scent still hung in the air. Finn knew he would have to train in the indoor arena for a couple of days. That was one of the benefits Caballo Stables could offer and his clients appreciated that Finn always put their horse's safety first. Finn had taken on a new yearling and it would be boarded at Lola Grande. It brought in additional income, but it also meant additional work.

Kit watched Finn take the newest horse over to the arena. He wanted to get in a training so he could take Sunday off. Kit's dad had invited the whole family for a barbecue. The men could visit while the women explored the Quonset for stored treasures. After the initial training and introducing Patches to his new stall, Finn stopped to talk to Rio, and they stood side by side watching Phoenix prance around in the far paddock. He was a superb horse who was high-spirited, but it was still too soon to let him take on his role as a stud horse. He was anxious, but Finn knew his dad would tell him to wait a little longer.

There was no mistaking the admiration and respect in Rio's voice when he said, "Your dad taught you well. He would be impressed by the fine young man you've become and how you have handled things over the last year. Your mom is also very proud of you." Kit and Trace had molded Finn into a fine young man.

After his dad died Finn had something to prove, this time to himself. Even though he homeschooled his last year of high school and kept Caballo Stables operational he graduated with honors. It had taken commitment and determination, and Finn knew his dad would have been proud of him. He had come a long way from the vulnerable youth who showed up at the ranch and thought he was stupid. Fate had pushed Finn into adulthood with both hands and Finn had become a man overnight. He couldn't have done it without the support of everyone, including Rio. "I didn't do it alone and having you here definitely helped. I'm glad to have you here. I think we all are even though my mom and you definitely got off to a bad start."

"That's putting it mildly."

They were distracted as Doc drove by on his way up to the house. He continued to drop by regularly on his way home from town. The two men exchanged courtesy waves. There was no longer any tension or awkwardness between the two men. They were civil to each other, but they weren't friends.

At first Doc dropped by out of concern, but Rio knew it was more than that. Rio's expression revealed a familiar trace of irritation. He knew what Doc's intention were, but Kit continued to confuse Rio. He actually thought there was something developing between himself and Kit. He knew she was as aware of the chemistry between them as he was. Rio's life had taken on more meaning since living here.

Rio often watched from afar. Today, he watched as Doc strolled up the steps to the front door. Kit greeted him warmly. Rio knew she valued their friendship even more with Trace gone but he knew the vet wanted more. Both Doc and Rio had strong feelings for Kit, stronger than simple attraction.

Finn and Rio remained standing against the rail. "I think Doc has a thing for my mom. I think Doc thinks you also have a thing for her." So did Finn. There was a hint of amusement in Finn's eyes.

The look Rio gave Finn was indifferent, "You know I don't care what people think, especially the good old vet." But he didn't deny it.

Doc was only stopping for a moment to drop off a parcel he had picked up for Kit in town. "It seems like Finn and Rio have formed quite the bond."

"They have but Rio also spends a lot of time with Benny. Kenzie has no time for any of us unless she wants something. Now that she has her learner's license, Rio has been taking her driving when he has time. I took her once and that didn't go well so I'm grateful to Rio. He has way more patience with her than I do."

Doc's heart hurt when Kit added that all the kids were turning more and more to Rio. Doc envied the family life they had and was unable to dismiss the feeling of loneliness that assailed him. Today he wished for a family of his own. He was very aware of his deep feelings for Kit. He had experienced an instant tug of attraction the day he met Kit, which was shortly after she had arrived at Valley View. Both he and Trace were intrigued but she only had eyes for Trace. Doc had quietly stepped aside but his attraction for Kit had never faded. He had only buried it. Because he had always been enamored with Kit he hadn't been willing to settle for just anyone. After Trace died, he kept trying to make his intentions clear with no success. He often wondered if he'd be more successful if Rio wasn't living at the ranch. Rio, the handy man, who could do anything and seemed to have fit nicely into their everyday lives.

The two men had sized each other up quickly when they first met and were polite enough to each other. Doc usually had an easy and relaxed manner but that often disappeared when Rio was around. There was something about the cowboy that irritated Doc. He wished he would leave. Rio's constant presence was an unexpected hurdle. When Rio first arrived,

Doc was glad he was staying at Lola Grande for protection. But he was still here, and the man had a distinct advantage. Doc was annoyed with himself due to the stab of jealousy he was feeling. He could see familiar sparks between Kit and Rio. They were easy to recognize. He had seen them many times between Kit and Trace. There was always a self-assurance about the cowboy that irritated him. Another cocky cowboy was in the picture. Doc had stepped away once. He wasn't about to do it again. Their relationship hadn't gone anywhere because he'd been respectful of her loss. It was time to show Kit the real Jim Parker.

Rio's mind was elsewhere while he walked over to the barn. Rio knew Kit and Doc had history and how close they were. He had watched them from a distance many times. He believed the vet's feelings were stronger than Kit's. Or was that wishful thinking? In the beginning, Rio tried to keep a safe distance from Kit, but it kept getting harder as he got to know her. Spending time around Kit, Rio found himself becoming more enchanted even though she exasperated him more often than not. He knew he was falling in love with her. He also realized he had competition. First it was with a dead man. Now it was with a determined long-time friend who wanted to be more than a friend.

CHAPTER THREE

One gets through the storms in life just like you get through seasonal storms. It had been a mild winter and Kit would take that as a positive sign moving forward. Signs of spring were everywhere, and everything had come to life. It was time to enjoy the rebirth that surrounded them. She frowned when she heard Kenzie and Benny going at each other upstairs. They usually got along but there were days like today when things seemed to take on a new intensity. They had been at each other all day and Kit was tired of it. She climbed the stairs just in time to see Kenzie trying to push Benny out of her room.

"Just because your room is a drab pigsty it doesn't mean you can come in my room anytime you feel like it." Kenzie loved her new room. Rio had spent hours helping her sand down a couple of her great-grandmother's furniture pieces that had been brought back from Valley View and when that was done Kenzie painted them. Kit helped Kenzie paint and wallpaper her room. Kenzie had spent hours online before choosing her new bedding. After that, it was a few trips to thrift stores where they found the perfect area rug that was the final touch that transformed her room. Kenzie had made it her own and together with her mom, they were able to balance the youthfulness and sophistication she was striving for. Kenzie didn't want Benny anywhere near her room.

Benny's nose was out of joint. He regretted not redoing his room now that Kenzie's was so nice. He hated his room, and he hated Kenzie because she wouldn't let him in her room. Today, the fight was on. Benny stood there stubbornly refusing to move.

Kenzie remained where she was, blocking the door to her room.

Benny turned to his mom and let out a moan of misery, "Kenzie keeps bossing me."

"Kenzie likes to boss everyone."

Benny glared at his sister as he continued to rant, "Tell her to quit."

Kit had experienced the teen years with Kenzie and Finn, but she had a feeling these next few years with Benny were going to be more trying, even though he was far from being a teenager. Today's episode was another example of what she had to look forward to. Kit was familiar with her daughter's dramatics but Benny's defiant behavior surprised Kit. Her little boy used to be so easy-going.

"This is Kenzie's room, so you need to respect her and leave." Kenzie grinned with satisfaction.

"Why should I?" Benny challenged childishly, refusing to leave. "Kenzie always gets her own way."

Kit lost her patience, "Both of you stop this right now. Go to your room, Benny."

"I told you it's Ben. I'm not a kid anymore." With a firm set to his chin, he refused to move. Benny was usually reasonable, but he could also be stubborn. A strong trait shared by every member of the Grayson family.

The hardening of the youth's jawline caused Kit to sigh. Benny was old enough to know his behavior was unacceptable and Kit said as much, "I said go to your room and while you're there you can clean it up. Don't come down until it's done."

Benny remained defiant, still too young to know when his mother had reached her limit. "I don't want to clean my room."

"Do it anyway."

With a scowl on his face, Benny stormed off with tear-filled eyes positive his mom loved Kenzie more.

"If you keep treating Benny like a baby he'll continue to act like one. It's time for him to grow up."

Kit's own temper got the better of her, "Your behavior wasn't exactly mature. I don't have time for this."

Kenzie didn't miss the note of disapproval but ignored it anyway. "You would have more time if you weren't always so busy lecturing us."

"I do not appreciate your attitude. Since you like your room so much, Kenzie, you can stay in there as well, and you can turn that music down. I can't believe what you kids listen to these days."

Her mother's face was so stern Kenzie didn't argue. She was old enough to know better.

Not knowing if either one of them would do as she said, Kit went outside. She needed a moment to herself. Tears of frustration blurred her vision as she wandered down to the corrals. It didn't matter that it was empty. She let her gaze wander to the pasture beyond where several of their horses grazed freely. Thick, dark clouds had rolled back in taking away the sun. There was a biting north wind, and the temperature had dropped. The gloomy sky fitted her mood. She was about to head in when she heard footsteps and turned expecting it to be Lola. Kit was sure Lola had heard Kit slam the door on her way out of the house. Instead, it was Rio.

He went and stood next to her and rested his arms on the top rail. "Are the kids getting to you? I heard the screaming match."

"Lately everything ends in an argument between Benny and Kenzie. It was uglier than usual and I'm always the one who has to deal with it. Why do I always have to be the grown up? Why can't I be the kid who gets to throw a tantrum? I should just ground them for life and be done with it."

Her own verbal tantrum made Rio want to laugh, but he knew better. "I would hate to be on your bad side."

"Who says you're not?" Kit had to admit that Rio teased her the same way Trace used to. Today it was annoying as hell, so she was unable to hide her flash of annoyance.

"Your kids are working out their emotions and sometimes they take it out on each other."

"You know this because you are drawing on experience?" Kit said sarcastically.

Rio refused to be offended, "I may not have had on-hand experience, but one can learn a lot by watching."

Kit immediately chided herself, "I'm sorry, Rio, that comment wasn't called for. I'm just frustrated."

They both turned when they saw Benny heading to the barn. Today, Kit and her young son were butting heads due to sheer stubbornness. Kit called him over. "I told you to clean your room."

"It's clean."

"You were in there for five minutes, so I doubt that."

"It's clean enough for me. If you don't like it you can clean it."

The insolent tone in Benny's voice affected Rio more than Kit. He took a step forward. Knowing Rio was about to say something Benny glared at him, "You're not my dad so mind your own business." The boy's tone was now belligerent.

Rio's voice was sharper than he intended, "Regardless of who or what I am you do not speak to your mother that way, or any other adult for that matter. You can apologize to your mother." Rio's voice held an underlying authority that Benny couldn't ignore.

Wiping the tears from his eyes with quick, angry strokes, Benny turned and fled.

Unable to keep the frustration out of her voice, Kit yelled after him, "This isn't over, young man."

Rio thought it best to take his leave as well, knowing he probably stepped over the line as far as Kit was concerned. He no longer felt like an outsider, but he continued to be on guard around Kit.

Instead, Kit placed a hand on his arm, halting his retreat. There was a hint of despair in her voice, "You said you have a degree in Social Services and worked with troubled youths. As you saw for yourself, Benny has become defiant and challenging. This isn't just about today. His behavior has been uncalled for on too many occasions. It's much too soon for teenage behavior but he's old enough to know better. I don't know what's with him these days. I have to find a way to reach him. Any suggestions?" Her young son's behavior worried her.

Kit usually had such pride when talking about her children. Today, Rio detected a note of panic. His reply was candid, "Benny's feeling neglected. You might not believe this, but he's missing his sister. She's spending more time with her girlfriends, and it will be worse next year when she's in high school. She doesn't have time for him, and Finn and I were extra busy through spring. Next year Kenzie will be in high school, and there will be boys who she'll spend more time with, and she'll start dating."

His uncanny insight surprised her but his comment about Kenzie dating panicked her. "Please don't go there. They're growing up too fast."

Rio's expression was concerned, "Father's Day is coming up. That's always a hard time for the kids, especially Benny. This is the second year that he hasn't had a dad." Rio had continued to step in for Trace, but he wasn't the boy's father. Knowing Trace had promised Benny he'd teach him about horses just like he had Finn, Rio had been spending some evenings with Benny doing basic training. Rio could recognize that Benny was also a natural with horses. He'd been taught how to handle them and care for them and when he was ready he would learn how to train them. Horses had to be handled with confidence and command and Benny was proving to be an avid student and fast learner.

Rio knew Benny was anxious to advance to a bigger and stronger horse. He had outgrown Tilly. She had been a great horse when Kenzie was little and for Benny to learn to ride on, but Tilly's time was done. Rio was wise enough to go through the proper channels and get permission from Kit. He was well aware that there were invisible boundaries that had to be respected. He was a little uneasy when he suggested, "We should give Benny something special to look forward to. Would you let him continue his training on Jasper? I'm pleased with the progress he's making so I know he can handle Jasper." He laughed at her look of doubt.

Kit hadn't missed the "we" but didn't say anything. It was important for Benny to have a strong male figure in his life. She responded with a weak smile, "I guess I haven't thought about it. I trust your instincts and you would know better than I would. Benny will be pleased so go ahead. I'll let you tell him." Kit knew Rio had a lot of the same values as Trace and continually gave Benny the encouragement he needed.

That pleased Rio as he left and went back to work.

Kit spent the rest of the day replaying the events that happened. Kit paused, realizing Benny wasn't her little boy anymore. She also kept thinking about her conversation with Rio. She knew her kids were normal siblings. Kit enjoyed the bantering, but the fighting kept getting worse. Benny didn't always understand their teasing so he would get mad or take it personally. Her immediate challenge was to figure out how to deal with Benny. Experience didn't make it easier because every child was different. Kit knew it was time for a family meeting.

After supper they met in the living room. Lola had gone to her place, respectful of what her role was. This was a time for the mother and her children. All three children were anxious. Their mom had been quiet all day, the kind of quiet that meant she was still mad. They were wise enough to sit without interrupting while she covered all the issues that had been happening recently, reiterating that their behavior was unacceptable. "Anger is never a good emotion." Kit had heard that enough in her lifetime and still struggled with it. She informed them how difficult it was being a parent because none of them came with a manual to follow. She remained serious, "I do my best and I may not always get it right, but I am the boss. I expect respect to me and to each other. The most important thing to remember is we are a family who love each other."

They were all solemn when she was done. Benny, now fighting tears, got up and hugged his mom. "I know I've been a jerk lately."

Kit squeezed him tight. He was still her little boy. "No argument from me. Let's try to be a little more tolerant with each other. Yelling never solves anything."

Knowing his mom wasn't mad anymore, Benny grinned mischievously and left, his own anger forgotten. He could be such an imp.

Kit's eyes warmed watching him go. He was the spitting image of his father and kept taking on more of Trace's mannerisms. In those treasured moments it was like having Trace back. Benny had the same charisma as his dad and was learning how to use it effectively. He was Trace inside and out.

Kenzie went over and snuggled up next to her mom. "I'll try to be nicer to Benny. You are a good mom, and we do love you." She also headed up to her room.

Finn wasn't too old to give his mom a hug, "It's starting to rain, Mom. I'll go lock everything down in case the wind picks up."

Kit stood at the kitchen window watching the steady drizzle. It was a much-needed rain. She sighed heavily. She knew the kids were still missing their dad. Kit understood; she was too.

Last night had ended well but this morning bedlam had erupted, and Kit was getting flustered. Lola had left at the crack of dawn. She was driving up to Edmonton for a conference and would be gone all week. The kids were running late and if Benny didn't come down now he'd miss breakfast. Kit called again. When Benny still didn't come down she stomped up the stairs and burst into his room believing his bad behavior from yesterday had returned and he was back to sulking. To her surprise, Benny was still in bed. One look at him and she could see he was sick. She crossed over and placed her hand on his fevered forehead.

Hearing Finn leaving his room she called out. He walked in and could tell his mom was anxious. "You and Kenzie can go ahead and have breakfast without me. Benny is sick, so I'm going to tend to him and try to make him more comfortable."

As soon as Kenzie was finished breakfast she popped into the room. She was scared to see Benny lying motionless in his bed. "Will Benny be okay? He looks really sick."

Kit tried to reassure Kenzie that Benny would be okay despite her own concern. His fever was high. She struggled to keep her own voice from breaking, "He'll probably be better by the time you get home from school. You better hurry, the bus will be here soon."

Finn kept coming in and checking on them throughout the day. "Have you eaten anything?"

"I'll get something later." She didn't want to leave Benny.

A few minutes later Finn appeared in the doorway with a fresh cup of coffee. He spoke softly, "Do you think we should take him to emergency?" He felt helpless.

"I'm sure it's just the flu. Maggie said Rhett was sick last week." Kit was grateful for the coffee but wasn't up to going downstairs to grab a bite to eat. Benny's fever continued to spike despite the fact she kept cooling him down. Kit headed back to the bathroom to wet down a face cloth to place on his forehead. When she returned she wiped him down, then gently covered him. All Benny did was moan. Every time he stirred she tried to get him to take a few sips of water wanting to keep him hydrated. His fever persisted. Throughout the day, Kit continued to provide the necessary comfort, but it was hard to watch him fight his illness.

As soon as Kenzie got home from school she ran up the stairs. Kenzie held Benny's hand as he slept. "Lucy Rose said when Rhett had the flu he was fine in a few days so Benny will be okay soon. Right, Mom?"

Kit was relieved to hear that Kenzie's voice sounded less anxious than she had earlier. When Kenzie offered to stay with Benny so she could have a break, Kit went down to grab another coffee. While she was in the kitchen she took time to have a couple of pieces of toast. It made her feel better. She knew Kenzie and Finn would make their own supper so she could sit with Benny.

After the kids settled for the night, she bathed Benny down hoping to bring his temperature down and make him more comfortable. Kit crawled up beside Benny and listened to his shallow breathing, his chest barely rising. Her touch soothed him, but he didn't open his eyes. Being a single mom was hard enough when everything was going well. Completely exhausted, she fell asleep beside Benny. When she opened her eyes, morning light was filtering through the window. Kit sat up and wiped the sleep from her eyes. Rio was sitting across the room with his long legs stretched out in front of him. She knew he had been there all night. His morning growth was visible, and he was wearing the same clothes as yesterday.

Rio smiled at her, "Benny's fever broke a couple of hours ago. He's been sleeping soundly since then. Why don't you go have a shower. I'll sit with him until you come back. Finn and Kenzie are both up and are downstairs having breakfast."

Relief rushed in and without hesitation Kit nodded. In the shower, she allowed herself to drift in thought. Rio didn't show his feelings much, but she was well aware of his caring nature. He would be a good father. She knew he loved her children, and she questioned her feelings for him. She was a little confused by her thoughts but chalked it up to exhaustion.

When Kit returned, both Finn and Kenzie were also in the room. They were desperate for assurance that their little brother was okay. Benny had fallen into a natural sleep and sleep was the best thing for him now.

"I believe young Benny is through the worst. I'm going to go to my place, wash up and get to work." They all left so they could get on with their day.

Kit knew she no longer had to sit with Benny but continued to check him throughout the morning. By noon, Benny thought he could get up but as soon as he tried the room spun, and he fell back into bed. He was weak and his face was still pale. Within a few minutes he was back asleep, but his breathing was normal. By late afternoon he was doing much better and came downstairs for supper. He was weak from the exertion but managed to eat a little. Kit was relieved that children could bounce back to normal so quickly.

CHAPTER FOUR

The school year had ended and tonight the Graysons were having a family barbeque to celebrate Finn's graduation from high school. He had vowed to graduate despite running Cabello Stables. Kit wasn't surprised he had graduated with honors. She knew he had something to prove to himself as well as his family. Kit knew Trace would be proud of the fine young man Finn turned out to be. Both the Walker and the Ortiz families were invited. Maggie Walker and Kit had been best friends since Kit moved to Alberta. Matt, Maggie's husband, and Trace had been friends since high school. With Trace gone and Rio living at Lola Grande, the two men formed their own friendship. The Walker children, Lucy Rose and Rhett. were the same age as Kenzie and Benny and had naturally developed their own friendships. Matt Walker had hired Rio's brother Hector when they immigrated to Canada. Anna, Hector's wife, and Lola were good friends. Lola had helped Anna learn to speak and write English. Cruz, their son, was Finn's best friend. There were strong ties between all of them. It would be an enjoyable day.

Benny and Rio continued to bond over the horses like Finn had with Trace. Rio was having a morning training session with Benny because of the afternoon barbeque. They chatted as they headed over to saddle up. "I'm a lot bigger than I was last year."

"You sure are, Ben." The young boy beamed. No one had ever called him Ben.

Benny was still a little in awe of Rio, "Why do you keep your hair long?"

"When I was younger and travelling around the country it would be months before I could get to a barber. So, it was easier to just let it grow. I braid it so it doesn't blow around or get in the way."

"Will you ever cut it?"

"I don't know. I suppose if an occasion calls for it."

"Thanks for setting up a training this morning instead of skipping it. It's times like this when I really miss my dad."

"I'm sure he'd be proud of you like I am." They watched as Finn walked by with Rebel and waved. Rio didn't miss the look on Benny's face. The boy's ultimate dream was to ride Rebel, who was Finn's horse, but only Finn was allowed to ride him. Rio patted Benny on his shoulder. "Maybe one day but today you will ride Jasper."

Understanding exactly what Rio meant, excitement lit Benny's eyes. He couldn't wipe the grin off his face even though he was nervous and eager at the same time because Jasper was a lot bigger than Tilly.

Once in the saddle, Benny focused on Jasper and settled down and Rio led them out to the training paddock. "We'll see how you handle Jasper by winter and maybe advance your training when we move to the indoor arena." Finn and Rio had talked and depending on how Benny did with Jasper he could begin training a yearling. Time would tell if Benny had the same skills as Finn.

Both Kit and Finn knew about today's training on Jasper. Finn joined his mom at the rail, and they watched from the sidelines. A note of pride became evident in Finn's voice, "Benny's a true Grayson. He has the same natural ability as the rest of us, and he has your stubbornness and Dad's tenacity. I appreciate Rio's dedication to Benny knowing I don't have the time. Benny still needs a lot of guidance, and I feel bad that I'm always so busy. We're lucky Rio lives here at the ranch. Rio's good with Benny, and he has a gentle nature with the horses. He has magic hands."

Kit smiled to herself. *Not just with the horses.* Every time he touched her, her body would respond.

They watched and chatted until the training was over. Rio's slow, steady movements reminded Kit so much of Trace as he walked over and joined them at the rail while Benny lead Jasper back to the barn to cool him down. Kit smiled at him, "You have a lot of patience with Benny.

Trace was never known for his patience, but he did have it when it came to training." Kit also appreciated the time and attention Rio gave Benny.

Rio and Kit's relationship had developed over time where they could mention Trace freely. Rio felt he was no longer competing with Trace Grayson or trying to fill his shoes. Rio valued the relationship he had formed with all of Kit's kids. Rio was confident in who he was and was becoming more comfortable on a personal level with all the Graysons. He was looking forward to the barbecue.

Kit didn't have time to chat, "I'm going inside so I can get things done before everyone gets here." It was the perfect day for barbequing and spending time with friends.

"I better head back to my place. I'm making homemade backed beans. I soaked the beans last night but it's time to work the rest of my magic."

"You know how to do that?" Kit asked in surprise.

Rio laughed at her expression, "I've become capable of doing many things over the years, sometimes out of necessity. If I wanted to eat I had to learn how to cook. The internet is a wonderful source for recipes. I enjoy cooking something different once in a while."

Lola and Benny now joined them. Benny, who heard the last part of the conversation, studied Rio closely, "Can you bake cookies?" Benny loved cookies.

"I don't usually bake but I did make a birthday cake once."

This man never ceased to surprise Kit. She wondered who he cared for enough to bake a cake for. He was a complex man.

Lola came to the rescue, "How about you and I bake cookies for tonight. Go wash up and come up to my place when you're done."

"Thanks, Lita. What kind will we make?"

"You decide before you come up." She knew oatmeal chocolate chip cookies were his favorite. She would get everything ready. Baking cookies was always a special time between the two of them.

"I better go and finish up my chores. I've cleaned out the stalls, but they still need fresh hay." Finn had taken time to watch Benny.

"I'll come help you as soon as I get the beans in the oven." Rio put a hand on Finn's shoulder as they walked away.

"He's a good man, Kit. Trace would like him." Lola also walked away leaving Kit alone with her thoughts. She hadn't missed Lola's meaning, but she didn't want to complicate things.

As usual the day was enjoyed by all, and the baked beans were a huge success. Rio hung around after the others left. He had nothing else to do so he stayed and helped Kit clean up. Knowing she was tired he called it a night when they were done. He had just settled in at his place when there was a gentle knock on his door. Rio was surprised to see Finn and wondered what was up.

"Do you have a minute, Rio? I need a man to talk to. I can't talk to my mom about everything."

Because of their relationship, Rio wasn't surprised to see Finn, but he was definitely curious. Rio led the way back into the house. shut off the television and they sat down.

Finn had become a mature and confident young man and had started to make time for a personal life. The tone of his voice was serious, and he looked uncomfortable. Dating was new to him. "I've been dating a really nice girl. I like her but I'm not sure how she feels about me. We seem to keep our relationship superficial, so I wonder if she's only dating me because her best friend is dating Cruz. I'm used to Grayson women who are open and opinionated. You always know where you stand with them."

Tonight, had taken an interesting turn. This conversation wasn't at all what Rio was expecting. What did he know about giving dating advice. Rio understood Finn's comment and nodded. Grayson women could be very intimidating.

Finn's mind drifted to Eden, a pretty long-legged brunette who was studious and serious about her education. She had a subtle sense of humor which Finn enjoyed even when she caught him off-guard with her teasing. Eden's friend, Daria, was the total opposite and Finn often wondered what Cruz saw in her. Daria was a sassy blonde who was high maintenance. A bit of the nose-in-the-air sort with a strong tendency toward snobbery. The poor girl had no common sense and was a total airhead at times. Finn sometimes felt out of the loop when they got together but he never regretted his commitment to Caballo Stables and Lola Grande. He did envy the social life Cruz often talked about.

Finn wasn't surprised when Cruz told him he wanted a higher education. When the boys were younger they had shared a love for horses and for a while Cruz thought he would like to do what Finn was doing. But as the years passed his interests changed. Cruz had always enjoyed school so had enrolled at the University of Calgary. Being his first year he would be taking general courses that would probably lead him to a career in business. Finn knew he would miss his best friend who would be starting university in the fall.

After sharing most of this with Rio, Finn added, "Eden has a sweetness about her, but her quiet nature can fool you. The girl has a fiery temper when she gets mad."

"You should be used to that." Rio had experienced the Grayson temper more than once. "Women are stubborn and unpredictable and sweeter than sugar when they want something," Rio cautioned with a grin. "I don't really know what to tell you. You'll get to know her better when you spend more time with her."

"We usually double date with Cruz and his girlfriend. I think Daria is the one who decides what we do and likes to be the center of attention."

"Maybe go solo one night, just the two of you. Take Eden to a nice restaurant that offers a more private setting. See where the conversation takes you. You can both find out more about each other. You can still double up with Cruz and Daria but once in a while you want time just with each other. I've been out of the dating scene for a while, but one thing never changes. You will never understand women. They have these unwritten rules they expect you to know. That's never going to happen because even if you think you have them figured out they'll change them if they want to. Thereby, establishing the belief that men are idiots."

Finn laughed. "Thanks for the advice or should I say warning."

*****

It was the end of a busy week and Saturday night. "I'm going to the city. Cruz and I are picking up the girls and we're going to a movie and dinner. I'll stay in town at Cruz's for the night." Cruz lived in a house close to the university that he rented with two other fellows.

"You've been seeing Eden for a while, but we don't know much about her. When do we get to meet her?"

Finn knew it was best to give his mom a little information knowing she would persist until he did. He wondered if all moms were as nosey as his. "Eden's family farms by Olds and mainly plant canola and some barley. Eden is committed to environmental issues. She's volunteering in a summer program in the city so she's living with Daria and her family who live in Calgary. It's more convenient than commuting."

"That's interesting but when are we going to meet her?"

Finn smiled and gave his mom a carrot, "Maybe at the Labor Day barbeque."

Kit knew it was time to quit prying.

Finn hugged his mom, grabbed his keys, and left. He was looking forward to an evening out. He'd been working hard for weeks and was ready for a break away from the ranch.

Kit was surprised to hear Finn drive into the yard a few hours later since his plan was to stay at Cruz's. "It's early, how come you came home?"

Finn shrugged in his typical off-hand manner. "Our plans changed. Eden wanted an evening with just us, so we separated from Cruz and Daria after dinner. I don't think they really minded. Eden had something important to tell me."

Kit's face paled. Was the girl pregnant?

"Eden is going to Spain in a few weeks. She accepted a full scholarship to earn an Environmental Engineering Degree. She will be gone for at least two years. Out of fairness to both of us, we wished each other the best and will move forward separately."

Kit breathed a sigh of relief, but she felt bad for Finn. "Are you okay?"

His expression softened as he forced a smile, "I will be. It was a bit of a shock. She's a nice girl and I wish her the best. We're still friends."

*****

The family was enjoying a leisurely Sunday breakfast. Kenzie, unaware of what had transpired the night before, opened up a new topic of conversation. "I think I'm old enough to start dating." She had outgrown her crush on Rio and was now interested in the boys at school.

Kit choked on her coffee. That came out of left field. "You'll be dating soon enough, but not yet."

"Who would want her?" Benny's teasing was an invitation to trouble.

As expected, his teasing annoyed Kenzie. "You can be so immature you little weasel."

Benny laughed. Lola tried not to. "Enough with the name calling." Kit made no attempt to hide her irritation, but it had no affect on any of them. She glanced over at Finn.

Finn got up and left saying he was going to saddle up Rebel and go for a ride, wanting to avoid everyone. He was in need of solitude but if he went to his safe place in the barn someone could seek him out thinking he needed to talk.

Kit understood Finn's need to escape, but now she had another difficult situation to deal with. Kit had accepted that her daughter wasn't a little girl anymore. They had many talks about dating and Kit had taken her to the doctor and got her a prescription for the pill. As a mother, she had taken the necessary steps leading up to dating, but she was not ready to let her start dating.

Kenzie refused to be daunted by Benny' s teasing and persisted, "Mom, don't ignore me, I'm serious."

"You're still too young," Kit declared abruptly.

Kenzie was disappointed with her mom's response, and she lashed out without thinking, "When is the right time, Mom? When I'm old like you and no one will want to date me?"

The snarky remark made Kit laugh, which made Kenzie madder. "Megan Ford is the same age as I am and she gets to date," she cried out in exasperation.

"Megan Ford doesn't live in this house," Kit countered.

"Well, I wished I lived at Megan's house."

"So do we." Benny was enjoying himself. Unfortunately, he was only making matters worse.

"Benny, that's enough." Kit was annoyed. Lola sat there amused, waiting to see what would happen next. Lola had undeniable admiration for Kit as a parent, but this morning had presented a new challenge, and she didn't think Kit was handling it well.

Kenzie sighed with impatience and turned to her grandmother, "Lita, tell Mom I am old enough." As usual, Kenzie wasn't about to give up.

Lola agreed but said nothing, wisely keeping her opinion to herself. Instead, she flashed her granddaughter a silent warning that Kenzie ignored.

Kit remained inflexible but Kenzie refused to give up. Kenzie would chip away until she got her own way. "I'm old enough and responsible. Dad would let me," she responded defiantly.

Kit hated it when one of the kids pulled out that card. Not having another parent for support meant butting heads more often. Kit knew that her daughter had no problem wrapping her dad around her little finger, but Kit knew Trace would have her back on this. Kit was tired of arguing over this, "What part of no don't you understand? This subject is over."

Unshed tears glistened in Kenzie's eyes. "Dad always said you were stubborn. I wish Dad was still here. He would let me go." Kenzie was in one of her moods and could go from one side of her emotional spectrum to the other in a heartbeat. "Instead, I have a mean and unfair mother."

Kenzie's remarks were becoming more personal. It was more difficult being a single parent, but parenting still had to continue. She felt Kenzie had no reason to get this upset. Her look was uncompromising. "It's rather hard to consider you dating when you continue to act like a child. If you want to be treated like an adult you can start acting like one." As soon as she said it she knew she had made a mistake.

Kenzie was about to retaliate, but one look at her mother and she knew better. Giving her mom a look of resentment, Kenzie stormed off, muttering under her breath. She knew her behavior was childish, but she didn't care. She knew it would be futile to argue any further.

Kit waited for Kenzie's bedroom door to slam, which it did. If her daughter wanted to sulk, fine. There was always one challenge after another. As a teenager, Kenzie was a bigger challenge than Finn ever was. It was more difficult to parent an outspoken daughter who was a younger version of herself. "As usual, Kenzie persists in arguing with me."

Lola had remained silent until now, "When your daughter wants something she never gives up. She's too much like her mother."

"Ornery and stubborn." It was more a statement than a question.

"To say the least. She is also spontaneous and quick to show her emotions."

There was a hint of annoyance in Kit's voice. "Stubbornness seems to be a strong Grayson trait with all three generations." They both started to laugh.

Kit sighed heavily as she poured Lola and herself another coffee. For some reason she felt she had to defend herself, "It's hard letting them grow up but it's the sensible decision at this time. I'm not ready for Kenzie to start dating."

"No, but she is. Your little girl is growing up. She's ready to spread her wings, not fly the coop. They won't always make the best decisions or the one we want them to make. Sometimes the lessons can be difficult but don't hold them back. They'll only learn by experiencing life. You can't continue to be over-protective because of what happened to Trace."

Lola's over-protective remark hurt. "I only want what's best for my children."

"Of course you do. Parenting is the hardest job we do, and it never stops, even when they're as old as mine. I still miss the special times I had with Trace and now that Riley is a parent our bond has become stronger. You are doing a good job. You have good kids; they are just challenging."

Kit groaned, "Lately, anything anyone says or does makes Kenzie mad, disgusted, or embarrassed. She has always been a bigger challenge than her older brother. I think Benny is taking after Kenzie rather than Finn."

"You can't protect them from life. You might want to lighten up on Kenzie."

Kit hadn't meant to over-react, but she really had been caught off guard. Kit frowned, knowing she hadn't handled the conversation with Kenzie very well. She understood Lola's point so agreed to think about it. She needed time to process this and maybe widen some boundaries with Kenzie.

Lola looked at Kit with a serious expression and responded with her usual directness, "Everyday logic often goes out the window when it comes to dating and I don't just mean with Kenzie."

Lola's comment resulted in an expression of displeasure on Kit's face. Kit usually appreciated Lola's input because she admired her mother-in-law. But there were times she felt Lola overstepped. She didn't appreciate the topic to include her dating. Or lack of.

Lola remained serious, "Since we're on the topic of dating, you know it's okay to go out with someone. It's been over a year since Trace died. You don't have to hide your feelings from me like you are from Doc and Rio."

"You don't know how difficult it is at times."

Lola smiled, knowing she was right. "So, you do have feelings for one of them?"

"It might even be more than that. I care for both of them. We all know Doc has feelings for me and if Rio has any he's keeping them to himself."

"Trace denied his feelings for you in the beginning. Maybe Rio needs a little encouragement from you."

Nothing was more complicated than considering a relationship when conflicting feelings were involved. "Things are fine the way they are for now."

"You should listen to the wisdom and experience of your elders. It's time to move on," teased Lola as she gave Kit an understanding hug.

Kit had no reason to be upset but there were times like this that her life was still difficult. "Do you really think it's the right time to start dating?"

"Neither Doc nor Rio are going to hang around forever," remarked Lola deliberately.

Kit's voice was indignant, "I meant for Kenzie."

"As she said, other girls her age are dating."

Lola had given Kit a lot to think about and it occupied her mind all day.

After supper, Kenzie joined her mom out on the verandah. "Can we talk?"

"Of course."

"I'm sorry for my behavior. I do miss Dad, but you are the best mom ever."

Kit appreciated that this was Kenzie apologizing for real and not sucking up. Maybe her daughter was maturing. Kit knew her daughter wasn't a little girl anymore. With that realization came another. "You caught me off guard at breakfast, but I've had all day to think about what you said. I feel like I lost my baby girl overnight. I know you're growing up, but I need a little more time to accept that. You will also have to learn to behave like the young lady you want me to think you are."

Kenzie teased back, her expression saucy, "Think fast. The boys are starting to gather around and flirt with me. When someone asks me out I would like to say yes."

Kit knew it was time to broaden the boundaries, but it was difficult having to make all the decisions. What if it was the wrong one? She had to laugh to herself. It wouldn't be the first time, and it surely wouldn't be the last. All she could do was rely on her instincts and do what she felt was right. She knew she needed to be a little more open-minded and listen to what the kids were saying. Having a daughter start dating was going to be much more difficult than when Finn started dating. She also had Trace then. Kenzie wasn't the only one struggling with change. Kit knew her life would become more complicated when she widened her own boundaries.

CHAPTER FIVE

School was back in, and Kit was glad to have their routine back. Even though the kids grumbled, she knew they were glad to be back at school. They had missed their school friends, one of the disadvantages of living in the country.

Finn's phone rang and he looked down at the unknown number. He hesitated a moment before answering. His face paled as he heard a familiar voice from the past. "Yes, I remember the address. I'll see you tomorrow at ten o'clock." He looked at his mom and swallowed hard. "That was Mrs. Sloan from the Foster Agency. She wouldn't tell me anything over the phone other than the fact it was important that we meet." He didn't have a good feeling about this. It had been years since they had spoken. "Don't worry, Mom. I'm sure it's nothing." Not quite meeting her gaze, Finn shrugged in his usual off-hand manner, pretending it didn't matter. Finn turned and walked out the door without another word.

Kit knew she would have to wait until he was ready to talk, but she was uneasy. What was so important that Finn had to go see Margaret Sloan? Was her son's life going to be turned upside down again? Kit knew better than anyone that you never know when a big change will happen in someone's life, so she was uneasy. Were they about to be thrown another curve ball that would change their lives again? Could Finn handle another big change in his life? Could any of them?

Finn remained troubled all day. Due to past experiences with the Foster Agency, dark memories kept surfacing. For the past few years, he had been able to bury the pain deep enough, but it all came back with the unexpected phone call. He thought he had left that life behind.

Finn was up early the next morning. He was anxious about what would happen today. He wasn't surprised to see his mom sitting at the table having coffee. He knew she was as anxious as he was.

Kit looked up, dark circles evident under her eyes. She hadn't slept well either. "Do you want me to go with you?"

Finn's voice was quiet but determined, "I'm fine. Mrs. Sloan is still in the same office, so I know the way. Besides, I have a few errands I can do since I'll be in the city." He was nervous but trying to stay positive. Worrying wouldn't change anything, but the fear of the unknown continued to take over once in a while. He poured himself a coffee to go and left. He hadn't bothered with breakfast.

Even though Finn had been adopted by the Graysons, he knew this meeting wouldn't be easy due to past experiences in her office, fear of the unknown being a constant reminder. At times it was still hard to let go of the past. He was experienced enough to know life could change quickly, and it wasn't always good. Finn was anxious as he entered Mrs. Sloan's office. He had to swallow hard, unable to suppress his fears. Her office didn't hold fond memories.

Margaret Sloan greeted Finn warmly knowing it took a lot of courage for him to come today. "It's good to see you again, Finn. I was so sorry to hear about the loss of your father. He was an honorable man."

Finn knew she was sincere but there was no need to waste time with social pleasantries. He would appreciate it if she would get right to the point. His face was solemn when she told him to have a seat. He took a deep breath, hoping it would help release the uncomfortable feeling weighing on him.

Margaret Sloan could sense his underlying fear. She had seen that expression too many times on the foster children she had met over the years. It was a result of the pain from past experiences along with fear of the unknown moving forward. Finn was one of the lucky ones whose story had a happy ending. Now there was another chapter to his story. Margaret stared for a moment at the young man who sat in front of her as she studied his face. The transformation was immediately apparent. Finn was only seven when he was orphaned and entered the system. She had never forgotten the day she met him, a frightened freckle-faced boy with piercing green eyes. The poor boy was so thin and too pale and trusted no one. He was no longer a scraggly kid who barely knew right from wrong. Nothing remained of the haunted, vengeful youth who believed living on the streets was better than living with the foster parents he had. Her decision made years ago had resulted in a wonderful success story. Finn had survived his foster years. Here sat a healthy, self-assured young man, not the confrontational youth who made impulsive choices based on bad decisions. He had successfully transitioned from the painful problematic phase of his young life into adulthood. Success stories like Finn's were what helped Margaret Sloan to remain in the position she was in.

When Finn gave her one of his intense looks she got right to the point. "When you're a foster child you always live with the fear your foster parents can give you back or the agency can send someone to take you away. As much as the agency tries to do their best, we don't always find the right fit the first time." When Finn went to the Grayson's she hoped he had found his permanent home. His was a real success story. Families seldom adopted their foster children. Finn was one of the lucky ones. "Usually, a foster home is never a permanent home. I couldn't have been happier when the Graysons adopted you after we removed you from the Ungers. Look how far you have come since then."

The look in the Finn's eyes had changed and the momentary flash of dread was evident. He had tensed at the mere mention of the Ungers. He didn't want old wounds opened up even though those days were long gone. The Graysons had taken away those fears years ago. He now lived a good life. "I've had years to get over it and now have a loving family." Finn had developed a lot of self-worth over the years but time with foster parents had ingrained a certain caution. Those early years had conditioned Finn to expect the worst. Finn raised a questioning eyebrow and drew a deep breath, "What's this about?"

Margaret understood the complexity of the situation moving forward. The young man's future was once again at stake. It upset her that she could be turning his life into chaos. How do you prepare someone for something like the news she was about to reveal? She hoped she was making the right decision. Margaret wondered what his reaction would be to what she had to say. "A man named, Duncan Barns, came to see me, and he says he's your biological father."

Finn was visibly shaken as he shifted his position. He drew in a shocked breath as the color drained from his face. He sat staring at the floor, unable to meet Margaret Sloan's gaze. Silence hung heavily in the air.

Margaret's face remained expressionless. She knew Finn needed a moment to absorb the shocking news he received. She hated the fact that she caused the look on his tormented face. Her words were direct when she continued, "I felt I had an obligation to inform you and let you contact him if you want to." Finn had the right to make that decision.

Finn hadn't expected this. Old fears resulted in a strong level of suspicion, but he had no reason not to believe her. His voice was barely above a whisper when he asked, "Why now? What does he want?"

She hadn't miss the nervous tone in Finn's voice. She left the question unanswered for a moment while she considered her response. Her only option was the truth. "He wants to meet you."

A familiar look darkened his face. His voice cracked with unmistakable emotion, "How did he find me?"

Margaret's eyes remained kind, but her words were candid, "Once you were adopted this information became public and there are so many ways to obtain information through the internet. He obtained a copy of your file from Child Services."

This information caused Finn's eyes to darken. Their conversation had stirred up unwelcoming memories and the ghosts from his past kept pushing their way through. For a brief moment the insecure child was back. His first instinct was to run. Finn understood the significance of what he just learned. In a heartbeat life changed and his world had been upended. This could have a big impact on his life. He knew from experience that life had a way of kicking you when you're down. Life had conditioned Finn to expect the worst but he sure as hell hadn't expected this. His expression remained intense. "I thought I was done with this."

Understanding the new emotions Finn was now having to deal with, Margaret wanted her parting words to be positive, "Finn Grayson, I am proud of the fine young man you have become. You are now the one who can make the decisions in your life. Only you can decide what is right for you and I wish you the best moving forward." She shook his hand as he left.

Her well wishes didn't help. This news had turned Finn's comfortable world into turmoil. His face was solemn when he left.

Margaret had prayed for Finn the day the Graysons left the office with Finn to take him home. She prayed for him again today.

Finn sat in his truck a long time before leaving. Fate had pushed him into adulthood with both hands but today he felt like he had slid back into the abyss of his childhood. Were more ghosts looming in the background ready to drag him back to his dark past if he contacted the stranger claiming to be his father? Finn was at a crisis point. Depending on how he decided to move forward could result in big changes that would affect the future of his whole family.

Finn was filled with conflicting emotions by the time he reached home. Even though he knew his mom and grandmother were waiting for him he headed directly to the barn looking for Rio. Finn was turning more and more to Rio, like he used to with his dad. No one was around so he sat down in his safe place. Since the arrival of Rio, a great weight had been lifted from his shoulders, and it felt good to rely on him. As a youth, he was used to struggling in silence but that had changed since he became part of the Grayson family. Did he have more family? Things had really changed since his meeting.

Rio had seen him arrive. After a few minutes he headed inside to see if Finn needed to talk. He could tell Finn was troubled. "What's going on, Finn? Whatever it is, it looks pretty serious. Talking usually helps." It might be good advice, but it wasn't something Rio did.

Finn took a long pause before confessing, "I would just like to wipe the past away. Life is never what you expect."

Rio thought he was referring to the fire and his dad's death, the traumatic event that had brought Rio to Lola Grande. Life had taken a dramatic change then. "I know it's been hard at times since your dad died. Trace was a good dad to you." Rio had heard nothing but good about Trace.

"He was the best, but this isn't about Dad." Finn opened up and told Rio about his meeting. "I had to learn to deal with change when Dad died. I will deal with this, too." Finn looked away. A moment later he turned back with troubled eyes. "Trust doesn't come easy, so I don't know what to do." Being a foster child for years, he hesitated to get too close to anyone. Other than family, he had only one close friend and now Rio.

Rio knew Finn was struggling, "You can't run away from your problems any more than you can ignore your past. It's always part of you. It can't be changed or undone."

Finn's mind filled with unpleasant images, his fears escalated as he imagined the worst. He was struggling with the decision that could change his life. His voice sounded a little panicked and full of doubt, "What if I ignore this and refuse to contact him?"

Rio put his hand on Finn's shoulder, keeping it real. "I don't think he'll give up. He did find you." Rio's dark eyes were filled with genuine concern, "Are you going to be okay?"

Finn shifted to look directly at Rio. He struggled to keep his voice from shaking, "Yeah. I need to go talk to Mom. I know she heard me pull in. I'm surprised she hasn't come out here to see what's going on."

"I'm sure she's been in the kitchen pacing, and if your grandmother is with her she's praying."

Rio's comment brought a brief smile to Finn's face because Rio was right. "What do you think I should do?"

Rio had always treated Finn like an adult, "Nobody can tell you what to do or what is right. You're of age to make your own decisions, but it's okay to give it some time. Talk to your mom and your grandmother. They are wise women."

With a gesture of resignation, Finn nodded. He knew he'd have to take care of this in his own way. His lips were pursed, his jaw rigid as he headed to the house. Life could sure change quickly. His mind filled with unpleasant images, his fears escalated as he imagined the worst. He continued to struggle with the decision that could change his life.

It had been a long morning waiting for Finn's return. It was even longer waiting for him to come in from the barn. Both women knew escaping was his coping mechanism and were concerned about what he was dealing with. They waited, knowing Finn would come in when he was ready. Meanwhile, negative thoughts began to overshadow common sense. Unexpected obstacles always add unwanted stress. "He's been out there a long time." Kit looked at Lola with such despair Lola took her into her arms.

An hour later, Finn walked into the kitchen. Kit figured her son had been talking to Rio.

Finn felt bad seeing the concern on their faces. He knew they were in for a big shock. Another serious conversation was about to ensue. He dropped heavily into the chair next to his mom, his face solemn as he struggled to find the words that could impact all of their lives. The silence was uncomfortable after he told them his devastating news.

Kit and Lola exchanged a glance, their expressions identical. They knew life could change quickly and it wasn't always what you expected, but they hadn't expected this. Kit stated the obvious, "That's shocking news."

In a ragged voice, Finn continued, "Trust me, I was just as shocked when Mrs. Sloan told me. I'm still trying to process this. It brought back a lot of unpleasant memories."

"Do you think he could be your father?"

Finn stared into his mom's eyes for an agonizing moment. "I guess he could be. The line for the father's name on my birth certificate was left blank."

Kit hated seeing the anguish on her son's face. Just when you think life is back to normal it changes. This put a new spin on life and definitely complicated things. At that moment Kit could relate to how her dad must have felt when she showed up unexpectedly and said she was his daughter. She knew about making hard decisions. That's what she had done when she came to Alberta looking for the father she was told was dead. She knew Finn needed to know just like she did. "I understand your reluctance. It's not easy to face your fears. I told you how I was scared to death to come here looking for my father. I can see why this man is doing the same thing if he believes he is your father. Ignoring this will not make it go away."

This was a challenging, possibly life-changing decision. "When I showed up here you told me choices we make can have long-term effects. I don't want this man to be my father," Finn said bluntly. Finn took a deep breath before asking, "What if he really is my father?"

Things will change for all of us. Kit's voice was heavy with emotion, "We deal with that just like we have dealt with everything else. Like a family."

Lola agreed, "Whatever lies ahead, we'll get through it." Kit and Lola shared an anguished look.

Finn had only one choice. "I have to contact him. We all need to know."

"That's a brave decision. Are you sure you don't want to think about this a little more?"

"There's no point in that. Waiting won't change the facts. Why are the right things usually the hardest to do?"

A sense of apprehension shivered down Kit's spine. She went outside, needing a moment. Were they once again going to have to deal with a big change? Kit knew she was strong enough to survive anything fate threw at her. Was Finn? When she saw Rio down at the corral watching the horses romp she headed over. Kit was concerned for her son. She hadn't missed seeing the fear in his eyes. Maybe Rio could tell her more about what Finn was feeling.

Rio watched her approach, saddened by her expression. He knew from experience that Kit was on a mission. He would respect Finn's confidentiality and still try to reassure Kit that he was okay.

They stood together discussing Finn's unexpected news. Kit was unable to mask her fear or hide her resentment. "When Finn first came here as a foster child I told him bad memories fade and get replaced with happy ones. All those dark memories have resurfaced. Why did this man show up now? What does he want from Finn?" Kit let out a distraught sigh, "We could all be in for a big change if this man is Finn's father. I know we can't always protect our children but my God this is so unexpected. This man better not hurt my son." A tear escaped as her eyes brimmed with tears.

"Parents can't always protect their children from getting hurt." When another tear dropped on her cheek, Rio gently brushed it away. "Finn is an adult. He has to make that decision, but he is confused and scared."

"So am I."

Rio's compassion drew him in. He circled his arms around Kit and held her against his chest. There were no words that would comfort her, so he just held her close.

Kit was touched by Rio's concern. It was a comforting moment. She really needed a strong shoulder to lean on if only for a minute or two. Even though Rio shared Kit's doubts and had his own misgivings, they had to respect Finn's decision. Kit knew this. How often had they had to embrace change. What was Finn going to have to face? "Fate seems to constantly change our lives in unexpected ways."

"It sure does." His life had certainly changed since he arrived at Lola Grande. Rio cared for the Grayson family, and he was falling in love with Kit. "Change is difficult, especially when it's not by choice." Rio watched Kit as she turned and walked back to the house. He turned back to the horses. Dealing with horses was so much easier than dealing with people.

Finn was troubled by the events of the day and remained withdrawn during the evening meal. His meeting had been unsettling. As soon as supper was done, he headed outside with both Kenzie and Benny. He decided he needed to spend some time with them. This was his family.

Lola stayed behind. "Do you know what Finn plans to do?"

"He's still struggling but he said he's going to contact this man. Whatever he decides, we have to be there for him and support that decision."

Later that night, Finn and Kit had another discussion in regard to this before Finn headed to bed. "I'm going to call him in the morning."

Kit sensed his underlying fear. Or was it her own? She leaned forward, her tone serious, "The choice you make can have long-term effects. Are you sure about contacting him? Once you make that call there is no going back."

With a gesture of resignation, Finn nodded. This was not a little thing that could be ignored and there was only one way to deal with it. "I have to meet with him." That was the only way he'd get the answers to questions that had been left unanswered for years.

Kit understood, they were about to deal with another complex situation.

Finn lay in his bed staring at the ceiling, his mind wouldn't stop. Questions resulted in more questions, and he had no answers. Memories he didn't want to recall took over. They grabbed hold and took Finn back to a dark time in his past. It was a long time before he fell asleep. An hour later, he woke with a jerk, his heart racing. His childhood nightmares were back. The fear of the unknown had been all too familiar. He kept struggling with the decision that could change his life. Eventually, he fell back into a restless sleep. He had left the light on.

The kids had already left for school by the time Finn came down for breakfast. Kit knew he hadn't slept any better than she had. "How are you doing, son?"

Finn ran his fingers through his hair, "I'm still confused and scared, but I haven't changed my mind." He had intentionally decided to wait until today before making his call. He didn't want to appear over anxious to a stranger. He also knew that once he made the call he had no control over what could happen. Finn held his breath waiting for his call to be answered. The stranger's voice sounded familiar, and his tone seemed rough. There was something about the man's voice that bothered him. Or was that fear taking over and misleading him? Finn's expression changed to one of apprehension. Past experiences had made Finn cautious but even though he didn't like the tone of the man's voice, he agreed to meet him.

"I don't want to inconvenience you. I can come to your place."

Finn remained cautious. He didn't want some stranger coming to Lola Grande. He agreed to meet him at a restaurant in Calgary. Finn's voice remained cool as he reassured him, "I won't change my mind. I'll be there at noon." The conversation with the stranger had been guarded and brief.

Kit had been listening to the one-sided conversation, "What did he say?"

"Not much, other than once he knew about me he had to find me. I have my doubts, but I have to hear his side of the story. I guess I'll know more tomorrow. I hope you understand that I need to know." Finn shrugged his shoulders, pretending he wasn't worried. He still didn't give an inch or show how much things mattered.

Kit heard the restraint in her son's voice. She knew he had struggled internally making such a huge decision. "I understand. I'll go with you if you like."

"Thanks, Mom, but this is between him and me."

Kit noticed the determined set of his shoulders. Further discussion would be pointless. Finn had made up his mind and nothing she said would change it.

The rest of the day dragged. Finn couldn't maintain focus while training. Fear seemed to be lodged in his throat and weighed heavily on him. Was there going to be another big change in his life? Change could be just as scary as an adult. Curiosity had nagged at him all day. For the hundredth time he wondered what Duncan Barnes looked like. Would he learn more about his mom? Needing to expend his nervous energy he headed over to the barn and began puttering in the tack room. He was too jittery to do much more than what came naturally.

CHAPTER SIX

Both Kit and Finn were anxious during breakfast. Benny was bugging Kenzie and for a change Kit didn't mind the distraction. Kenzie and Benny didn't know what was going on. There had been no reason to upset them until decisions were made and facts confirmed. Right after breakfast Kit hustled them out of the house to catch the bus hoping to have a couple of minutes alone with Finn. "Are you sure about meeting this man?"

"I am."

Kit hoped for his sake he had made the right decision and repeated her offer to go with him.

"I'm not a kid anymore, Mom. Besides, this is something I need to do on my own." He forced a smile, knowing how anxious his mom was. No one knew what was going to happen today, so he dreaded what lay ahead. Even though he wasn't meeting Duncan Barnes until noon he knew the time would only drag if he stayed home. He would do a couple of errands once he got to Calgary since he didn't get them done the day he went in to meet with Mrs. Sloan.

"As your mother I respect your decisions and offer my support based on them. You are an adult." Worry clouded Kit's expression as she watched Finn drive away. It was going to be a long day of waiting. She was wise enough to know life could quickly change and it wasn't always what you expect. She wasn't sure what they were in for.

There were so many emotions surging through Finn as he sat waiting in a corner booth that offered some privacy but allowed him a view of the door. Finn promised himself he would give the man a fair chance. He knew it was easy to judge others based on past experience. Or to judge them knowing little or nothing about them. He would try to remain open-minded when they met.

Finn allowed himself to gaze at the other patrons in the restaurant, but he looked over every time someone came in. Time dragged and the man was now half an hour late. Maybe he wasn't going to show. Five minutes later Finn said to hell with him and got up to leave. He looked toward the door one more time. A sudden feeling of panic caused his chest to tighten. Finn's face was deathly pale, his mouth dry, and he ran his tongue nervously over his lips. He knew right away who the man was standing in the doorway. Finn shot an uneasy glance toward the imposing man and regretted his decision. A ghost from the past had become real. The man in the doorway wasn't a stranger, Finn just never knew his name.

The man's gaze shifted as he scanned the room and made eye contact. Finn's whole body was tense, his heart racing. His knees were weak, and his hands that he had slipped into his pockets were shaking as he attempted to recover his composure. He took a deep breath as the burly man approached. When he got closer, Finn's stomach turned because he could smell the man's body odor, and he was sure he'd been drinking.

Duncan Barnes hadn't changed much but time hadn't been kind to him. His hair was long and greasy, thinning at the top and his unshaven whiskers were gray. Faded jeans were tattered above his scuffed shoes and his beer belly hung out below his faded t-shirt where he carried cigarettes in the pocket.

"You have to be Roxy Doyle's son. I'd recognize you anywhere." Before him was a young man. The last time he'd seen Finn Doyle he was a scrawny boy.

As soon as the man spoke, his gruff voice made Finn flinch as it triggered a flashback. He had heard that voice too many times raised in anger toward his mother. It confirmed his belief as to who the man was. Finn hated it when his mom brought men home. Finn remembered he hated this man the most because he was the one who often abused her. Finn's immediate reaction was one of mistrust, so his feeling of unease intensified. This was going to be harder than he thought it would be. Finn stared at him without responding and sat back down, glad they were seated near the back and away from most of the patrons. Finn didn't smile but managed to meet his gaze, "I'm Finn Grayson now. I was adopted when I was a teenager by my foster family, and you must be Duncan Barnes."

"That I am, but everyone calls me Duff."

Here he was sitting face to face with a man claiming to be his father. Finn stared hard at him. He saw no sign of family resemblance, but Finn knew he took on the looks of his mother. Finn got right to the point, "I always thought my mother didn't know who my father was. There was no name on my birth certificate. So, what makes you think you're my father? Why are you here and what do you want?"

The questions were valid, but Duff wasn't prepared for Finn's directness. He was such a meek boy when he knew him. Knowing he couldn't escape the inquisition, his eyes darkened. He leaned back in his chair, "Every father deserves the chance to get to know his son. Tell me about yourself." Verbally, the man was smooth, but his manner was bold.

Finn fixed his gaze on Duff. Feeling no connection to the man, he ignored the question. He was curious about this man who he didn't trust. "I'll let you start, and you can begin by telling me why you think you're my father," he said deliberately.

Duff had a cold and detached attitude especially when confronted. He hesitated a moment before answering, "Your mother knew as soon as she realized she was pregnant that I could be the father and so did I, but so could a hand-full of other men. I doubt if she knew for sure. I told her there would be no child support from me. Shortly after Roxy told me she was pregnant I took a job offshore with an oil company. When I came back to town I reached out to Roxy, and you were already five. She still swore I was your father. It was obvious Roxy had gotten hooked on drugs. She was a mess but so was I, so we'd spend time together. She spent time with anyone who would give her drugs."

When Duff saw their waitress he called out, "Get over here, Missy." As soon as she reached their table, Duff blurted out his order, "I hear there's nothing better than Alberta beef, so I'll have your steak rare with a loaded baked potato and a starter salad. You can bring me a cold beer right away." Finn ordered a Caesar salad. He didn't know if he could manage to get a bite down. He also ordered a beer with the hope it would help calm his nerves.

As soon as the waitress left, Finn threw Duff a challenging look and asked him to justify his continued absence. Not getting any reply, Finn's voice took on a hard edge, "How did you find me and why did it take so long?"

"I didn't know what happened to you after Roxy died. The trail to find you was difficult because you became a ward of the government. It was easier once I found out you were adopted."

Finn looked at Duff, his intense green eyes unable to hide the torment he experienced from years of abuse. He decided to share a few of his unpleasant memories, not for sympathy, but rather for clarification. Resentment poured out, "After my mother died I entered the system, essentially the government became my legal guardian." His expression remained set and hostile. Finn would never forget the day his mom died, a traumatic event that changed everything. "I'll never forget the fateful morning I woke up and went to find my mom. I walked into the living room, and she was lying on the floor, and I couldn't wake her up. She just lay there cold and unmoving. I was a seven-year-old boy looking down at the lifeless body of my mother. I was really scared because I didn't know what was going to happen to me. That day, I was taken away by strangers, too young to understand what was happening." That was the beginning of suffering caused by others. He learned tough lessons. He also learned he couldn't trust anyone.

Life changed when he was fostered by the Grayson family. They were honest and fair and never abusive. Thanks to the Graysons he knew that what happened with foster parents was on them, not him. The Graysons helped him with his low self-esteem and aggression, but he remained strong-willed. Finn broke out of the painful memories he had not wanted to live through again. Conflicting emotions played across Finn's face. He had endured a lot in his young life. "You grow up fast when you're an orphan. I'm not that scared little kid you knew years ago. I learned when you have the right people around you and know you're safe, trust can be rebuilt."

"Well, you can trust me, Finn."

Finn did not trust him for one minute, and he didn't want to show this man how vulnerable he had become. This conversation had opened old wounds. His face remained masked while wondering what else the man had to say.

Duff resorted to the blame game, "It's too bad Roxy loved drugs more than you." Duff actually sneered. He was well aware of her life and how she died. "Your mother lived a destructive lifestyle. I could never control Roxy."

Finn's voice rose with indignation, "Not even when you hit her? I was too little to stop you when you slapped her around, too little to protect her." Finn didn't like the fact that he let this man get to him and that he had exposed his raw emotions. Finn was unable to hide the pain he had buried for years, and his guilt resurfaced. He had never been able to help his mother. Finn took a deep breath for control, but he wasn't sure how much more he could endure. He could hate his mother but no one else had the right to say bad things like this.

Duff shrugged off Finn's accusation, offering no explanation. This arrogant man was deaf to Finn's words just like he'd been deaf to his mother's cries when he was hitting her.

Finn boldly held his gaze. "You never said what you did was wrong. According to you it was all my mom's fault."

"It was; your addicted mother was a mess." The real Duncan Barnes was emerging, so his voice had a hard edge.

Here was another person telling him how bad his mom was. Finn refused to let Duff's words hurt him. The last words his mom said to him were, "I love you, Finnie," as she tucked him into bed and kissed him goodnight. This was one of the good memories he continued to hang onto. He had done his best to take care of his mom, but he had failed. The fact that he failed still bothered him.

Finn knew his mom loved him, but she failed as a mother. His mother had continued to neglect him with her selfishness and addiction. He learned at a young age you can only depend on yourself. Finn felt a strong pang of regret. He really didn't know much about his mother, so he had hung on to the image of the mother he wished he always had. Controlling his feelings took a great deal of effort. He had to will himself to keep the pain buried deep. His mom did the best she could. It took all of Finn's willpower to maintain eye contact, as he gave Duff a doubtful look. Being older and with more life experience, he knew it wasn't all his mom's fault. He was sure the man across from him had been a bad influence.

"This all happened years ago. It was a bad time for both of us." Picking up on Finn's underlying anger, Duff lowered his voice and changed his tactics. "The choices I made back then were wrong. It was due to the lifestyle we were both living. I've changed. I've turned my life around and I need forgiveness."

Their conversation was interrupted when the waitress brought their meal. Throughout the meal, Duff kept up an endless banter without really saying anything. Finn didn't know if the man was nervous or just liked to talk. It irritated Finn, probably because he was nervous. There was no way he could relax. Duff kept drilling Finn with questions without much success. "You seem to have done well for yourself. Look at you now, you survived nicely."

"Not every child is born into a loving, protective environment. It's amazing what having loving parents can do for you. They restored my faith and gave me a life I'm proud of. They taught me good values and the importance of hard work. I'm a cowboy who works on a ranch."

Bull shit. You're family are landowners, and you run a successful business. Duff had done his research. He waved the waitress over. The poor girl came quickly to avoid a scene. "Put your hand on my back. Do you feel a bump?" The embarrassed girl shook her head. "That's because I'm not a camel. I can't go all day without a drink so bring me another beer." His voice was getting louder, and he had become more belligerent.

Finn felt sorry for the waitress and asked for their bill as well. He'd had enough of Duff's attitude. The man's behavior was beginning to grate on his nerves. Suddenly the music seemed too loud, just like the man in front of him. Finn decided it was time to end this meeting, "I want a DNA test done."

Finn's directness caused Duff's manner to change, his expression now closed and tight. Duff glared at Finn as he shifted in his chair and snorted at the DNA request. "I have documented proof."

The gruffness in Duff's voice made Finn frown deeper but he remained unconvinced. He knew better than to take him at his word. Thanks to the internet documents were easy to create. In fact, Finn had a feeling he was being lied to. Like his dad, Finn took nothing at face value. He had grown to be a confident young man who couldn't be intimidated. Finn was unwilling to let it go. The atmosphere became more tense.

A muscle twitched in Duff's face. He was less than impressed by Finn's insistence. Duff had picked up on the tell-tale signs of doubt on Finn's face earlier, but his manner remained evasive. Duff's voice rose emphatically, "Are you serious? I am your father."

Finn would prefer to have nothing more to do with this man. He faced Duff and looked him squarely in the eye; his manner remained cold. He cleared his throat before speaking, but he didn't show any sign of weakness. Finn wanted to make this situation clear, "That's yet to be determined. I can't simply take your word for it. I want my own DNA test done so I have my own proof." Duff's expression hardened, once again surprised by Finn's directness. "I'm sure you understand and can appreciate the value of documented proof of paternity. I'll call you again when I get the results."

"That will take days. Can't I see you before then?"

Finn's look never wavered as his eyes narrowed. Today, he was in control. He interrupted before Duff could continue, "I'm busy." He didn't want to get involved with a man like Duncan Barnes.

Duff realized this meeting hadn't gone well, "I planned on sticking around for a few days anyway." For a change, Duff actually spoke the truth. He was hoping to find out more about Roxy Doyle's son. Finn hadn't shared much whenever he was asked a question. All of Finn's answers were vague.

When the waitress brought their bill. Finn dropped his share on the table. Duff finally pulled out his wallet when he realized Finn wasn't going to pay for him. They walked out together. As soon as they were in the parking lot, Duff reached for his cigarettes and lit up.

Finn didn't want to spend any more time with Duff but he wanted the cigarette butt so he could take it for testing.

Duff took a couple of quick drags, then threw his cigarette to the ground and ground it out with the toe of his shoe. Finn bent down and picked it up. His gaze never faltered as he placed it in the napkin he had taken from the restaurant. He needed to know for sure if this man really was his father.

Finn had done research on DNA testing. Kits were available and results could be emailed but the internet wasn't always reliable in the country. He decided to have a reputable company do the testing and mail out the results even though it could take as many as seven days. It would be the longest week in his life, but having a physical copy would prevent either one of them questioning the results. "I'll call you when I get the results." He watched Duff shrug his shoulders and walk away. Finn put his hand in his pocket and felt the napkin. He had what he needed. Nothing could be resolved until he had the report. That's when a lot of things could change.

It was a relief when he climbed into his truck. Finn rested his throbbing head against the back of the seat and closed his eyes. The meeting had been stressful. There had been so many unexpected moments that tormented him because his past kept surging back. Finn was devastated by their conversation. It brought back the ugly time growing up with his mom. The older he got the more he resented his mother's lifestyle. Addicts not only hurt themselves. They hurt the people who love them the most. Finn hated the bitterness he still had for his mom. People like Duncan Barnes only made it worse.

Finn's mind was reeling by the time he got home. He parked and headed straight to the barn. He still needed time alone to process everything. Everyone had seen Finn drive in.

Rio went over to the barn a few minutes later. He didn't know what was going on, but he could see something was bothering him. "Are you okay?"

"I need to be alone" Finn replied with a snap, declining to go into details.

Rio turned and left knowing Finn was dealing with something difficult, and it wouldn't be fair to pressure him.

It seemed like forever before Finn made his way into the house. He hadn't failed to notice his mom's concerned look. He still wasn't ready to talk. It had been an intense day, and his mind had been reeling for hours. "I don't want to talk right now."

Knowing the struggle going on within her son, Kit had to let it go. As a mother, sometimes all you could do was wait and pray. Finn would talk about it when he was ready.

Before going to bed that night Finn joined his mom in the living room. He needed the comfort of his mother's words. She always knew how to make her children feel better. "I'm sorry I was abrupt earlier. It was a very trying day."

Kit knew this wouldn't be an easy conversation.

"I stopped wondering a long time ago who my dad was. Besides, I had a real dad." They both smiled knowing he meant Trace. "Now things have changed. What if he really is my dad?" The anguish was evident in Finn's face when he confessed, "I don't want him to be my dad. I get the feeling he doesn't care about anyone but himself or what he can get from someone else. I'm not sure what he really wants but I don't trust him." In a ragged voice Finn shared everything, including the fact that he was having a DNA test done. He had stopped and dropped it off at the Canadian DNA Services Inc. before coming home. They would just have to wait. Nothing was resolved.

Kit had to ask the hard question, "What if he is your father?"

Finn knew he had to be prepared for the worst. His voice was flat, "Duncan Barnes is a stranger who may have provided his sperm to give me life. Even if he is my father, he abandoned us and abused my mother. He implied it was her fault for the way he acted toward her. He took no accountability whatsoever. Whatever the result, I know the past can't be changed, but this man will never be a part of my future."

*****

The week passed slowly. Finn had been withdrawn and kept to himself, and lines of anxiety were evident in his face. "I'm going to town to do a few errands." He would pick up the mail knowing the DNA results should be there.

Kit gave Lola a sideways glance. They both knew the real reason he was going to town. They were all anxious knowing this could change all of their lives.

"I'm going to go and garden for a while." Lola hoped it would help pass the time. She was working around the yard when a strange vehicle pulled into the yard. She felt the hair on her neck rise and knew right away who the unexpected stranger was. The man's arrival was such an intrusion, and she braced herself as the man approached. There was no way he had been invited. Despite her displeasure, she maintained her composure.

Kit had seen the stranger drive in and quickly joined Lola. No man intimidated either one of them but there was strength in numbers.

"Beautiful country around here but it sure gets windy." The man's voice was deep and dark. Buddy, who stood next to Lola, growled.

Lola stood facing him and stared Duncan Barnes down. She had learned to size people up quickly and her dislike for him was instant. "And you never know what the wind blows in."

Duff didn't miss the sarcasm, and there were no social pleasantries extended. A hostile look crossed his face making it clear that she had struck a nerve.

"You are on Grayson land uninvited. State your business."

"I came to see my son."

Kit bristled at his tone and her posture remained rigid. It took incredible effort to speak in a controlled voice because his showing up had unnerved her, "That has not been determined, Mr. Barnes. You might be his father, but I am his mother."

Duff smirked as his shifty eyes darted to Kit, "You can't stop me from spending time with Finn once he gets proof that I am his father."

Kit hadn't missed the veiled threat and felt a sense of dread. The last thing she wanted was for this man to know how unsettled she was, and she wished Finn was back from town. She saw Rio heading to the indoor arena and tried to wave him over, but he passed by before she could get his attention. Kit was now trembling from the unpleasant exchange. She took a couple of steps back while Lola held her ground.

Lola was quick to confront him, "How did you know where Finn lived?"

After his meeting with Finn, he'd followed him out to the ranch unseen. He was impressed by the actual size of the ranch. Recalling the conversation with Finn, he was not expecting this. He watched from the road for a while, impressed with the outbuildings and set up. On his way back to Calgary he stopped in town and made some general inquiries and once he got back to his room he did a lot more research on Lola Grande, Caballo Stables and C&G Ranching. "Folks around here are real friendly and quick to help a stranger. Even more so when you drop the Grayson name." *It's interesting what you find out when you start poking around and the folks in town were so kind.*

Kit shook her head in disbelief. How brazen could a person be? She could understand why Finn didn't like this man. She didn't either. *Please don't let this man be Finn's father.*

Duff clenched his jaw, his eyes narrowed, and his smile was forced. He was tired of their attitude, "I didn't think anyone would mind me dropping by. Where is Finn?"

Anyone who knew Lola knew better than to cross her. Duff didn't know what he was in for now that he had provoked her. She'd had enough of the man's arrogance and was about to ask him to leave when Finn's truck pulled into the yard.

When Finn saw Duff talking to his mom and grandmother, he froze. He was unable to deny the fact that the man's appearance here unnerved him. He was hoping to look at the DNA results before having to share the news with anyone, especially if it was bad news.

Everyone's head turned as Finn left his truck and headed over. They stared at the large brown envelope in his hand. Kit felt sorry for her son. So much depended on the results and there was no going back once he opened it. They had no control over what would happen next.

Finn gripped the envelope. There was no sense delaying the inevitable. He took a deep breath for control and was surprised he was able to keep his voice steady, "I guess it's time to find out." His hand shook as he broke the seal. Would life continue to be cruel for Finn?

Finn pulled out the results and fought to hold back his tears as he silently read, 'No Match'. Finn stared at everyone but said nothing. The expression on his face was masked and they all wondered what the results were. Finn turned to Duncan Barnes, intentionally holding the man's gaze, and spoke with undeniable authority, "Since you are already here, it will save me having to contact you. According to the information here, you are not my father. Based on that, I never want to see or hear from you again."

Duff shot Finn a suspicious look before he grabbed the paper to make sure and cursed out loud, "I figured it was worth a try since it was possible. I ran into some old friends and Roxy's name came up. I decided to look you up once I had more information on you. It's too bad for me but you sure landed in a pile of roses. A lot better than the pile of …"

Finn's eyes flashed and he cut Duff off before he could continue, "You are a vile human being." He had lost the fight to keep the anger out of his voice.

Kit and Lola looked at each other. A profound look of relief crossed their faces as tears of relief filled Kit's eyes. Lola took control and quickly interjected, "If you step one foot on our land again I will have you arrested for trespassing." She hadn't missed the open hostility in the man's eyes and thanked God he wasn't Finn's father.

Kit's expression matched the coldness in her eyes. She didn't bother to mask the disgust in her voice when she added, "You played with my son's feelings, and you couldn't care less. You are despicable."

Duff's face hardly changed expression even when he saw the look of resentment in Finn's eyes. He wasn't intimidated by Lola's threat but today hadn't played out like he hoped. He turned and walked away.

Even though the confrontation had passed, it took them a few minutes to recover from the unpleasant encounter. They remained standing where they were until the final dust had settled as Duncan Barnes drove away.

Kit hated what that man had put them through. Kit knew this hadn't been easy for Finn. It hadn't been easy for any of them. Some of the stress lines disappeared from Finn's face as if he had been released from an invisible load. "Thank God he's not my father." The fear in Finn's voice had been replaced by relief. He whistled to himself as he walked away.

CHAPTER SEVEN

Kenzie, who usually chatted continuously during meals, was quieter than usual and had been sulking for days. Kit wondered what was up and knew a talk with her daughter was necessary when she continued to snap at her brothers for no reason.

Benny finally retaliated, tired of his sister's behavior, "What's your problem?"

"I don't have a problem?"

"You've been moody and rude for days and we're all tired of it." This reprimand came from Finn as he got up and headed toward the door.

"Instead of sitting there bickering you can go and get ready for school."

"I'm not going to school." Kenzie stormed off and escaped to her room.

Kit was right behind her. "Okay, young lady, what's going on? Are you having problems at school?" Familiar with Kenzie's dramatics, it could be anything.

Kenzie's manner was always confident, but peer pressure was a powerful force. Kenzie had been excited having reached a new milestone and moving on to high school. She expected a smooth transition and was eager to make new friends and learn new things while bringing along the typical teenage enjoyment from her junior high years like hanging with her friends and talking about boys all day. Instead, high school brought huge changes that shook Kenzie's confidence. "A new girl, Vanna Parkhouse, has transferred here from Calgary. Her dad is the new town foreman, and her mother is a corporate lawyer. A real clique has formed around her. I tried to be her friend in the beginning, but for some reason Vanna took a dislike to me. I haven't done anything to her, so I don't know why Vanna's being mean. Yesterday she called me a fatherless country bumpkin." Kenzie had spoken so softly Kit could barely hear her.

Kit struggled with her own anger. It was such a cruel thing to say. "She probably realized you're one of the popular girls and considers you a threat. Her mean girl behavior stems from being insecure, immature, or jealous, which often results in bullying. Bully's like the control they have over others. Girls like her manipulate others with fear of exclusion and backstabbing. What makes this new girl so special?"

"Vanna's pretty with long blonde hair, petite, and outgoing to the extent of being perky. She is vain, a total snob, and is nothing more than a spoiled rich girl. She thinks she's superior to all of us country kids. Vanna was the head cheerleader at her school and has taken on that roll at our school. I don't understand why anyone would want to jump and prance around in a mini skirt and scream 'Go Team Go' but cheerleaders are always the popular girls in high school. She is a great addition to the cheerleading squad but rules over the others. They renamed themselves the Shimmer Squad and of course Vanna is team captain. It's obvious she took dancing for years. Most of the routines focus on her being center stage since she choreographed them. Her followers all belong to the cheerleading team and Lucy Rose is one of them. I'm glad Lucy Rose made the squad because she really wanted to. That's all she talked about all summer. That's her thing so I am happy for her, but it's like she changed once she became a cheerleader and became part of the pom-pom clique. They're this generations version of the mean girls led by Vanna Parkhouse." Tears smarted Kenzie's eyes as she blurted out, "That whole group of girls treat me like I've got the plague, and Lucy Rose is hanging with them instead of me. She's barely spoken to me in weeks. It didn't take puppet girl long to let Vanna control her strings." Her friend's actions had really hurt her. Kenzie blinked hard but she was so overwhelmed by misery her tears spilled before she could hold them back. "They told Lucy Rose that I didn't want to hang around with her and I was tired of her being my shadow. Why would they lie and why would Lucy Rose believe them?" Her closest friend felt like a traitor who had betrayed her.

Seeing the hurt behind the words, Kit didn't know what to think about Lucy Rose's behavior. The girls had always been best friends and did everything together. Kit took her time before answering, wanting to choose her words carefully, "Lucy Rose is a little messed up right now because she's trusting like you so why wouldn't she believe them? You've both started at a new school and the popular girl befriended her and she wants to fit in just like you do. She doesn't want to be rejected or criticized. That kind of pressure can be powerful and hard to resist. Lucy Rose isn't as strong as you. She's sensitive so it makes her an easy target for being controlled. In time she'll find out what the new girls are really like. As her friend, give her time and let her know that she's still your friend. I know it hurts when someone you love, like a best friend, disappoints you."

"Vanna's confident and cunning. She enjoys humiliating others, but her followers don't see it."

"Or they choose to ignore it, so they fit in, or so Vanna doesn't turn on them."

"I told Lucy Rose that Vanna would sacrifice her in a heartbeat to make herself look better. She said I was just jealous." Kenzie was confused and upset with her friend.

"Lucy Rose is still your friend. She will figure it out for herself and realize what this girl is really like. It takes some a little longer than others if they are insecure and not comfortable with who they are. They want approval from others, in this case the popular girl at school. She'll soon realize how superficial these girls, especially Vanna, are and appreciate the true friendship the two of you have always had."

Kenzie was finding no comfort in her mother's words, "You have no idea what it's like dealing with mean girls."

Kit gave her daughter a reassuring smile, "I understand better than you think. I was a teenager once and I had no dad, and I didn't have a mom who loved me and was there for me. Instead, she was part of the problem, and I had to deal with bullying on my own. It's sad that it's still a problem. There's nothing wrong with you. Continue to be yourself and trust in yourself. Don't change who you are just to fit in. People will like you for who you are and to heck with those who don't."

Kenzie let out a sigh and nodded. That's what she had always done but was finding it difficult to do it now.

"I'm sure you're not the only one they treat this way. When a leader isn't getting the result she wants from others she'll turn on her own. For now, surround yourself with your other friends. I'm sure not all of them are part of that group. I understand your anger but at school you need to manage your emotions and not let them take over. I know it's not always easy but try to ignore these girls and walk away."

"I do and I no longer want Vanna as a friend, but I wish Lucy Rose would see her for who she really is. Vanna enjoys humiliating others, but her followers don't see it."

Kit hated the dejection she saw. Teenage girls could be so mean. "Their behavior is unacceptable. Is there a teacher or guidance counselor you can talk to?"

Kenzie was less frustrated. "There is and I will talk to someone at school if it gets worse, but I think I can handle this on my own. For now, I'll put up with their stupid high school antics and figure out how to deal with this. I'll be okay, Mom, but growing up isn't always easy."

"No, it's not my darling daughter. Not at any age. We just do our best and stay true to ourselves." Kit remained silent for a moment. When she spoke her tone remained serious, "It's important for you to understand there will always be challenges in our lives. Right now, it's the girls at school. I even have challenges. I have one right now because my daughter is hurting, and I hope I found the right words to help her. I don't have all the answers, Kenzie. We just do our best. Is there anything else bothering you?"

"Isn't that enough!"

Kit flashed Kenzie a compassionate smile, "I meant is school going okay otherwise?"

Lightness returned to Kenzie's voice. "School is fine. I've actually been thinking about journalism after I graduate so I'll see what courses will help me next semester. I'm also trying new things. I'm taking Drama this semester."

"That should be a good class for you. You've had years of practice being a drama queen."

That made Kenzie laugh, which lightened the mood. "I guess I have. I'll be nice to Lucy Rose. She's still my best friend. As they say, it's a new day but I better hurry if I want to catch my bus." Kenzie was stubborn, not insensitive. She was also raised with good values and her fairness kicked in.

Kit gave Kenzie an understanding hug. She knew her daughter would never let anyone back her down, but Kit was still concerned. She'd invite

Maggie over for coffee so she could find out what was really going on. Kit knew how devious teenage girls could be. There was probably more to this than Kenzie was sharing. If there was a bigger problem, she couldn't stand by and allow it. It was also possible Lucy Rose was struggling just like Kenzie but was afraid to say anything. One crisis after another. She sighed heavily as she returned to the kitchen. The anguish with Finn seemed to be over but today presented new concerns. There was always something to deal with.

*****

A few weeks later things were back to normal between Kenzie and Lucy Rose, and they were again best friends. Also, a couple of the new girls began spending time with them and there was a sleepover coming up on Friday night. Kit was relieved this drama had passed but she was experienced enough to know there would be others, and they would also resolve themselves in time. Hopefully, she would have a reprieve for a while. That didn't happen. Kit was caught completely off-guard when Kenzie bounced into the house after school with a burst of excitement, "Gunnar Adams asked me if I would like to go to the movie with him."

"I hope you told him no."

"I said yes. I hope you will too. Please, Mom. We want to go to the movie in town next Saturday. I like him and he likes me, too. Please say, yes."

Despite Kenzie's pleading look, Kit remained firm, "We've had this discussion before, you're still too young to date. Subject closed."

"You're not being fair." Realizing her mom wasn't going to give in Kenzie let out an exasperated sigh and stomped off.

Kit decided she also needed a moment so headed outside just as Lola was on her way over. They headed back into the house and Kit told her about the disagreement she had with Kenzie over dating and waited for Lola's reaction.

"This will only continue to be an ongoing clash with your daughter. This requires a little give and take on both sides so you might try working out a compromise. I thought you would have learned that by now. I know it's easy to react and respond instead of taking the time to communicate and have a conversation that allows both of you to be understanding. Have you let Kenzie have her say and listened to her point of view? Whether you like it or not your little girl has grown up. You can't keep holding Kenzie back. She's ready to enter a new stage in her life."

"If I say yes, there's no going back." Kit knew Lola wasn't trying to interfere, she was offering a more objective point of view. Kit immediately chided herself for her earlier abruptness with Kenzie who was beginning to show signs of maturity. Youth allowed one to remain stubborn. Being more mature, Kit went up to Kenzie's room to talk and get some information about Gunner. She went and sat down beside Kenzie who was curled up on her bed. "I realize you are growing up, so I have to get used to the idea of you dating. I would like to know more about your Gunner Adams."

Kenzie sat up hoping her mother had changed her mind. "Gunner and I are in a couple of classes together, including Drama. He's considered a jock, so I was impressed that he was taking Drama. Sometimes we have lunch together. Gunner reminds me of dad, quiet until he has something to say. He has a subtle sense of humor that not everyone gets. Kind of like our family."

Kit gave her daughter a questioning look. "How old is he?

"He's just a few months older than I am. He's very motivated for his age. He worked all summer and is saving up so he can buy his own vehicle when he turns sixteen."

At least he sounds responsible, thought Kit.

"Sorry for the attitude. You're not the only one who has been doing some introspective thinking. It's time for me to change my behavior if I want you to see me as someone who is mature enough to date."

"You are charming, interesting, bright, and always a challenge. I don't want you to change. Just take a moment sometimes to think before you react. You might have more success when negotiating or defending something. We'll leave it there for now."

Kenzie was disappointed that her mom hadn't actually said she could go out with Gunner, but she remained hopeful.

The evening meal was much more pleasant than breakfast had been. Both boys went out to the barn after supper and Lola agreed to a second cup of coffee. Kenzie was about to leave when Kit stopped her; it was time to widen the boundaries. "I've taken time to think about you dating. You aren't a little girl anymore and I have to see you for the young lady you are becoming. I've decided to let you go to the movie with Gunner." There were still tell-tale signs of doubt in her face as she relented.

Kenzie squealed with delight as she gave her mom a huge hug.

"Don't get too excited. I don't want to be over protective but there are a few conditions. I'll drive you into town and we'll meet Gunner at the theater."

A mortified expression crossed Kenzie's face, appalled by her mother's comment. "Really! A chaperoned date! That's ridiculous." Kenzie's groan was probably heard in the next county.

Kit couldn't resist teasing, "I promise not to sit next to you, just a couple of rows back." She couldn't contain her laughter, "I'll drive you to town and you can meet Gunner at the theater. I'll go have coffee somewhere and I'll pick you up when it's over."

Kenzie fought the urge not to retaliate but lost, "So, it's your way or no way."

"You'd be best to listen to the wisdom and experience of your elders," Lola declared before she got up and left. Both Kenzie and Kit looked at her, not sure who she was talking to. Usually very direct, Lola could be rather ambiguous at times, so you had to think about what she said.

Kit smiled at her daughter, "This is a first step for both of us. We want to enjoy this new experience together, so this is the way it is this time." Her little girl was crossing another threshold.

Knowing she had to appreciate that much, Kenzie thanked her mother and ran up to her room to text Gunnar. Saturday night couldn't come soon enough for Kenzie. It would come too soon for Kit.

*****

Kenzie was experiencing unfamiliar anxiety, but she knew it was natural on the first date. She spent the day facing a wall of uncertainty, the most important was deciding what to wear. She lost count of how many times she changed her mind before she was ready to go.

Kit and Lola had to blink twice when Kenzie walked into the kitchen looking so pretty and grown up. She was wearing a short denim jacket over a maxi-dress and her comfortable cowboy boots were replaced by a pair of fashion boots. She had blown her hair straight and it hung to her shoulders.

Mixed emotions overtook Kit. Kenzie was a young lady. Gone was her little girl and despite the fact that this was only her first date, one day she would lose her daughter to a fine young man. Life was moving forward so fast. She blinked hard and smiled at her daughter, "You look beautiful. Are you excited?"

"Beyond words, Mom. Thank you again for letting me go."

Kit knew Kenzie was nervous. She had to admit she was a little nervous herself. She didn't remember being nervous like this when Finn started dating. Maybe it was different with a daughter.

Lola hugged Kenzie, "Just be yourself and have fun, honey."

"Let's go, Mom. I can't be late."

Kit grabbed her book on her way out. It was going to be a long evening passing time in a coffee shop. Kenzie was excited and giddy driving in, so she talked non-stop. Kit was excited for her and hoped it would be as exciting a date as her daughter hoped for.

"There he is," Kenzie said as they parked down the street from the theatre. Kenzie was out the door before Kit could tell her to have a good time. Kit sat and watched misty-eyed. Gunner Adams wore new jeans, a black t-shirt, and a school team jacket. Kit was impressed that he wasn't wearing the customary ballcap, but his dark hair was a little longer than most. They looked so cute as they held hands walking through the doors to the theater. She waited until they were inside before she got out and walked to the coffee shop. She opened her book, hoping the story would help her escape. Time passed quickly as she was drawn into the story by the devious main character. Kit had just returned to her vehicle when she spotted them standing on the corner once again holding hands. When Kit honked, Gunner walked Kenzie over and opened her door, politely greeting Kit before he said goodnight. Kit was impressed. She watched as he walked back across the street and got into a car driven by a woman Kit guessed to be his mother. She looked over at Kenzie but refrained from commenting. Instead, she asked about the movie.

"We both really enjoyed it. Gunner wants to take me out again." She sat back against the seat and smiled.

Kit smiled back. Tonight, had been a special night for her daughter. "You've entered a new phase in your life. It can be just as scary as it is exciting. The important thing to remember is I'm always there for you."

Kit remained outside when they returned home. She leaned against the verandah post thinking about today. Having allowed Kenzie to go to the move with Gunner was a big step for both mother and daughter and there was no going back. Past experiences prepared her for the fact that it would be difficult to rein Kenzie in because she was like a young race horse when you opened a gate. Understanding and communication would be more important than ever moving forward.

*****

Kit let her gaze drift to the activity in the training corral. It wouldn't be long before all training sessions would be moved to the indoor arena. She was proud of Finn who had grown into a confident young man. There were times she thought he worked too hard so was grateful that Rio often stepped in to help where he could. It was nice having Rio around in many ways. She lifted her eyes to the darkening sky. Autumn was definitely in the air. Drifting clouds overhead cast moving shadows across the lawn. Yesterday's westerly wind had cleared most of the trees of their leaves and they now carpeted the lawn. Days were getting cooler with fall coming to a close. She turned as Benny came out the door. He was currently her everyday challenge. Knowing it would rain later she grabbed him before he could go over and watch Finn train. "I want you to get a rake and a few garbage bags and clean up the front lawn."

"I'll do it later."

"It's going to rain soon, so I want you to do it now," Kit said firmly.

"Why do I have to do everything?" he complained, folding his arms across his chest in an open act of defiance.

Kit could do with a little less attitude from him. A clap of thunder boomed as a steak of lightning flashed across the sky. "Just do it instead of complaining and stack them along the drive so they can be collected and taken to recycle." It was times like this when she was still resentful of fate, and it made her angry that Trace was gone. Trace's death had left her to cope with everything. The kids, their questions, their anger. Her own anger at the injustice of it all. She took a deep breath. Sadly, this was her life, and she had to deal with it.

Rio heard most of the exchange. He walked over and stood next to Benny, "Go get the bags and I'll grab two rakes, and I'll give you a hand.

We'll be done in no time, and you can still go watch Finn. We can throw the bagged leaves into the back of the work truck, and I'll take them to recycle on my way to the city." Rio had become more than hired help and unknowingly stepped in as the father figure her kids were missing. Benny still had a bit of hero worship in regard to Rio.

Kit objected, "That's Benny's job. Kids need responsibility."

"Of course they do, but there are times they appreciate a little help," Rio said good naturedly. "I'll head out as soon as we're done but I won't be back until late."

Kit knew better than to ask why he was going to Calgary. It wasn't any of her business. He always had time for the kids, but he didn't let others get too close. He was very private.

CHAPTER EIGHT

The days had gotten shorter, the feel of winter was in the air and there had been snow on the mountains for weeks. One never knew what kind of winter Alberta would have so it was best to prepare for the worst. The early forecast was for a long, cold winter. Despite the weather being unpredictable, life had been relatively normal, a welcomed change in the Grayson household.

The weeks kept flying by. Thanksgiving had come and gone and here it was December. Kit hummed to herself as she puttered in the kitchen waiting for the family to gather. Christmas was only a couple of weeks away. Benny no longer believed in Santa, but it didn't mean his list was any shorter. Kit was looking forward to Christmas break as much as the kids were. She smiled as the kids began to file in and greeted Lola warmly when she joined them. Tonight, Kenzie's high school Drama class was putting on a play they had written.

As soon as they were inside the school, Kenzie took off to get ready. The whole family hurried inside so they could get front row seats. They laughed as hard as the others throughout the performance. Kenzie was one of the lead characters and was in her element performing in front of everyone. The play was a comedy of errors, not all of them scripted. Kit recognized Gunner, who was enjoying himself much more than Benny had in his concert the night before. Benny's was the typical school concert. It had been obvious Benny was less that impressed with having to participate but he knew all the words and actions to the songs and sat quietly while other classes performed.

After the concert Kit tracked down Kenzie who was chatting with Gunner and his family. Introductions were made and after a polite chat Kit got Kenzie's attention. "Your brothers and grandmother are waiting at the door so it's time to leave. Gunner, you, and Kenzie were exceptional and carried the others when the occasion called for it. Well done." Kenzie would have preferred to stay longer but it was still a long drive home. She smiled at her mom and said goodbye. Kit was still amazed when Kenzie showed her maturity. It sure made life easier.

Everyone was in a festive mood driving home. "The weather is going to be nice on Sunday. How would you boys like to go and cut down our tree? Last year's was way too big so keep that in mind when you pick one. Kenzie and I will bake cookies, and I'll put on a pot of chili for supper."

"I'll bake buns up at my place." Lola though it would be a good time to let Kit and Kenzie have some mother-daughter time by themselves.

"It's a deal. Can Rio come with us?" asked Benny.

"If he wants to."

Benny's grin was wide, "He does. I already asked him."

Kenzie loved the festive season. "Can we start decorating the house?"

"I'll pull out the decorations tomorrow and we can start anytime but like always, the tree won't be decorated until Christmas Eve." The Grayson family's tradition was to decorate the tree on Christmas Eve and listen to Christmas music and share memories.

"Will Rio be having Christmas with us this year?"

"No, Rio will be spending the day with his family."

Benny looked dumbfounded, "I thought we were his family."

Kenzie nudged her brother, "We should adopt him," she teased.

Lola smiled. *Or your mother could marry him.*

Kit had no problem reading Lola's mind. "I've already invited Rio for Christmas Eve, and he said he'd spend both Christmas Eve and New Year's Eve with us, and we can welcome the new year in together." That appeased the kids.

Finn had become quieter than usual. Christmas had never been his favorite time of year. He had too many unhappy memories from his childhood. He'd go back to school after the holidays, and the other kids would be excited sharing what they got, especially from Santa. He would make something up because Santa never came to his house. Most years there was no Christmas at all, no tree, no decorations, nothing unless he made something at school and his mom hung it on the fridge. Once he entered foster care he understood what the kids at school were talking about. The homes he lived in were decorated and there was a Christmas tree with presents underneath. There was always something for him. Everyone else would have a stocking hung on the mantle but he never had one of his own because he really wasn't family, and they never knew if he would stay.

When the topic changed to New Year's, Kenzie had to ask, "Why do people make New Year's resolutions? Lucy Rose says she's going to lose weight. She's always concerned about her weight, especially now that she's a cheerleader."

"I guess some people want to start the new year doing something positive. For them it's an intention or commitment to achieve a goal like losing weight which is a typical resolution for many. Exercising more is another one."

"It sounds like a set-up for failure and disappointment."

"I agree with you, Kenzie. Very few reach these types of goals. After a few weeks they fall into their old ways. Following through is too difficult."

"Well, I don't need to make any."

"You should. You need to spend less time on your phone," teased Benny.

"And you should spend less time annoying me."

"Why don't we all try to be a better person in a positive way, not just to begin a new year but to begin every new day." The kids looked at each other and rolled their eyes.

*****

The tree the guys had chopped down had been brought inside. Benny had helped Finn put it in the stand and it stood in the corner by the fireplace ready to be adorned. The house had been decorated, and the stockings were hung. Once the tree was decorated the presents would be placed underneath. There were even gifts for Rio this year. Right after supper, bedlam erupted and the kids took off, the adults right behind them. Rio had joined them for supper and was as excited as everyone else. For a while there was chaos everywhere in the living room, but the end result was stunning. Now that the kids were older the tree took on a more uniform look. Kit smiled. She missed those years when the kids were little. The decorated trees told a story of their own with clustered decorations on the lower branches and tears when ornaments got broken. Like every year there were still tears of laughter and the occasional tear of sadness as they decorated, but they were all giving thanks as Benny hung the star on the top of the tree.

Finn looked around the room, glad to be part of this family. He looked over at the mantle and there was his stocking hanging beside all the others. His eyes came to rest on Rio and wondered what his Christmas's were like. When they were sitting around the fire having hot chocolate and popcorn he decided to ask.

Rio sat back, totally unprepared. He decided to share his last Christmas. "The Christmas before I came up to Canada I was travelling around South America and that winter I was working in Caracas, the capital city in Venezuela. They have a very interesting tradition at Christmas time. The week leading up to Christman there is a daily church service called Misa de Aguinaldo, which is Early Morning Mass. In Caracas it's customary to travel to church on roller skates. It's a holiday tradition that began in the fifties when roller skating became popular. The concept of the holiday tradition was that kids could use the skates they would have received as gifts during the year." Benny started to laugh. "You can laugh, Ben, but it's the truth. From December 16th to December 24th, they close some of the roads until 8:00 am to provide worshipers with a clear passage to church so families can skate together safely."

"Did you ever roller skate with them?"

"No, I passed on that tradition. I value my body too much to risk an injury doing something foolish."

"Does Santa come on Christmas Eve like he does here?" Rio had caught their attention, and they all wanted to know more.

"He does. In fact, most of their traditions are similar to ours. They play traditional Christmas music, and families will set up a nativity scene. They decorate artificial trees, and many of the trees get handed down as family heirlooms. Firework displays are very popular. One of their unique traditions is that before going to bed on Christmas Eve the children tie one end of a piece of string to their big toe and hang the other end of the string out the window and wait for Santo Clos to come. The gifts are brought by, Nino Jesus, and San Nicolas."

"Why do they hang the string out the window?"

"Skaters passing by pull on the string. Nobody could give me a real reason as to why they do it. It seems odd but that's their tradition."

"What's the most unusual Christmas you had?" Finn was still curious, wondering if they compared to his.

"Are you sure you want to hear another story?"

They quickly nodded; they were always fascinated by Rio's stories.

Rio had so many different experiences due to his transient lifestyle, but he knew which one he would share. It marked the beginning of his journey. "Okay, if you're sure you aren't bored I'll tell you about my friend Babe. I met her the year after my mom died. She was on old lady who lived alone in the wilderness away from society. Most people would call her a hermit or a recluse. That's often a person who lives a solitary lifestyle usually due to religious reasons but for her it was how she had grown up."

"I left home when my mom died. I was angry at my dad because I felt he had always chosen work over family and wasn't there for my mom. I was struggling with his choices and my own. Like Babe, I needed solitude. I bought my first camper van and headed south, drawn to the Sierra Madre del Sun mountains. I had no destination. I just kept driving, hoping to escape the heartache I wanted to leave behind."

The adults listening to Rio understood. The younger ones were anxious to hear more about Rio's adventure.

"I had somehow taken a wrong turn driving through the mountains, but I kept driving anyway. I rounded a bend and saw smoke. Concerned it was a fire caused by a lightning strike, I kept going further into the bush to check it out. There was no road, just an overgrown trail but I kept going because of the smoke still rising from the trees. When I got closer I realized it was coming from a weather-beaten shack that was tucked away in a small clearing."

"As I pulled up, an old lady was sitting on a wooden chair on the small front porch holding a shotgun. It was like right out of a movie and just like in the movies I slowly got out of my van showing her my empty hands and explained why I was there. I was going to leave but when I saw her struggling to walk into the house due to a twisted knee I went to help her.

By then it was starting to snow, and she told me to stay until morning. It was a week before the weather cleared and I was snowed in."

"That first night we talked for hours. She told me her name was Babe. She said it probably wasn't her given name but that's all her parents ever called her. Her dad died when she was young, and her mom taught her how to be self-sufficient. Their house was sturdy, but rustic. It had no electricity, no running water, and no indoor bathroom. When she was only fifteen her mom died due to pneumonia. Babe continued to live there alone in isolation. She had learned life skills growing up with her parents and knew no other kind of life. She would have been lost living in civilization. The property had a well and was within walking distance of the river and there was a rain barrel next to the house. A make-shift chicken coop provided eggs and meat. She would also snare wild rabbits and small game and there was a small area where she grew vegetables. She was self-sufficient."

"I stayed with her all winter, I cut and stacked enough wood to get her through another winter. Years of harsh weather had damaged the house, and she was unable to do the necessary repairs to maintain it. I did odd jobs inside her house like resealing the windows and when the weather allowed I repaired the roof that had been leaking for years. I cleaned the chimney and wood-burning stove in the living area as well as the wood-burning stove in the kitchen."

"There were no clocks, no calendars, nothing that we use to keep track of the passing of time. She said she didn't need them because if you pay attention to what's around you, there are signs everywhere. The sun gets up every day and sets every night. Whenever there was a full moon, the next day she would go out to the old tree in the back and make a notch. I asked her how old she was. She gave me her quirky grin and sat back, "Older than yesterday." One day I counted the notches in the tree. By my count, she was in her late seventies, but she was fit and healthy. She told me there had been no birthdays to celebrate after her mom died. She said she simply celebrated every new day, grateful to have another one. She wasn't an educated woman, but she was wise beyond measure. She always gave me something to think about. I shared a lot with Babe. She was a good listener."

"One night, I was surprised by a knock on the door. She opened the door and in walked a massive man loaded down with supplies. He was an old trapper who would come by a couple of times a year to check on her. He'd bring her wild meat and basic staples to get her through until his next visit. It made me feel better knowing there was someone looking out for her. He stayed for two days, catching up and trading tales. I sat there listening, fascinated by both of them. I understood what he said the morning he left. He thanked her for her hospitality but if he stayed longer he would be intruding on her solitude and way of life. He was looking at me when he spoke. I knew what he was telling me. Babe smiled at him and patted his weathered cheek and thanked him for his visit."

"I remember the morning before I left. Babe was sitting outside listening to the sounds of nature which was music to her ears. I could tell she was waiting for me. By the look on her face I knew without her telling me that the time had come for me to leave. Babe got up without a word and went back inside. When she came out she had a whittled feather. Her pastime was whittling, which is an art of using a knife to carve shapes out of wood. Over the years, Babe had become very adept at whittling. She made a lot of her own utensils, but she was also artistic. She had whittled the feather which represented a connection to spiritual realms. I knew it was the feather that hung in her kitchen window above the sink. It had been whittled from white birch which symbolizes hope, and fresh starts. She told me it was time to continue my life's journey on a new path now that my struggles from my past were fading away. She handed me the feather and said my guardian angels were close offering their protection and guidance. She told me bird feathers symbolize freedom, both mental and physical. When a feather falls to the earth it is considered a sacred gift from the sky and the Creator. Feathers also symbolize respect and honor. She told me to take it as a gift. It has hung in my camper window ever since. I didn't know how to thank her. I surprised her by baking her a cake and we pretended it was her birthday."

So that was who he had baked a cake for. There were times when Rio was a confusing man to understand. He continued to surprise her in many ways, but she was also learning how spiritual he was in his beliefs. She always thought of him as complex. In truth, he believed in the simple things in life.

"I know she appreciated what I did for her, and I know she was glad when I left. I think I stayed more for me than for her." Rio had found an inner piece by the time he left. Over the years he had thought of her often and he learned new things as he travelled to different places. He looked at people in a different light and judged less. He had even begun to see his dad in a different way and could accept him for who he was. He looked around the room. That time in his life was an important part of his journey and his journey had led him here.

They could have listened to his stories all night, but time had passed unnoticed. "I'm sure I've outstayed my welcome and Santa won't come until you kids are in bed. Merry Christmas." He didn't often display his affection, but he hugged them all when he left.

Kit walked him to the door. "Merry Christmas, Rio. Pass our greetings on to your family when you see them tomorrow."

"I will." Rio left with mixed feelings. He felt the Graysons were as much family as his own. He had come to love this family.

CHAPTER NINE

January had come in like a lion and it was roaring across the land. The month had been long and cold. Kit always felt when they turned the calendar page to February the worst of winter was over, but they were in for another storm starting today. Nobody was in a hurry to head outdoors despite having to go to school and feed the horses. Kit had taken the time to cook a hot breakfast, which usually only happened on the weekend. She was feeling guilty knowing she could stay inside her nice warm house. They had just sat down to eat when they were surprised by the knock on the door.

Rio was very respectful of the Grayson family routine, so he never disturbed them unless he had to. "Last night I had a call from my dad's brother. I have to leave for a while. Our dad died and I have to go back to Mexico. We didn't know he was sick and sadly he died alone." Rio was unable to hide his guilt. "I need to make funeral arrangements and settle his estate. I want to leave tomorrow and drive down so I can bring back some of our father's things. Hector, Anna, and Cruz are flying down once the funeral arrangements are made." A shadow crossed Rio's face. He was concerned about what he might discover when he got there. The phone call from his uncle indicated things hadn't been good between them and their dad had fallen into hard times. He wouldn't say why. Dealing with additional guilt he continued, "I realize what an inconvenience this will be." It troubled Rio that Benny would feel disappointed and let down. Rio had been giving up a lot of his personal time for Benny and his training. It would likely come to an end during his absence since Finn would have an additional workload. Rio hoped he wouldn't be gone too long, but he didn't know what he'd find when he got to Mexico.

"How long will you be gone?" Kit asked, while Benny looked away, unable to hide his disappointment.

"I don't know, but at least a few weeks since I'll be driving."

This vague comment frightened Kit and left her feeling empty except for the many unanswered questions filling her mind. Kit knew he was keeping something from her. What wasn't he saying? A heavy silence fell between them.

The tone of his voice became more serious. "I need to sort things out while I'm there."

Kit's face paled. *What kind of things?* A chill ran down her spine. Did he have to sort out more than his dad's stuff? Was it more personal than that? Kit was too afraid to ask.

The timing was bad, but Finn couldn't change that. They would work out the challenges while Rio was gone. "I'll come find you after breakfast and we can decide what needs to be done today. It will be more challenging around here with you gone but we'll cope."

Rio nodded, excused himself, and left.

The atmosphere was somber as they finished breakfast. They would miss Rio. A strong bond had formed between Rio and the kids. Kit reluctantly admitted it wasn't just with the kids.

After Benny and Kenzie left for school, Finn went to find Rio. There were a few things that couldn't wait, and it would go faster if they worked together. Knowing a storm was blowing in he wanted the tractor with the attached snow blade filled with gas. The forecast wasn't for a severe snow storm, but the wind could cause drifts quickly.

"I'll be back as soon as I can." Rio felt bad about leaving but it was better that it was now and not during the busy spring season.

Finn was glad to hear that. Even though spring was their busiest time there was always work to do on a ranch. Everyday chores needed to be done year-round. He would manage but it meant a heavier work load. Finn groaned when snowflakes began to drift through the air. It was only a matter of time before the storm hit. Throughout the day the weather worsened. There was a raw wind sweeping down from the high country and the temperature dropped.

Kit looked across the yard and saw Rio hooking up the trailer to take bales out to the pastures for the horses before the snow became heavier. Finn and Rio worked diligently, doing what they could before dark.

Rio had been invited for supper. Kenzie and Benny chatted away about school which helped ease the tension. When supper was done, Kenzie and Benny both hugged Rio before they left the kitchen. Finn went with Lola up to her suite knowing Kit and Rio needed time alone.

Rio didn't want to go to Mexico, but it was like his mother was calling him from her grave. He knew he had to do the honorable thing and bury his father next to his mother. "I was able to spend time with my mother during her illness. It was a special time for both of us. Dad and I may have lived under the same roof but all he did was work from sunup to sundown. Looking back, I think work was his escape. He didn't know how to help mom. I have to go back to Mexico to honor my father." There was a look of regret in his eyes. It was going to be hard to leave, even for a little while. "I better head home. I want to get an early start."

"It's nasty out there. Safe travels." Even to her own ears, her words sounded forced. She wanted to conceal what she was really feeling.

"It's supposed to let up by morning," Rio said as he grabbed his coat. He studied Kit's face for a long, tender moment. Unable to stop himself, he pulled Kit into his arms, "I have to go." He turned and left.

Kit let him go, unspoken words hanging in the air. She couldn't bring herself to say goodbye. She watched him go with sadness, knowing she would miss him.

Winter had closed in. It had snowed all night, and the land was covered in a thick blanket of snow. There was no sound outside but the howling wind. Rio was glad he had his winter tires put on. He had experienced more than one Alberta winter. The early morning air was bitterly cold, and he could see his breath as he exhaled. It was still dark when he finished loading his van but the kitchen light was on in the main house. He knew Kit would be sitting at the kitchen table with a cup of coffee. He knew he should have said something more to Kit last night. Another regret. He would miss her and hoped to be back soon. Rio was anxious about what lay ahead for him, and it wasn't just because of the weather. He was nervous wondering what he would find out when he got to Mexico. Since moving back to Mexico, their dad had only limited communication with both of his sons and only if they called him. He always said everything was fine, but he kept the calls short. Both Rio and Hector were concerned. Rio again glanced at the main house. With an air of finality, he climbed into his van and drove away.

Kit heard him drive away. She got up and looked out the window. She could see the tracks where the van had been parked. It had stopped snowing during the night and by daylight the sun was shining on glistening snow. Kit didn't know what she was feeling but the silence that remained with Rio's departure was eerie. He had just left, and she already missed him. She welcomed the stirring of her family.

Finn was busy all day clearing snow from the yard. Lola was in her suite, the kids were at school. Everything was normal but for Kit the house was too quiet. She went outside to shovel the driveway and sidewalks before the kids got home from school. Doc pulled in minutes later. Snowflakes clung to her long lashes when she greeted him.

"Give me that and I'll come in for a coffee as soon as I finish up." His last client had cancelled so he got away from the clinic early. Doc noticed the camper van was gone when he pulled into the yard. "What's up? Where's your hired hand?"

Kit quickly explained why the van was gone.

When Rio first arrived, Doc was glad Rio was living on site. He provided protection for the family during the early months as the Graysons dealt with Trace's death and the rebuild, but he was still here. Doc hoped Rio would never come back, and Kit would forget all about him. Maybe then things would get back to normal.

CHAPTER TEN

Kit knew it was early without looking at her bedside clock. She was sleeping poorly because she couldn't get Rio out of her head day or night. She closed her eyes, fighting the desolation that continued to torment her while struggling with his absence. It wasn't due to the fact that he was away from the ranch; it was because of the man himself. She was missing Rio and felt an intense sense of longing since the day he left. She got up and went and stared out the window. It was still dark, but it was time to get on with her day. It would be another busy one.

After breakfast Kit turned to Lola, "Do you know when Hector and his family are coming back from Mexico?"

"They got back over a week ago. I talked to Anna yesterday. Hector said Rio stayed because he had additional business to take care of. You know the Ortiz brothers, they don't share more than they have to. They haven't heard from him either, so they're as confused as we are."

Kit had a sick feeling in her stomach and was unable to push away the wave of unease. "Well things are getting more difficult around here without him. Finn is exhausted and you and I can't do all the work Rio used to do."

"Hopefully it's for just a few more days."

Kit shook her head, "I'm beginning to wonder if he will come back." There hadn't been any contact from him since he left, which was over a month.

Lola watched Kit with troubled eyes. "Don't go there. We're all distraught these days, but we don't need to jump to conclusions. I'll feed the horses before I go to town for groceries." They were reeling from Rio's continued absence, and it made things harder for all of them, especially Finn. They were doing their best so Finn could keep up with his training. Everyone, including Benny were pitching in but it wasn't enough. The Graysons weren't afraid of hard work but with Rio gone there was more work than they could do. What they needed was a full-time man working at the ranch.

Kit couldn't bring herself to believe Rio wasn't coming back but the nagging voice in her wouldn't let it go. Rio had always lived a transient lifestyle before he moved here. Was he missing his freedom? Maybe it drew him back while he was away, and this was the excuse he needed to stay away. He had fulfilled his commitment to the Grayson family, so there was nothing to keep him here. Kit didn't want to jump to conclusions, but the nagging thought persisted. After Lola left, Kit crossed the yard and headed over to Rio's place. Even though she felt uneasy when she opened his door, Kit went inside and looked around. Everything was neat and orderly. She was bewildered when she saw Rio's cell phone lying on the nightstand. She felt more confused than ever. Was it intentional? Was this a subliminal goodbye note? The few personal belongings in the living quarters could easily be replaced. Had Rio misled all of them? It frightened her where her mind had just gone. She turned around and left, closing the door with more force than she intended. She tried to shake off her black mood as she headed home.

Supper was another depressing affair. It wasn't just the adults looking for answers. "I miss Rio. I hope he comes back soon," Benny said, eyes enormous and troubled. He was missing Rio who had become a father figure to him.

An expression of doubt showed on Kenzie's face, and she asked the question everyone was asking themselves, "Did Rio leave us? The Ortiz family has been back for a long time." They were desperate for reassurance.

Kit knew where their apprehension was coming from. Their dad said he would be fine but died in the fire. Kit understood those fears too well herself and knew what it was like to wait for someone to come home. How many times had she done that waiting for her mother when she was little. Kit wanted to give them the reassurance they were looking for. "I'm sure Rio has a good reason for not contacting any of us, so we just have to wait."

Benny wanted to believe her. "How come he hasn't come back?"

Kit heard the yearning in her young son's voice. She kissed his anxious face. She couldn't help but worry about Benny. The kids were feeling abandoned, and his absence was affecting them, but Benny was becoming more of a challenge than ever. Finn looked lost and vulnerable, a look reminiscent of his youth. She probably looked no different. "Rio said he was coming back so I'm sure he will." Kit tried to make her voice sound more optimistic than she felt. She didn't know what else to say. She knew Rio didn't care about what other people thought but he did care about them. This was out of character. She couldn't understand Rio's continued absence any more than her children could. Her words didn't comfort any of them. They were all tired of waiting for Rio to come home.

*****

Another week passed and still no Rio, and nobody had heard from him. Kit stared out at the mountains that usually brought her peace. The mountains at this time of the year offered a spectacular backdrop. The snow-capped peaks made the sky look bluer and seemed to physically bring them closer. It presented a picturesque feeling of peace, but life was in turmoil for the Graysons. Kit's eyes drifted across the yard. Buddy was sniffing around where Rio's van had been parked. *He's gone you stupid dog.* Kit felt stupid herself for being mad at a dog. *I miss him too.* She remembered how they had waited for Rio to show up when he first came to Lola Grande after the fire. Here she was waiting for him again. The man was insufferable. Kit continued to struggle with her own anger due to Rio's continued absence.

Kit went to open the back door when she heard a kick and Finn called out. His arms were loaded with wood. Kit meant to do it, but she got distracted when Benny needed her. Parenting was still her full-time job.

"That's a heavy load you're carrying, son."

"It's not too bad. I'll bring in another load after I stack this."

"That's not the load I'm talking about," Kit said pointedly.

Finn tossed his mom a defiant stare. There was no time for one of her "meaningful" conversations. "I need to finish this."

"You don't need to do everything yourself."

"Well, I don't see anybody else doing it."

Kit hated hearing the sarcasm but refrained from responding. She grabbed her coat and went out to help. When they were done Finn stayed inside to warm up. Kit's tone was serious, "Graysons have never been afraid of hard work, but I have learned when to ask for help. We need to stay on top of things, but we aren't so things are piling up. We need extra help until Rio comes back. I'm going to talk to my dad. We aren't able to do this on our own anymore."

Finn was also concerned about the future and strain lines were showing on his face. He needed another supply of hay bales, but he didn't have time to drive over to Valley View. He knew someone from there would bring a load over, but he was stubborn like his mother and didn't want to ask. Besides, it wasn't just a matter of getting the load. It needed to be unloaded and stacked when it got here. He felt he was letting everyone down and his dad would have been disappointed in him. Finn pushed his hand through his hair in frustration, "I'm glad to have you and Lita but I wish dad was here."

Kit didn't take offence. She felt the same way. The challenges continued to be difficult, and Trace wasn't here. Neither was Rio. Where the hell was he?

Finn turned to his mom, "Don't you get tired of being strong?"

"I have no choice. I can't lay down and say I give up."

Finn's anger toward Rio was turning to resentment. Rio was letting them all down and he couldn't care less. "It's only going to get worse," Finn said as he grabbed his coat and hat and left. He still had to muck the stalls that weren't done yesterday, and he wouldn't have time to do them in the morning. He had too many other things to do and he had to go look at a new colt which could mean a new client. He should be excited, but he was too exhausted. He hadn't been this tired since his dad died. It seemed like there was always something else to do. Everything seemed to take longer these days and sometimes there just weren't enough hours in the day. He was beat by the time he returned to the house. He took a quick shower hoping to revive himself. It helped, but not for long. He joined everyone for supper but was almost too exhausted to eat. He was too tired to go out to do more, so he escaped to the living room. An hour later Kit woke him and told him to go to bed.

The next day dark clouds closed in, and there was a biting north wind contributing to the growing cold. Another strong gust of wind took Finn's breath away as the wind slapped snow in his face. He pulled his collar higher and braced himself. The weatherman had forecast heavy snow for the foothills. The weather worsened during the day as the storm closed in. The snow was swirling, drifts already forming across the yard. The last thing they needed was another snowstorm. The temperature had dropped even more by the time he returned to the house.

Later that night Finn joined his mom in the living room. She quickly muted the television. Finn was struggling because of all the responsibility. Responsibility may build strength of character, but it wasn't always easy. He felt he'd been responsible ever since he was little. Finn's face took on a serious expression. The boy's look was heartbreaking for it told a story of its own. He had lost his mom; he had lost his dad. Had another person he loved abandoned him? Just like the night his dad died, the feeling of being forsaken returned and for a moment he reverted back to that little boy with deep fears. Experience should have taught him better. People he loved always left.

Kit couldn't bear to see Finn lost and vulnerable. She knew her son was devastated knowing Rio might not come back. She couldn't hide her look of concern, but she had to be real with Finn, "I know you're hurt because we haven't heard from Rio."

Finn was preoccupied as he nodded, "You warned me he might not stay when we hired him. I guess once a free spirit, always a free spirit."

Kit was thinking the same thing. "The truth isn't always easy, but I think the time has come and we have to be realistic and accept that Rio may not come back."

Finn thought long and hard before responding, "Rio isn't fair. At least when Eden left she had the decency to be honest and upfront. Rio lied when he said he wouldn't be gone long." He'd been lied to before. That's why he had no dad.

"Sometimes life isn't fair."

"Life is never fair for some of us," Finn said bitterly.

No, it isn't. Kit hadn't missed the sound of defeat in Finn's voice. The poor boy was confused and desperate. "Disappointment exists for all of us. It hurts more when it comes from someone you trust." Tears stung her eyes, anger and hurt mixing together. Kit lowered her eyes but there was no way to hide her misery. Rio had to come back.

The snow worsened as the night wore on. This was not what they needed. By morning, the storm had come and gone, but the drifts were high. Finn didn't even know where to start. He was pulled from his thoughts as the troops drove in, his grandpa in the lead. The community had pulled together to help. They were all there, BJ, Matt, Hector, Cruz. "Riley will be here later. He's taking a few bales to the horses on his way over." Finn was beyond grateful.

Cruz slapped his buddy on the back, "Dibs on the tractor with the plow." Cruz had been home for the weekend and decided to wait a couple of days before driving back to the city. It would be easy to catch up on his classes since most of it could be followed online.

The Graysons were speechless. All of these men had left their own places to help them first. That's what community was all about. Neighbors helping neighbors in their time of need.

*****

Kit threw another log on the fire and curled up in the chair. She grabbed a blanket, wrapped it around herself, and stared pensively at the dancing flames. Her mind was on Rio. She had experienced such deep loneliness when Trace died, and she was feeling that way again. She questioned Rio's feelings. She questioned her own feelings. When she got up to stoke the fire, she grabbed the poker to shift the logs. Suddenly the sparks were flying everywhere because she was stabbing at the coals in anger. She hated Rio for not coming back. She started to cry in frustration. It wasn't fair that Rio had the ability to turn her life upside down. *Damn you Rio. Why haven't you come home?*

Finn had taken a much-needed break and was meeting up with Cruz for supper but said he'd be home early. It was now closing in on midnight and Kit was worried. It was out of character for Finn not to call if he was going to be late. She let out a weary sigh. You worry no matter how old your kids are. A few minutes later she got up and began to pace, often looking out the kitchen window hoping to see headlights. It was well past midnight when she heard vehicles. One was Finn's, the other one Cruz's. She wondered what was going on.

Even though Kit was relieved, she was dismayed when she saw Finn stumble out of the passenger side of his truck. Cruz stepped out from behind the wheel and hurried over to help his staggering friend. Daria remained in Cruz's truck. Finn refused to make eye contact with his mom, determined to just walk inside and head up to his room. He put his hands in his pockets, stumbled, and would have fallen if Cruz hadn't grabbed him. Cruz looked extremely uncomfortable but stayed to make sure everything was going to be okay.

Kit had never seen Finn like this. She put a restraining hand on his arm, but he pulled away and swayed. She had to control her temper with effort, "Well, aren't you in fine shape." She had a good idea where this act of defiance was coming from. The fact that Rio hadn't returned had been Finn's breaking point. "You're lucky Cruz was there for you tonight."

Finn's response was slurred as he turned and looked at his friend, "My buddy isn't like his Uncle Rio who isn't there for anyone." There was so much hurt behind the anger. Finn's eyes were cold, his expression hostile and his disjointed ranting continued, "I was right when I said you can't trust anyone. Damn, Rio. I let myself trust him like I did Dad." A scowl darkened his face as angry words continued to spill out, "Rio's not coming back because he's a liar." Finn gave his mom an intense stare. His expression hardened, "The foster care system screwed me up years ago and you would have thought I would know by now that you can't count on anyone."

Despite hearing Finn's resentment, Kit's own anger escalated, "So, Rio hasn't come back; deal with it."

Finn's mouth was set in a hard, thin line and his expression remained set and hostile. "Yeah, you already told me." Finn was a tormented young man. He was mad at Rio and tonight he was taking it out on everyone.

Finn was obviously more affected by Rio's absence than she realized. Kit wasn't really sure how to deal with Finn, but she didn't deserve his attitude, and she wouldn't stand by and allow this behavior. The tone of his voice was unacceptable. "Let's get something straight right now. Enough with the attitude."

Finn lifted his shoulders in a defiant shrug. "Whatever."

Kit knew she was wasting her breath so there was no point in letting this continue. Her tone changed, now laced with frustration. "Get to bed, it will soon be daylight." It would be useless to get into it tonight.

Finn turned to leave, anxious to escape his mother's wrath. He just wanted to go to bed and avoid further conversation. When she didn't call him back, he felt he'd been given a reprieve. He had sobered enough to know this wasn't over. He knew his mother's anger would only fester.

Cruz felt he had to defend his friend, "I'm worried about Finn. Usually we share everything, but lately he's been withdrawn. He's been like this ever since Uncle Rio didn't return when we did." Cruz handed Kit the keys, "As soon as I saw Finn I knew he was already drunk. I called Daria to come get us so she could drive my truck while I drove Finn's. He kept drinking while we waited for her to arrive. By then, he was wasted."

"Thanks, Cruz. You've aways been a good friend. Please thank Daria for me."

Cruz valued the friendship he had with Finn. "There's nothing to thank me for. Friends take care of each other."

"Bless you, Cruz. I owe you for this."

"Finn's struggling right now. That's what tonight is all about. He's really mad at my uncle." No other explanation was necessary.

Kit could barely breath. A wave of sadness washed over her, replacing her initial anger. She had to ask, "Have any of you heard from Rio?"

Cruz shook his head. He knew his dad was concerned, but he didn't say anything. Nobody could understand why Rio hadn't come back.

Kit's anger toward Rio intensified. Tonight wasn't all Finn's fault. "I hope you aren't driving back to the city."

"No, I talked to mom. We're staying there tonight."

"We all need to get some sleep. Good night."

Cruz was as glad as Finn was to make his escape.

Kit tossed and turned when she went to bed, wondering how Trace would deal with this. She knew he wouldn't let Finn lie around tomorrow. He'd drag him out of bed and work his ass off. Finn wasn't a kid anymore, and he was still living under her roof. Rio had let her son down. Now she was mad at both of them, and she was disappointed with herself for losing her temper in front of Finn's friends. Nothing was right anymore. Feeling like she was a failure, the tears came. It had been a long time since she cried herself to sleep.

Finn groaned when he looked at the clock beside him. His head pounded but he knew better than to roll over. He wondered if his mom was intentionally making a lot of noise in the kitchen to punish him. Knowing he could no longer stall for time, stealing his nerves he left his bedroom and headed downstairs. Not knowing what to expect, he reconciled himself to the fact he'd be subject to his mom's wrath. He could only hope she had settled down since last night, but he doubted it. He was apprehensive as he entered the kitchen. He knew the hearty breakfast, including fried bacon, was to make a point. He held his tongue, but his stomach turned. There was no way he could get food down. He sipped on his coffee.

Kenzie knew exactly what had happened last night and couldn't resist giving her older brother a cheap shot, "You don't look well, Finn. Are you sick?"

Finn was in no mood for her teasing but knew better than to retaliate.

"I'm sure Finn is tired since he had a very late night. Or maybe he had something in the city that didn't agree with him. I don't think we have to be overly concerned. I'm sure it was something he ate or drank, and drank, and drank." Kit's voice was heavy with sarcasm.

Finn's eyes narrowed. "I'm fine," he lied, as he sat there comatose and gray and hungover as hell. He didn't appreciate the sarcasm from either one of them and knew his mom's anger hadn't disappeared.

Kenzie was enjoying herself at her brother's expense. "I think Finn is lying. He looks like crap." Kit was annoyed and amused at the same time, but it didn't lessen her anger towards Finn.

Lola smothered her laugh. Benny didn't get the sarcasm and sat wide-eyed and close-mouthed. He was used to his mom getting mad at him or Kenzie, but never at Finn.

Mealtime remained tense. Finn sat in discomfort enduring his mother's glares. When he couldn't take it anymore, he got up to go to work. Or at least to the barn where he could hide out until he felt better. He knew he wasn't up to training. He wasn't up to anything. He also hoped to avoid his mom's lecture. That was short-lived.

Kit stopped him before he reached the door, "I did not appreciate your attitude last night. You and I will talk after supper." She knew it would be useless to get into it now. She was still too angry.

Great. He knew his behavior was inexcusable. Now he had to worry all day about what she would do for punishment. Finn didn't bother to go in for lunch. It was late afternoon before he felt human again and couldn't believe he had managed to avoid his mother all day. That was probably part of her conniving punishment. He fared better with supper and was able to eat. If he thought breakfast was tense, supper was even worse. He got up as soon as he was done hoping to escape.

Kit motioned for Finn to sit back down. She had no intention of letting this go, "You can just sit there and listen." Finn sat back down while everyone else scattered. Finn braced himself. "I thought you'd be over the rebellious stage by now."

Finn met her gaze with defiance as he attacked back, "I wasn't rebelling."

Kit's temper snapped, "So what the hell was last night all about? You were so drunk you could hardly stand up."

"I thought a drink would help me feel better. It didn't, so I had another. After that I didn't care anymore, but I guess there isn't enough booze to drown the pain because it's still here."

It was the break in Finn's voice that caused Kit to take a deep breath to bring her anger down. Kit made no attempt to hide her disappointment and wasn't sure how to deal with this. Even though his pain stabbed through her heart, parenting had to continue, and unacceptable behavior still resulted in consequences. He may be an adult, but his actions impacted his younger siblings. "For your information, parenting isn't always easy either. You still live under this roof. Kenzie and Benny need to know my rules are the same no matter how old you are. What you did last night was unacceptable. You exercised poor judgement and were irresponsible. Alcohol isn't a way to cope. It didn't change a thing, did it? I realize this is a hard time for us, but life can only beat us up if we let it. We are Graysons. We are strong and we are survivors. There will always be difficulties in our lives. That doesn't change when we're older. We just learn to cope better." Kit watched her son with growing concern because she knew there was more to it than this. "This isn't just about Rio, is it?"

Finn looked his mom squarely in the eyes and replied honestly, "I feel I've been responsible since I was just a kid living with my mom. I'm tired of carrying so much responsibility. I'm physically exhausted."

Kit took a moment, searching for the right words. It was time for a serious talk. "Life changes our lives in unexpected ways. Nobody knows that better than you and me. We have experienced major changes that were out of our control, and we have always survived and moved forward. I think maybe it's time to consider hiring another employee because we need help now. We can no longer keep our lives on pause."

Finn turned to his mom. The pain in his voice was evident as he stated his truth, "I hate Rio for leaving us." He had been turning more and more to Rio, like he used to with his dad. This wasn't the only reason he was missing Rio. It wasn't only the burden of Lola Grande that was weighing on Finn. With Rio gone, Finn had no time to spend with Benny and Kenzie. He wasn't worried about Kenzie. She kept busy with her friends and school activities, but he could see Benny withdrawing more and more.

Kit had managed to bring her anger with Finn under control. Despite hearing the frustration in Finn's voice, Kit continued, "There's nothing I can do about it so you will just have to deal with it. Look, Finn, we don't always know why people do what they do but we still have to try to do our best under the circumstances. What you did last night didn't help any of us."

Finn became very quiet as his guilt surfaced. He knew the stern lecture was deserving. Finn shifted uncomfortably, "You made your point, but nothing makes sense anymore. Not since Dad died."

Kit was troubled by the events of yesterday and she didn't always know what to do either. She felt a twinge of shame as her own guilt was beginning to surface. She knew there were times when she could have handled things better instead of letting her anger get the better of her. She understood Finn's actions, but she couldn't condone it. Finn had to be held accountable for his uncharacteristic behavior. He may be an adult but that didn't change things.

Finn knew he had messed up. He let anger override common sense. He was lucky Cruz was there for him. His own guilt was strong. His behavior last night wasn't fair to his mother. He knew she was also struggling. His hangover was gone but he felt worse than ever knowing he had acted irresponsibly and scared his mother. He leaned forward, his hands between his knees as he hung his head. "I'm sorry I worried you. I know actions always have consequence."

Kit made a decision that was out of character, "You've been suffering enough. We'll chalk yesterday up to experience and bad choices." Kit just hoped he had learned his lesson.

"I'm letting you down."

Kit heard the desolation in Finn's voice. She hesitated before stating, "It's Rio who let us down."

"You're right about that," Finn said bitterly.

Kit decided it was time to talk to her dad. The work at Lola Grande had been barely manageable. Spring was here and the work load had already increased, and they were still short-handed. When Rio was here every day things ran smoothly. Things got done and they didn't need outside help. Decisions were getting difficult. Did they ask her dad for even more help, or did they hire a new employee and count their losses? Rio had promised to help break Bandit, one of their own colts, this spring. Finn had a new client's colt that he would be training as well. Rio had been a handy man to have around, and he was a hard worker. And now he was gone. The ranch required constant attention. Rio knew it was the busiest time of the year, and he still hadn't come back. What the hell was going on with Rio?

The next morning Kit called her dad. Kit appreciated being able to turn to him for help. Like he promised, he was always there for her. He said he'd go check the fences himself and haul feed to the horses. His full-time employees and the newly hired wranglers had their own work to do. Kit was grateful for any help and knew this would get them through the worst of it. At the end of the conversation, he stated the obvious, "It appears that Rio may not return. If he doesn't show up soon you will need another employee."

Kit knew her dad was right. "Why should we wait. We can't keep relying on Valley View for help. Spring is your busiest time just like it is ours. I'll tell Finn we need to start looking." By the time she hung up her gratitude turned back into anger. They should never have been put in this position. Rio should have had the decency to let them know he wasn't coming back.

After supper, Finn headed to the door. "I have to get a few more things done."

"Can I help?"

There was resentment in Finn's tone, "I don't think anybody can." Finn's face darkened due to the fact he was feeling like a failure. He was unable to get everything done even though his days continued to stretch into fifteen-hour work days. He knew his dad always managed so why couldn't he?

"I talked to my dad this morning. I think it's time to admit that Rio isn't coming back, even though he said he was." Promises were broken before. Kit needed to be honest with both of them, "He's been gone too long without a word to anyone." She felt sorry for her son. So much had changed in his life over the years and here they were again faced with another big change. Kit drew a deep breath before saying, "I agree with my dad. I think it's time to look for a replacement." They couldn't keep up with the daily workload.

A weary sigh escaped as Finn nodded reluctantly, knowing they were right.

"It's not the first time we've had to work through a sudden change in our lives. You and I have done this before, and we can do it again. It's just harder when you feel it's because someone you trusted let you down."

Finn hadn't heard such bitterness from his mom since his dad had died. He'd talk to both Riley and Matt to see if they knew of anyone looking for work. Even a part-timer would help. As much as they tried the everyday chores were piling up. Some of the stress lines disappeared from Finn's face but the anger at Rio remained.

Kit also had to accept that Rio wasn't coming back. If he really was gone, they would figure out how to live without him whether they wanted to or not. She refused to slip into depression, but she unknowingly began building her protective shell. She should have known better than to complicate her life with another man. She didn't deserve the heartache.

*****

Seven weeks of being away from Lola Grande was taking a toll on Rio. It had taken too long to settle his dad's estate. Paying off the gambling debts was the easy part. Unfortunately, finalizing his dad's estate was consuming his time. Rio knew his dad had a will, but it was in the house with all their documents, including the deed to the property. The problem was he was denied entry until all outstanding debts were cleared, including the house taxes that were in arrears. He had spent weeks dealing with lawyers and it seemed like no one was in a hurry to obtain the legal documents required so he could gain entry. Problems compounded the delay. He discovered the bank trustee failed to issue a transfer of property, so he had to go to court to have the bank release the certificate. The documents needed to be validated so they could sell the house. This was all causing Rio undue stress. More time and more money. Rio didn't bother Hector with the details since there was nothing he could do.

Every day he kicked himself for forgetting his phone. Had he know how long this was all going to take he would have purchased a new one, but he expected to be back weeks ago. He sighed knowing Finn was probably working too hard with him gone. All of them would be.

Kit was always at the forefront of his mind. Rio admitted his feelings for Kit were much stronger than simple attraction. This was rather surprising since they seemed to be at each other so often. In the beginning it was like every encounter resulted in conflict and he tried ignoring her with little success. Kit was trouble from the get-go. She continually challenged him, but he had learned how to deal with it. Kit irritated and attracted him at the same time. Spending time with Kit, Rio felt himself becoming more enchanted than ever, even though she exasperated him more often than not. Kit was more than beautiful. She was a woman with many fine qualities. She was smart, hard-working, as well as strong-willed and independent. Rio discovered she was intelligent and had a sense of humor to go along with her quick wit. He had also discovered her stubbornness trumped everything. He laughed out loud. That would never change, but his life definitely had. Up until he left he didn't realize there was this void in his life.

A faraway look darkened Rio's eyes. Kit wasn't always easy to understand but Rio guessed that was women in general. The feelings he had for Kit scared him because he never felt anything like this before. He was in love with her but was unclear about her feelings for him. He knew she had feelings for Doc but were those feelings due to years of friendship and comfort? He decided to make his intentions clear to Kit when he got home, and no one was going to get in his way.

Rio remained serious. He knew Kit would never entertain a casual relationship. She would want the full commitment of marriage. He was ready to commit and become a father to her children. Prior to coming to Lola Grande, he didn't really know anything about kids. He'd never spent much time around kids until now. The Grayson children were already a part of his life. Rio was relaxed and at ease with all of the children. Spending time with Kit and her children made him long for a family of his own. This was the family he wanted. He wanted to be a permanent part of their family. Would he be able to fill that role? Yes, he was ready for that role.

The kids were so different. Kenzie was a spitfire who was full of life and loved attention. She was strong-willed like her mother and wanted to exert her independence. Rio liked spending time with Benny, who was a young boy wanting a father figure. He knew he could never fill Trace's shoes, but he wouldn't mind taking on that role. Benny was at such an impressionable age, always curious and eager. Then there was Finn, more man than boy. Rio was ready to settle down in more ways than one. This realization was more comforting than it was disturbing.

Rio faced reality as he returned to the present. Now that the financial part of the estate was settled, he no longer had to stay. His uncle would look after the house until it was sold. He had already finished packing up the personal effects he wanted. A faraway look darkened Rio's eyes. He had promised he would be back soon, and he had expected to keep that promise. He would leave in the morning, but there was still the return drive. He had to focus on that instead of thinking about Kit. Rio wished he were home. He thought of Lola Grande as home.

CHAPTER ELEVEN

Genna and Baxter Rodwell sat beside their daughter's bed. It had been five days since the accident that had resulted in Laurel Easton to be lying in a private room in the Missoula hospital. Their daughter had survived a horrific car accident just north of their ranch in Bitterroot Valley. Even though the accident happened closer to the town of Hamilton, the ambulance took her straight to Missoula because of her head injury. She had slipped into a coma before they arrived at the hospital. The doctor confirmed there was brain activity, but Laurel remained unresponsive.

Genna would never forget the night her husband took the phone call and the nightmare events that followed. According to the police it was a head-on collision caused by the other driver being in Laurel's lane. Due to heavy fog, it was understandable how it happened. Laurel's husband, Sam Easton, their four-year-old daughter, Gracie, and the driver of the other vehicle all died at the scene. Laurel was the only survivor. Nothing could have prepared them for the traumatic news of their massive loss and the comatose state of their daughter.

Genna had remained at her daughter's bedside since the accident, refusing to leave. She needed to be there when her daughter woke up and had to face the fateful facts. Baxter was making the two-hour commute daily because he had to go home at night to tend to things at the ranch. Sitting together in the private hospital room, Genna and Baxter would watch their daughter closely, hoping for any sign of change. Laurel continued to lay there, eyes closed, lifeless. There was never any change.

They couldn't understand why their daughter wasn't waking up. Genna prayed for a miracle. Her faith was a simple faith. It was the one thing that got her through the darkest times, but she was being tested every day. *God, stay with me. I'm feeling overwhelmed and tired, completely overcome with an enormous amount of fear and I'm emotionally exhausted. You are my strength. Do not forsake me now. Please bring our daughter back to us. The accident has taken too much from us already.*

Genna was tired of listening to the endless ticking of the clock behind her. Time passed even slower after Baxter left to go home. The monotonous hours dragged. Genna's head throbbed due to worry and her eyes burned from fatigue. She closed her eyes and nodded off. It was another restless night.

It was early morning when Genna stirred and she managed a weak smile when Baxter walked in. She was glad to see him. He was her strength. Today he was there earlier than usual. "Is everything okay?" Genna frowned. Nothing was okay in their lives since the accident. "Has it warmed up outside?"

"The air is so cold you can see your breath when you exhale. Would you like to take a break now that I'm here?"

Genna shook her head. She couldn't bring herself to leave her daughter's bedside. His wife's somber face was more than Baxter could bear. "I'm going to get a coffee. I'll bring you one and an order of toast."

Genna nodded and watched Baxter leave. She always thought her husband looked like Sam Elliott, the classic image of a western cowboy. Their daughter's accident had aged him. His shoulders now sagged as if he was carrying a heavy load that was draining the life out of him. Genna felt it too. Baxter was struggling because of the deep anguish he carried. He said fathers were supposed to take care of their children and he couldn't make his daughter better. As she waited for his return her thoughts drifted. Genna always wondered what he saw in her. She was never pretty and always a little heavy. Her attraction was her bubbly personality and generous smile she had for everyone. The years had added more weight, and she was what one would kindly describe as plump. Baxter called her cuddly. Short graying hair framed her friendly face that had aged overnight. These days she felt dowdy and tired.

Genna leaned forward and gently caressed her daughter's cheek, wondering when Laurel would open her eyes. She didn't know if her daughter heard her, but she talked to Laurel anyway. "It's time to wake up," pleaded Genna. Laurel didn't stir. Did her daughter even know her husband and daughter had died in the accident? Sam's parents had them cremated but were waiting to hold the funeral until Laurel was discharged from the hospital. This was a traumatic time for all of them.

Genna was distraught when Dr. Nolan Maynard walked in with Baxter. He had been in and out every day since Laurel had been brought in. Genna couldn't hide the concern in her eyes as she turned to the doctor, "Laurel just lies there. Why won't she wake up? Our daughter's life is ticking away."

"Right now, it's like your daughter's brain pressed the pause button. The good news is there is no reason Laurel shouldn't have a full recovery when she does come out of her coma. There is nothing we can do for her right now but wait."

The Rodwells shared an anguished look. The doctor hadn't brought much comfort. The rest of the day passed the same as the day before, nothing changed. Baxter left to go back home, promising to come back as early as he could tomorrow.

The next morning, Genna found herself more restless than usual. She wasn't used to the hustle and bustle around her, both inside and outside the hospital. She was ready to return to their secluded ranch. She walked over to the window that looked out over a large parking lot. People were coming and going, bundled in heavy winter wear. Even though it was early, the lot had already been cleared of the freshly fallen snow from last night and was filling with vehicles, each one representing a story of its own.

She heard the nurse's cart go past the door and turned to God in morning prayer. She prayed for the staff. They were facing each day knowing they would have an impact on people's lives while hoping they were making a difference in their hour of need. *In God's name I pray you give us the strength and compassion to deal with what you have planned for us today. You know how much I'm struggling, I fear the unknown and I'm angry that this happened, Please give me the courage to endure and accept whatever your plan is. I continue to wait for you to answer my prayers. Please let Laurel wake up.*

When she was finished praying, Genna sensed a change in Laurel and looked over to see her daughter's eyes were open and looking at her, but they had no life in them. Even though she was awake she hadn't spoken so Genna had no idea when she came out of her coma. Genna rang for the nurse, not knowing what to do. Within minutes the doctor arrived. Baxter was right behind him.

Dr. Maynard studied his patient closely, "I'm glad to see you're finally awake. How do you feel?" When Laurel turned her head, the movement caused her head to throb and for a moment the room spun around her, and her body ached all over. Getting no verbal response, Dr. Maynard frowned and turned to the Rodwells, "I would like the two of you to leave while I examine your daughter. I'll join you when we're done."

Genna and Baxter retreated into the corridor to sit in the empty chairs in the hall. Genna reached for her husband. They held hands as they waited while the minutes dragged by.

Laurel was confused as she watched them leave. *Why am I here and what happened?* With effort, she attempted to focus her thoughts. As the numbness slowly ebbed, harsh reality took its place. The fog in her head cleared and she began to remember. Laurel stared into space as memories took over. She and Gracie were excited because they were picking Daddy up at the Missoula airport. Dr. Sam Easton was a doctor who sometimes worked for Doctors Without Borders, an organization he strongly believed in. They provided humanitarian medical care to areas in conflict or in countries affected by epidemic diseases. He had volunteered before, but this was the first time since they had their daughter. Laurel wasn't pleased even though Sam had only committed until they could find a permanent replacement for the doctor who had taken ill. The week before he was to fly home he called with upsetting news. Laurel was shocked when he said he was extending his tour for another three months which took him into the new year. The relieving doctor's arrival was delayed due to a family crisis and Sam felt he couldn't abandon his team. Laurel strongly supported Sam and his dedication, but she believed he could have said no, and they would have brought in someone else. Her disappointment was taken over by anger. It upset her that he chose not to be home for Christmas with his family but what upset her more was that there was no discussion. He made his decision without talking to her first. It was another case where his wants came first with no regard to his family. This added to an already strained marriage. Her parents offered to postpone Christmas, but Laurel declined. Vengeance may have been a minor factor in her decision, but it was more about Gracie. Christmas was so commercial, and it was everywhere, and Gracie was at an age that it was meaningful to her. It wouldn't be the same as celebrating it by themselves when Sam was back home. Even Sam's parents supported her decision.

Sam, Laurel, and Gracie lived with Laurel's parents at their ranch. Because of Sam's dedication to volunteering and unusual hours, it made sense to live in the renovated wing in her parent's expansive home. Laurel and her parents had always been close, so it was a comfortable arrangement.

Laurel hated driving in winter because the weather could be so unpredictable, but luck was on her side. The sky was overcast but the roads were clear. She made good time, and her heartbeat quickened when she saw Sam waiting for her at the designated pillar. Laurel knew she would have to give Sam time to adjust to being home again, but big decisions had to be made moving forward. It was time to commit to their marriage and focus on their family. She also wanted to have another child.

As excited as Sam was to see them, Laurel could see he was exhausted, so she offered to drive home. Sam gratefully climbed into the passenger seat. Even before they got out of the city both Sam and Gracie had fallen asleep. Laurel was glad once she was through Hamilton, now it was only a short drive home. A few miles down the road, Laurel was surprised at how quickly the weather changed and it was miserable. A troubling wind had sprung up and the fog was beginning to roll in. At first it was a patch now and then, but she knew it was always denser in the coulee. It quickly closed in and surrounded her, and the visibility was almost nil. It was eerie quiet. Laurel felt her chest tighten and suddenly there was a horrible bang and then silence. Laurel had no recollection beyond the moment of impact.

Laurel lay in a state of shock as she closed her eyes to shut out the fragmented images now floating through her mind. She shook her head to escape the visions that kept disappearing into the fog. Aware of the heavy silence in the room, she shut her eyes tight. *I'm in a bad dream. Dense fog keeps closing in around me and consumes me. I'm in a living nightmare.* She tried to cry out but there was only silence. Her memory became as foggy as the night of the accident. Then there was only darkness as she felt the room close in around her.

Dr. Maynard took her hand, pulling her back to the present, "I'm going to bring your parents back in." The doctor's face was unreadable when he approached the Rodwells. Dr. Maynard sat down beside them, "Physically, your daughter is fine, however, she won't speak. Instead, she has retreated into herself. The human psyche is very delicate. I believe she is suffering from traumatic mutism which I believe in Laurel's case is a coping mechanism. I would like her to remain in the hospital today for observation."

Baxter's jaw tightened as he and Genna shared a confused look.

Dr. Nolan didn't want to give them false hope, "When someone comes out of a coma and we recognize traumatic mutism, it usually lasts only a few days, but there have been cases where it has lasted for months. It's not that she's refusing to speak, she may feel physically unable to speak. I'm sure this is temporary, but I can't tell you when Laurel will speak. It's up to her so all we can do now is wait. We will do a few tests and monitor her throughout the day. I know this has been a shock. I suggest you both go home and get a decent night's sleep. I'll check Laurel again tomorrow morning and if we don't find anything wrong and nothing else changes she will be discharged."

They stared at the doctor in disbelief. Nothing he said made any sense, but they were now fully aware of the severity of the accident. Genna's face crumbled and Baxter dropped his head into his hands. They had been completely tormented by the news.

"She seems to have some recall of what happened, but we don't know how much she remembers. We have to give her time."

Baxter could only stare at the doctor. Genna's words came out in an anguished whisper as she asked, "How can we help her?" They were both experiencing the same fear and uncertainty.

The doctor took a few minutes and explained what to expect, keeping it simple. He answered their questions about medication and told them to call his office to set up a follow-up appointment when she regained her speech. Baxter closed his own eyes tight when Genna broke down crying. Baxter's heart twisted painfully as he pulled Genna into his arms. His family was his life. He turned away, not wanting her to see his look of despair. Once they had composed themselves they returned to Laurel's room. Not knowing what Laurel remembered, Genna took her daughter's hand. "There's something we need to tell you."

Laurel didn't respond, she just lay their lifeless. Whether it was the tone of her mother's voice or another moment of clarity, she knew her husband and daughter had died. The events of the accident remained jumbled in her head, but the reality was clear. The cold look she gave them was frightening. There was nothing to say. Sorry wouldn't help. The dull pounding in her head intensified. She closed her eyes, overcome by sadness while filled with an incredible sense of emptiness. A vital part of Laurel died too. Suddenly more memories assaulted her, and they hurt more than the impact of the other vehicle. She willed herself to block out the images as she struggled to deal with the onslaught of emotions. She lay motionless, fraught with guilt. *I killed my family.* She didn't know the accident wasn't her fault.

They stared down at their daughter's tormented face. Without Laurel saying a word, they knew she knew. Such a tragic time. Just then the doctor entered with the nurse to begin their tests. Baxter and Genna said their goodbyes and left. Hopefully, they would bring their daughter home tomorrow.

The next day Genna and Baxter were at the hospital early but were asked to wait until after the doctor completed his rounds before going in to see Laurel. Knowing it would be at least an hour, the nurse at the desk suggested they go down to the cafeteria. More waiting. There was nothing they could do so they returned to the elevators. The doctor was coming out of Laurel's room when they returned.

"Based on the test results, there is nothing further we can do for Laurel. I have told her about her discharge, so she has had a few minutes to adjust to the thought of going home. As I told you yesterday, everyone deals with a traumatic experience in their own way. I think it would be best not to mention the accident until Laurel's ready to talk about it. Laurel can't seem to communicate verbally so I suggested she start a journal."

As glad as they were to be taking their daughter home, the Rodwells were filled with confusion. "We don't know what she's thinking or what she actually remembers, so how do we help her?"

"Try to live your lives as normal as possible and try not to treat her any differently. There will be two prescriptions you can pick up on your way out. One is for pain, the other is for sleeping pills in case she has trouble sleeping at night. I sincerely hope you see a positive change in Laurel when she gets home. It may be the trigger she needs for her to talk."

Genna couldn't hide her concern, "I don't know if she will be able to cope; she's still so fragile." She prayed they would be granted the strength to get through these trying days. For now, all they could offer Laurel was supportive sympathy.

They thanked the doctor and returned to Laurel's room. Genna had brought fresh clothes from home and helped Laurel to dress. Laurel was so pale it only emphasized the dark shadows under her eyes. "Are you ready to go." With a gesture of resignation, Laurel nodded.

The drive home was silent and not due to Laurel's mutism. Baxter and Genna were also silent, anxious about how Laurel would react when she got home. Due to her delicate state and being confined indoors for days, Laurel was a mere shell of herself. She found the clear blue sky too bright and the traffic too loud as they headed out of the city. Laurel dreaded going home. There would be no Sam or Gracie to greet her. She had killed them. She was a widow and no longer a mother. The throbbing in her head intensified as they turned off the road and drove up to the main house. Nothing had changed. Gracie's little bike she had been riding before they left to pick up her daddy was parked next to the garage. Laurel should have felt something, but there was only numbness. Nothing seemed real. Genna felt bad. She should have moved it out of sight. Baxter parked in the drive and grabbed Laurel's overnight bag and followed the women into the house. Genna and Baxter could only imagine how difficult this was for their daughter.

Deep emotions flowed through Laurel as she entered, and her dark thoughts followed her in. Silence encompassed her. *The house is deadly quiet. Pun intended. Reality at its cruelest.* On her way to her room, she had to pass by her daughter's room. Laurel closed Gracie's door without going in. Her dad had already taken her overnight bag up to her room. Laurel took it off the bed, placed in in the closet and climbed into bed. Feeling hopeless and empty, she was too emotionally exhausted to cope. A wave of depression washed over her. The haunted look was back. *I deserve to be confined to a life of silence, endless purgatory while confined to my room.* Unknowingly, she had sentenced herself based on her guilt. Mental and emotional fatigue set in. That's where she stayed for the next two days. She would have stayed there forever but she had a funeral to go to.

*****

The funeral for Sam and Gracie was difficult for all of them. The sight of Gracie's ceramic urn next to her dad's was heartbreaking for everyone in attendance. Laurel sat like a statue during the service and remained dry-eyed and lifeless.

The Rodwell family chose not to attend the Celebration of Life. The Easton family took Sam and Gracie's ashes to be buried in the local cemetery next to Sam's grandparents. There was closure for Sam's family. None for the Rodwells as they took their daughter home. Their daughter didn't deserve this, but it didn't change the facts. Their only daughter was a widow, and they were all she had left. Laurel wasn't the only one who had lost something precious. Her parent's loss and grief only contributed to the tremendous guilt Laurel already felt.

Genna tried to comfort Laurel when they got home. "Sometimes it's difficult to see past our grief. It will take time to adjust but you will learn to live without them. God doesn't give us sorrow without the strength to bear it."

Laurel's eyes filled with a silent plea, *Leave me alone!* She turned and walked away. Laurel heard her mom call her back, but she ignored her and fled. As soon as she was in her room, Laurel put her wedding ring in her jewelry box. It could stay locked away with the rest of her life. She was numb as she lay on her bed staring into space. She couldn't escape the misery that continued to overwhelm her, while guilt remained her constant companion. Laurel shook her head to escape the dark visions. It didn't help.

Genna went to check on her daughter and found her curled up in her bed. It hurt her to see her like this. Genna sat down next to Laurel and stroked her hair. Laurel rolled over so her back was to her mom. No words were necessary. Genna got up and left and went looking for Baxter. When she found him in his office, an open bottle of Jack Daniels sat on his desk in front of him. Suddenly it was too much for Genna and she broke down.

Baxter rose and took her into his arms. Both parents were at a loss as to how to help their daughter. They were still dazed by what happened.

As soon as her mom left, Laurel got up and crossed over to where she had thrown her overnight bag. She opened it and pulled out the journal her mother had bought. Dr. Maynard said it might help if she wrote down her thoughts and feelings. She would try anything to rid herself of the pain. She grabbed her journal and began to write.

My name is Laura Easton, and this is my journal. I was married to Sam Easton, a gifted doctor. We had a beautiful daughter named Gracie, who was only four. She was innocent, adorable, and full of life. I killed them. This is unbearable. I cannot speak of the unthinkable, a life without Sam and Gracie. This cannot be undone. They are gone forever. I'm guilty of taking the lives of others. I should have died with them. I'm dead inside. That's fair. I won't allow myself to cry. There are not enough tears to drown my sorrow. I can't shut out the pain that tries to fill the emptiness inside me. My world keeps closing in around me like the heavy fog, bringing back flashbacks of dark memories. I want to scream but I know if I start I won't stop. I can't ask for forgiveness, so I have nothing to say. I can't deal with my life anymore. I can't escape. This is too hard to live with. I wish I were dead.

Laurel shut the journal and put it in her nightstand. The gathering darkness outside her window reflected her mood. She sat in the chair beside the window and looked out into the darkness. She was filled with an incredible sense of emptiness and the familiar ache came. Laural was once a devoted wife and a loving mother. Now she was neither. This was her reality. Giving into fatigue, she climbed into bed. Laurel refused to take the sleeping pills the doctor had prescribed for her. She lay staring at the ceiling as sleep continued to deny her an escape from her reality. *Mom says it helps to pray. Now I lay me down to sleep, I pray the Lord my soul to keep. If I should die before I wake, my prayers have been answered. I want to die. Oh, God, please let me die.*

Laurel closed her eyes bringing the darkness she deserved. The light had gone out of her life. Finally, sleep came.

CHAPTER TWELVE

L ife had changed for all of the Rodwells. It was evident every day now that they were home. The days passed slowly as life remained strained. Laurel wasn't the only one suffering. Knowing this was a period of adjustment, Genna and Baxter tried to remain positive, but they were having their own difficulties coping. No matter how difficult this was they were grateful their daughter survived but Genna was concerned. Laurel hadn't stepped outside her room since she had returned home except to attend the funeral. Genna kept praying for a miracle as she continued to turn to her faith in prayer. *Please heal Laurel within, help her overcome the fears that are preventing her from recovering her voice. Grant me the patience to be there for her and Baxter. He struggles in silence, but he needs your help even though he may not ask for it. Guide me through my own challenges.*

Physically, Laurel was fine. Mentally, she was lost in her own fog. She remained lifeless, an empty shell with no spark of life. Laurel had fallen into a deep depression and couldn't find her way out. The accident had killed Laurel's natural exuberance. It had been buried along with her family. She had no purpose so there was no reason to get up. It was just another empty day, and she couldn't fill the emptiness. The shadows under her eyes weren't as dark but her eyes remained dull and haunted. She remained distant and spent her time alone in her room, unable to deal with the grief that continued to torment her. There was no escaping the dark memories that haunted, the guilt that suffocated. Her room, once her sanctuary, was now her prison. She had given herself a life sentence so remained locked away. Her numbness was slowly ebbing, making room for more guilt. At least in her room, she didn't have to see the despondent looks on her parent's faces.

Genna and Baxter Rodwell had always had a close and comfortable relationship, but Laurel's accident had taken a toll on them as well. They were struggling through every passing day. Genna was more irritable than usual, "Do you realize we no longer talk normally. We've taken to whispering between us, so we don't upset our daughter. We have to go back to living our lives like we did before the accident."

Baxter had to agree but didn't know how, so he tried to excuse Laurel's behavior, "Laurel is still having a difficult time."

Genna had reached her limit of empathy. Her voice was resentful, "We all are, and we are continuing to live in her nightmare. She doesn't care that this is affecting us, so things are going to change starting right now." She went and knocked on Laurel's door. Knowing there would be no response she went in. Laurel was still in bed. The emotions of the last couple of weeks caused Genna to lose control and snap at her daughter, "You can't keep spending all your time alone in this room. Starting today you will join us for every meal. I suggest you shower and get dressed and be downstairs for breakfast in fifteen minutes. Bad things happen that we have no control over. This is something that will not go away and life still goes on. You have no choice but to face the challenge of a different life. You have always been a strong woman and you still are so pull yourself together."

Laurel knew her mom was right, but she had fallen into a dark place. She felt she deserved nothing better than to imprison herself in her room.

"We have all had a hard time since the accident. The accident wasn't your fault, and you survived for a reason." This was the first time anyone had mentioned the accident. Genna turned and left.

Hearing the anguish in her mother's voice had affected Laurel, but it didn't change anything, so the guilt remained. *Of course it was my fault. I was driving. I survived because God is cruel.* She turned over and remained in her room.

The next morning Laurel joined her parents for breakfast. Hunger pangs motivated Laurel to leave her room. Her mother had been true to her word, so Laurel hadn't eaten since yesterday. Genna was glad to see Laurel had showered and washed her hair. She looked better but her expression was hostile. Genna's remained unsympathetic. She was grateful to see any change in her daughter.

*****

Genna's faith was being tested every day and she continually prayed for the strength to endure. She thought it would get easier. She thought she was prepared for this, but she didn't know what to do anymore. Even though Laurel now joined them for meals, it didn't make things better. In fact, it added tension around the table. They ate in silence. They did everything in silence. Genna felt like she was walking on egg shells, always choosing her words so she wouldn't upset Laurel or Baxter. Genna understood the magnitude of Laurel's loss, but she couldn't understand why she refused to talk.

As soon as the meal was over, Laurel got up to go to her room. Even though Laurel hated it when she and her mom fought, it didn't stop her. She had learned to fight back in a different way. Her fights weren't verbal, but she knew how much it hurt her mother when she walked away. She knew she wasn't just punishing herself when she escaped to her room.

It had been a more trying morning than usual for Genna. It was disheartening knowing it would be another day of silence. It only frustrated Genna more. Unable to hold her temper, she erupted in anger, "Enough is enough. Speak to us. There's no reason you can't. You can't keep shutting us out. Are you doing this to punish us?" If it was possible, it became even quieter in the room. Genna was tired of the quiet. "Your father and I have had enough. He may hide his grief but it's there. That's why he leaves the house all the time." Suddenly it was too much. This time Genna was the one who went to her room and closed her door.

Her mother's actions shocked Laurel who was used to her mom's calm nature. Her mom's actions just now hurt her, and she realized it was the first time she felt anything for someone else since returning home. Today had shaken her but it didn't change the facts. She had killed her family. This was her reality, and it wouldn't change. Laurel chose to remain isolated and silent in her shroud of guilt.

Once Genna calmed down she went to Laurel's room. She had spent every day encouraging Laurel to talk to no avail and got right to the point, "I know this hasn't been easy for you. It hasn't been easy for us either. The gift of life is often taken for granted until it's almost taken from you. Sam and Gracie died, you didn't. You are still here by the grace of God. You survived for a reason. God doesn't give us sorrow without the strength to bear it. We just have to pray for his help and guidance. I'm going to get groceries. Would you like to come along? It will do you good to get out of the house." Genna knew the answer before Laurel shook her head. Their daughter had no interest in life.

It had been a difficult day. Her mom's strong words still hurt, but Laurel was unable to pull herself away from her dark thoughts. Laurel couldn't accept what happened, and she couldn't deal with the fact that it was her fault. How could she be expected to pick up the pieces of her life. Guilt had such a firm hold. Laurel continued to struggle with her grief and the familiar ache came over her. That night she opened the bedside drawer and grabbed her journal.

Writing in my journal is supposed to help. It isn't working. I wake up every morning to face another day of misery. I feel numb, petrified, and always guilty. They say bad memories fade in time. That may be true, but guilt never goes away. A hundred years from now won't change the fact that I killed my family and destroyed all of our lives.

I know this has been difficult for my parents. I know their sadness. By locking myself away, Mom and Dad don't have to hide their heartache and disappointment from me. In one day, I destroyed their lives by taking the lives of others. More guilt to carry to my grave.

I know Mom keeps praying for me. She prays for everyone. Why? What good does it do? To be honest, I'm sick and tired of Mom's praying. God allowed this. I want nothing to do with him. Why would a loving God be so cruel? She tells me to keep praying. Fine. I pray tonight I will close my eyes and there will be no tomorrow. I don't deserve to live. I should have died along with the others. But life goes on whether I want it to or not. As I said, God is cruel.

*****

Genna was feeling beaten down and today it was more than she could cope with. She was tired of being strong for everyone. Not knowing how to deal with it anymore, Genna called Dr. Maynard's office and made an appointment for herself, and he agreed to see her right away. Laurel

Easton's case was one he had never dealt with before and it was still an open file.

Dr. Maynard greeted her warmly. Expecting a positive update, he was disappointed when Genna confessed in anguish, "I thought Laurel would have talked by now, but she hasn't spoken a word. There is no communication at all other than a nod or a shake of her head and the occasional indifferent stare. At first she wouldn't get out of bed, then she wouldn't leave her room. Now I insist she have her meals with us but as soon as she's done she heads back to her room where she spends most of her day. She's become reclusive. She's not coping; she's escaping. I feel she has locked herself away in more ways than one. Why is she still like this? You said she would recover sooner than this. Why won't she speak?" Genna's eyes glistened with unshed tears. "None of us can live with this unhappy lifestyle and be okay. There must be something more you can do," Genna pleaded.

"As I explained to you and your husband, Laurel's trauma is an emotional response to the distressing experience of a terrible event. In Laurel's case, we know it's a result of the accident. She's working through her inner struggle. Has she been writing in her journal?"

"How would I know, she hasn't said anything. I'm sorry. I know sarcasm isn't the answer, but Baxter and I are so frustrated. I believe she is writing."

"You may find it hard to believe but that is a very positive step for Laurel." That gave Genna a glimmer of hope. "If she hasn't regained her full memory, she may still think the accident was her fault."

"Should we go into details with her?"

"No. Her recovery can't be forced. She needs time to deal with the accident itself and with what she lost. I know it seems like it has been a long time but in reality it hasn't. Healing of the mind often takes longer than healing of the body. Give her more time."

Genna looked at the doctor with distressing eyes, "Her continuous withdrawing has made this extremely difficult. Day after day, nothing changes. Laurel never leaves the property even though I invite her to go with me. How can she function in the real world when she has no desire to do anything?"

"Laurel is either punishing herself by confining herself to her room or she feels that's her safe place. As we discussed before, there is nothing you can do but be there to support her. Nothing will change until she is ready. Laurel is afraid of something, and it's holding her back. It's still an ongoing struggle for her, but life won't allow her to stay locked away. Something will trigger her, and you will have your daughter back. Laurel is going to be all right. I promise."

Genna's doubts remained as she left his office. She knew she had to be strong, but she was tired of being strong. On her way home she pulled into the first church she saw. She couldn't go home yet. She entered and sat in an empty pew. It was times like this that it didn't matter how old you are you wish you could talk to your mother. Her mom had been gone for years but today she felt her mother's presence and a sense of calmness settled over her. Her thoughts drifted to happy times filled with happier memories. She remained lost in those memories for a long time. Finding peace, she knelt down and prayed, once again relying on her faith.

When Genna got home the house was quiet. It was always quiet. She found Baxter in his office staring into space. "You were gone a long time. What did Dr. Maynard have to say?" They knew they could talk freely since Laurel was in her room like usual.

Genna's troubled eyes met his and she shook her head sadly, "I have nothing new to report. Dr. Maynard says Laurel will talk when she's ready, but he is surprised it hasn't happened. He said to give it time and assured me Laurel is going to be fine. There's nothing he can do, so now it's up to us. We've been at a loss for months, but something has to change."

Baxter's own frustration surfaced because he was unable to help his family. "What exactly do you suggest we do? We can't force her to speak. Let's do what the doctor said and give her more time."

Genna couldn't hide the resentment in her voice. "How much time do we give her?"

"As much as she needs." Baxter didn't know what else to say.

"You don't understand how hard this is," Genna retaliated, unable to keep the dejected tone from her voice. She had taken offense to Baxter's casual response.

"Of course I do. It's just as hard on me." He turned to leave. When Baxter couldn't deal with things he would escape to the barn or go chat with Darius, their long-time hired hand.

Genna had no escape. She could no longer hold back her frustration, "Fine, walk out like you've done ever since this happened while I spend every day in this house living with the silence." She hated what was happening to this family. It was hard to live with the unhappiness that surrounded them every day. It was wearing on all of them. "Laurel hasn't come to terms with anything, and I don't believe it can happen here. I think a change of location will give Laurel what she needs to heal. We can't make this go away, but we can change things by moving."

Baxter's response was louder than he intended, "What the hell, Genna, did you lose your mind on the way home?"

"No, I found a possible solution instead so you can listen to me instead of leaving."

When Laurel heard her parents raised voices she stepped into the hallway hoping to hear what they were talking about. She'd never heard them speak to each other like this. As surprised as she was by their conversation, it didn't matter what they decided. It made no difference to her. Besides, what choice did she have. She had put them in this position. There was no change of expression on Laurel's face as she stepped back into her room.

A shadow crossed Baxter's eyes as he heard the despair in Genna's voice. He wasn't used to any type of comeback from his wife. It showed the stress she was under. He had been surprised by her outburst but knew she was right.

With annoying insistence, Genna continued, "Every day is overshadowed by what happened. There is too much sadness here. Sam's family said they didn't blame Laurel for the accident, but they did. They severed all ties with our family the day of the funeral. It's time for happiness, but it isn't here. Are you happy, Baxter?"

Nobody was happy anymore. Baxter threw her an exasperated look and shook his head.

"Give it some thought." Life as it was no longer existed for them. None of them could live with the unhappiness that surrounded them every day and be okay.

Baxter gave his wife a concerned look. "I can't believe you actually think moving will help?" He was unable to keep the irritation out of his voice. "Moving won't change anything."

"How will we know unless we try. Staying here certainly hasn't changed anything. Laurel seems to just get worse. Her eyes always have that haunted look, and she doesn't care about anything anymore."

"We have to be strong."

"I'm tired of being strong. I think it is time to make a change." She gave her husband a pleading look which he couldn't ignore. "God is guiding us. He has a plan, so we have to have faith."

God isn't listening. "Moving would be life-changing for all of us. Can Laurel handle another change?"

"She isn't handling her life now. This gives us hope." Genna started to cry. Everything seemed hopeless. "I keep praying to God for his guidance. With his help we will know what to do. We'll know when it's right."

"If it's right." Baxter saw no reason to move.

"We just have to keep praying."

Baxter was unable to hide his frustration, "Go ahead." *It hasn't helped so far,* thought Baxter, but said nothing. He'd given up praying. The silence between them was heavy. It had been an intense conversation. "I'm going out and I'm not escaping. I need time to think about this." Baxter turned and left. He needed to talk to Darius about the possibility of moving. He hoped Genna hadn't gotten her hopes up.

The hurt faded from Genna's face, now replaced with optimism. She went into the office and typed in, "Rural Listings in Alberta, Canada". She had felt her mother's presence ever since she stopped to pray in the church and believed this was the path to follow.

His agreement appeased his wife for now, but Baxter knew this wasn't the end of it. He needed to gather his own information on a few things. Baxter let out a heavy sigh and went to find Darius. A move would affect him too. Baxter found Darius mucking the stables. "I have something to tell you."

"Yes, Sir?" Darius had always addressed Baxter formally and Genna was always Ma'am. It was different with Laurel. He had called her Missy since the day they brought her home from the hospital, and it was so endearing that no one ever asked him to call her by her given name.

Baxter explained that due to their current situation they were considering selling the ranch and moving. "It will be life-changing, but you are welcome to come with us."

"My life changed before, it can change again." The Rodwells had been a part of his life from the day Baxter brought him home to the ranch. This was his family. He had severed his ties with his own family and lifestyle many years ago. There had been no contact with them since the day he left because he was considered a defector. "I have no family here." His voice was flat, without expression. Darius had never talked about his family and never considered returning to the Hutterite colony after he left.

"So, it's settled. If we decide to move, you will come with us." Darius nodded. There was nothing else to say. Baxter recalled the day he met Darius. The boy was walking along the shoulder of the highway. He stopped to pick him up and give him a ride to his colony. Baxter wasn't surprised when he said he had just defected and wouldn't be going back. He was still clean-shaven, so Baxter knew he wasn't married. He also knew the youth would be overwhelmed in the real world, so he offered to take Darius home with him until they could decide what to do. Darius never left and lived with them since he was fifteen. Darius was more family than an employee, living year-round in the bunkhouse. He managed the horses and would oversee the part-time employees who were brought in during busy times.

It took time before Darius would open up about colony life and his decision to leave. His colony was a highly structured society that was devoutly religious. The older children were allowed to attend high school, but Darius knew that once he graduated he would continue to live a lifestyle of submission and his role in the colony would be assigned. Their colony farmed, raised livestock, and produced manufactured goods for sustenance. All members were provided for equally. Boys worked from a very young age, learning their place in the colony. Men had more privileges than women as well as more obligations. Each adult was assigned their responsibility. For years, the Hutterites did not trust the outside world and often feared it. Over the last couple of decades there was increased exposure to the outside world. His colony welcomed new technology to maintain state-of-the-art operations with computerized equipment. Darius knew a life on the colony was not for him. Most often it was the young men who defected. Being an intelligent young boy who was curious about life, he became unhappy with the communal lifestyle, so he chose to transition to the outside world. He knew he would miss his family but not the lifestyle.

Baxter spent the rest of the day wandering around the ranch deep in thought, ending up in the secluded area behind the house. It had always been his personal place of refuge from the time he was a boy. This was his home, passed down to him from parents who had settled here and put down permanent roots. Baxter knew Genna couldn't understand the emotional conflict he was facing. He had to simplify his thoughts and wrap his head around moving. They wouldn't be changing their lifestyle, just their location. Genna said there was nothing holding them here. His wife was wrong. This was the only home he knew, the place where he was raised. The place where Laurel and her brother Cameron were raised, and where Gracie had lived her short life. Cameron had made his own life based on his career and now lived with his family in Florida.

Baxter wasn't concerned about selling their own ranch. Their neighbor, Neville Iverson, had expressed interest several times. His offers were becoming very tempting; even more so considering their lives were in shambles since the accident. Maybe a dramatic change was what they needed. This was a lot to think about.

*****

Baxter was sitting in his recliner with his eyes closed. "Are you okay, Baxter?" Genna wasn't sure if he was awake since he never napped during the day.

"Just taking a break," he answered, but didn't open his eyes.

Genna was concerned as she returned to the kitchen where she puttered until she heard him stir. When she went back in, she had a tray with tea and cookies.

Baxter gave his wife a skeptical look, "Are you trying to butter me up?"

"Yes, I need to talk to you." She went over and got her iPad and sat next to him. "Don't interrupt until you hear me out. Traumatic events test our faith, but I have never stopped praying for a miracle. I think my prayers have been answered. When I saw this listing and read the listing details I knew it was an omen when the word laurel popped out."

Baxter looked at his wife in disbelief, "For God's sake, Genna, it's in Alberta. That would be a dramatic move considering we live in the state of Montana. You are talking about moving to a whole new country. It's an extreme move."

Genna was prepared for his reaction. "I told you not to interrupt and don't be close-minded. I did some research when I saw this listing and they referenced the laurel trees. The spiritual meaning of laurel is a strong spirit that reminds one of their strength and desires. It encourages us to continue believing in ourselves. The laurel is considered a lucky plant that balances emotion, and the leaves attract happiness and prosperity into the home."

"I can see the owners have incorporated the laurel shrubs around the gazebo." The hedge made an effective private screen. She knew it would minimize the noise and wind and provide year-round interest for the surrounding gardens. She had grown up hearing about the fragrance of the laurel leaves in the air. Genna loved to garden and could see all sorts of possibilities to beautify the landscape. "Our daughter was named Laurel in honor of my family. It's a sign, Baxter. I know this will be the place that heals her."

"You and your signs." Baxter didn't believe in such things.

"This is the perfect place. It's located in south-western Alberta, close to where my grandparents homesteaded. It looks like a piece of paradise." She clicked on the video so they could view the property. Horses grazed in fenced pastures, the grass thick and green, a majestic mountain range in the distance. The horse facility was impressive. "The view is breathtaking. You can see forever. There's even a stream that runs through the property where willow trees stand tall along the bank." The stately home looked exquisite, but it had a look of being cold and impersonal. Genna was sure it was due to being vacant.

"This would be a huge move. Transporting the horses alone would take a lot of work on both sides. There is a lot more to consider than just the physical move itself."

Genna reached over and grabbed the binder next to her. She had done research on obtaining permanent residency and had contacted the listing realtor who had provided a list of contacts for organizations, family doctors in the areas and a recommended veterinarian.

Baxter wasn't surprised but definitely impressed. Obviously, Genna had been on a mission for days. She had done a lot of research to back her case to move to this location.

"We can leave everything bad behind."

"We will also be leaving Cameron and his family behind."

Genna shook her head, it wasn't an issue. "We see Cameron and his family only a couple of times a year, if that." Their son had taken a corporate job a few years ago and a promotion resulted in a relocation to Miami. They were settled there but there was no guarantee that he wouldn't relocate again. A move oversees was always a possibility.

Baxter looked over the listing in greater detail. He had to admit the property was stunning. "The horse facilities are extraordinary, but we'll be cutting back on our stock if we move. We would only transport our personal horses. Neville wants to buy the rest of our stock if we sell to him."

This told Genna he was listening. Feeling encouraged, she continued, "I do understand this would be a big change and we don't know how Laurel will respond. We can only hope we make the right decision."

Baxter continued to point out obstacles, "It won't be easy."

"Do you think it's been easy here since the accident? Besides, our lives changed months ago. They changed the day of the accident."

Genna's somber face was more than Baxter could bear. He couldn't resist the silent plea in her eyes. The accident had already resulted in big changes. What was one more if it would help their daughter? He would do anything for his wife and daughter. "I'll call Neville and see if he still wants to buy our place. If he does, and we can work out a deal, you can contact the listing realtor for more information."

Genna felt the stirring of hope. She strongly believed a change was necessary or their daughter would be lost to them forever. They would work out the challenges and learn to deal with the changes.

A few minutes later, Baxter called Genna from the kitchen. He had just gotten off the phone. "I spoke with Neville, and he will purchase our ranch."

"Why does he want our property so bad?"

"The location is ideal for what he has planned. They want to expand their own ranch. With the addition of ours with the horse facilities they would be able to provide an all-inclusive adventure for getaway vacations.

By the last phase, it will offer a choice of daily events for weekend getaways or full vacation packages. When they are done it will also be run as a Bed and Breakfast. Their son and his family will live in our home and run the business. Horseback riding and trail rides will became part of the vacation packages. They want to offer their guests a true experience to the western way of life, an exhilarating experience in the great outdoors. Guests can explore the countryside that offers some of the best scenic views. They plan on making major changes to our ranch, but I guess they can do whatever they want once they own it."

"There will be big changes ahead for all of us." A profound statement from Genna. She felt a surge of optimism. She place her hand gently on Baxter's cheek, "Fate is a powerful force. So is faith."

*****

Once their own purchase was completed they renamed the Alberta listing, Willow Downs, because of all the willow trees surrounding it. Due to the preliminary work by Genna the purchase went smoothly, and they applied for permanent residency. They were in the system, and everything was moving forward.

Baxter was feeling better about the move. "I spoke with Dr. Jim Parker, the local veterinarian. He gave me a few sites to check out on how to move forward to bring the horses across the border. Once I have more details about the date of the move, I will call him again. He said he'll come out to the ranch the day after we arrive to check the horses."

With a note of encouragement, Genna shared more about their plans with Laurel, "You know my mom's family homesteaded in Alberta. She moved to the United States when she married my dad, but she would often tell us stories about growing up there. She'd tell me about the laurel trees and their beautiful fragrance. You were named Laurel because of her stories. I'm excited to move back to Alberta. The ranch we bought is close to our original homestead. When the listing included a reference to the laurel trees in the description I knew it was a sign." Genna's voice softened, "We think it's too difficult for you here. Of course, even if we move there will be difficult adjustments to make."

Laurel got up and walked away. She had her own thoughts that she needed to express in her journal.

My parents are doing everything and anything to prove they love me. I don't know how they can still love me. Mom says we're moving to Alberta. Rather drastic if you ask me. They don't get it. How will moving somewhere else make things better? It doesn't matter where we live. Nothing matters anymore. I shut myself away to shut out the pain, but it follows me. I can't escape this nightmare. There is nowhere to hide from the pain. Moving won't change that. It will follow me, but I am glad we're moving away from here. My future is bleak. I have to face my future alone. There's no Sam. There's no Gracie. And there sure as hell is no God.

CHAPTER THIRTEEN

Kit usually welcomed Maggie when she dropped by. They had been best friends for years and had helped each other through more than one crisis in their lives. Maggie had been her strongest support when Trace died, even when Kit was at her worst and had turned her away. Kit was again struggling with the recent events in her life so today she wasn't up for a visit.

Maggie picked up on it right away, "Everything okay?"

"Everything's great."

"You're in a mood."

Of course she was. She'd been suffering for weeks. "I'm not good company today. I haven't been sleeping well."

Maggie watched the play of emotions on Kit's face. Seeing deep sadness in Kit's eyes, she guessed it was more than that. "I'll come in anyway. We'll have coffee and you can tell me what's made you upset, or should I say who?" That was Maggie, direct and straight to the point.

Kit's eyes were troubled as she told Maggie about Finn's recent drunken escapade. She was still mad about it. "Finn was irresponsible. In fact, it was plain stupid. It could have been so much worse if Cruz hadn't been there. I know Finn feels he's failing us because my dad has to help us but it's not his fault. We couldn't continue to carry the full load of running Caballo Stables while trying to keep up with the everyday duties at Lola Grande. Finn's been overworked and stressed for weeks due to Rio's absence. I can't excuse his behavior even though I can understand why he acted out like he did."

Maggie had always been outspoken, "Don't be too hard on Finn. I'm sure he's as angry as you are that Rio hasn't come back. Besides, it's Rio you're mad at so don't take it out on Finn."

Rio's failure to return really hurt Kit, and she was unable to hold her anger, "Finn is as angry as I am, but he decided to act out. Benny isn't any better. He's been acting out for weeks. Benny hasn't really gotten over his dad's death and now Rio has suddenly left. Another important person in his life is gone. That's a lot for a little boy to try to deal with."

Maggie understood, "Even Kenzie is beginning to wonder if Rio's coming back. She's been talking to Lucy Rose." Maggie had her own misgivings but wisely kept them to herself.

Kit's anger had been festering for weeks and today it spilled over, "Rio's continued absence has affected my whole family. He said he was coming back so why hasn't he?" Kit could always talk to Maggie when she couldn't talk to Lola. Kit was struggling with her feelings with Rio still being away. Maybe Maggie knew when he'd be back. Hopefully, Hector told Mike or her something. Not knowing anything was eating away at Kit. "Has anyone heard anything from Rio? Has Anna told you anything?"

Maggie heard the unhappiness in Kit's voice. "Hector and Anna don't know any more than you do. Just like you, they knew Rio had to stay longer. Maybe everyone's over-thinking this. He must have a valid reason for not returning yet." Maggie didn't tell Kit they were all getting concerned.

Bitterness crept into Kit's voice, "He was probably drawn back to the freedom of a nomadic life to fill his need for adventure. and nothing and nobody can hold him down. I should have known better. I knew he was a nomad." Kit had trusted him when he said those day were over, but some people never change. Or maybe he was missing his old life in Mexico and decided to stay there. She didn't know what to think any more. Did his dad's death make it convenient, and he didn't have to say goodbye? He probably enjoyed stringing her along knowing how gullible she could be. She had played and replayed every scenario. Defeat was evident in her voice, "Maybe he's not the man I thought he was. He could have had the decency to at least say goodbye to the kids. It isn't fair he had the ability to turn our lives upside down like this. I don't know what will happen to my kids if he doesn't come back. It really is a possibility because he has no deep roots here."

Maggie frowned, her friend was losing it. She tried to reassure Kit, "Of course he does. Hector and his family are here and all of your family. Try to be patient even though I know that doesn't come easy for you."

The ranting continued, "I know he left his phone behind but surely he'd have access to another one. Or he left it behind on purpose so no one could track him down. He probably never planned on coming back, so that's why he took his van. He could have flown like the rest of the family."

Unaffected by the indignation in Kit's voice, Maggie countered, "You told me he drove because he had to go through his dad's stuff. I'm sure both Hector and Rio wanted to bring some of their parent's personal items back. With his dad gone, there's no reason for Rio to stay in Mexico. Both Rio and Hector have made new lives here."

What Maggie said made sense. "One minute I'm worried about him. The next minute I hate him for hurting my family. We're done waiting for Rio to come back so Dad is helping while we look for a replacement. I couldn't care less. The truth is I'm glad he's gone. I knew he was bad news when he showed up. He's a loner who only cares about himself."

Maggie was surprised to hear this, but she tried to reign in Kit's anger by reassuring her, "Now you are talking crazy. It's obvious Rio cares for you and your family."

That comment reignited Kit's anger, "If he does he has a poor way of showing it."

Maggie had to close her eyes to keep them from rolling and ignored Kit's rant. It was all too familiar. Unaffected by the resentment in Kit's voice, Maggie asked, "What's going on between the two of you."

"Nothing. How can there be? He isn't here; he's MIA." Kit voice continued to rise the more she vented. "He's here one minute and gone the next."

"A year and a half is hardly a minute," teased Maggie.

Kit's lips formed a tight line. She didn't appreciate her friend's attempt at humor, and she did not want to discuss the subject of Rio any more.

Maggie would have been better off letting it rest, but with true form she continued, even though she was pushing the boundaries of their friendship. She knew Kit had feelings for Rio and guessed Rio felt the same way. "You know Rio loves you."

Kit had the decency to look away, but she wasn't ready to give in. She told herself she didn't care. She wasn't dealing with her anger, and her stubbornness prevented her from being honest. "Well, I hate him. I have shed too many tears over men. From this day forward I am saying to hell with all men. I don't need the grief and heartache that comes along with them." The words had caught in her throat forcing tears to her eyes, but she managed to hold them back. It was one thing to say something and another to mean it. She was struggling with her feelings for Rio. Bitterness broke into Kit's voice as her frustration surfaced, "Fate can be such an ugly force. It has attacked me all my life. Maybe Rio was brought into my life to torment me. Fate brought him here, let him get close to me and the kids, then took him away." Kit sounded miserable as she gave Maggie an exasperated look, "I'll just learn to deal with this like I have had to learn to deal with everything else. To hell with Rio Ortiz."

Maggie waited for the tirade to pass. She was used to Kit's rants, especially when it came to men. "You better snap out of this. You've been like this before and it's not good for anyone. They say absence makes the heart grow fonder."

"It's actually pissing me off." There was enough snap in Kit's voice to terminate the conversation. Maggie ignored it.

Kit knew she was being unfair to keep snapping at Maggie. She was mad at Rio, not her, but Rio wasn't here. If the man ever showed up, she would tell him exactly what she thought of him. "We don't need to discuss this any further" She didn't trust herself to say more.

Throughout their friendship they had conversations that developed into arguments, but it never affected their friendship. Like always, Maggie kept it real. She chose to be honest but took a deep breath before continuing, "May I tell you something without you getting mad?"

Kit gave Maggie an exasperated look. They had known each other too long for Kit to be offended. "No promises."

"It seems to me your initial reaction to Rio was very much like your reaction to Trace when you met him. Tell Rio how you feel when he gets back."

"I'll tell him a lot more than that if he comes back."

"You may not want to admit it, but you love Rio and Rio loves you. I don't know why Rio would love you? You're hard-headed, stubborn, and temperamental. What's there to love?"

Kit couldn't ignore the truth of what Maggie was saying, but she was too stubborn to concede and sighed in exasperation, "Then why hasn't he come back? Maybe he loves his old lifestyle more. It doesn't come with a nagging woman with three challenging children."

Maggie flashed her a compassionate glance. "He's been a good influence on you and your kids in many ways. He's become a part of Lola Grande."

Kit nodded, not trusting herself to speak. Maggie's words were like a dose of reality. She had let Rio into her life. Kit couldn't deny her feelings and she smiled as she remembered the first time they kissed. Lying was futile so she confessed dismally, "You're right as usual. What am I going to do? What is it with cowboys? How come I keep being drawn to them?" There was such sadness in her eyes as she confessed, "I am in love with him. I should have known better."

Kit had spent the morning pouring her heart out. Maggie had always been someone she could confide in. She realized she felt better. Talking to Maggie always had that effect on her. With her composure somewhat restored she apologized, "Sorry to dump on you. I wasn't planning on a pity party today."

Maggie made a disbelieving sound, "No, you're not. Besides, that's what friends are for. I'm sure Rio will be back soon."

Kit hoped Maggie was right.

Knowing Kit had withdrawn, Maggie refilled their coffee mugs and sat back down. Maggie knew it was time to back off. Their visit continued, both intentionally leaving the topic of Rio behind them.

"Doc stopped by on his way home yesterday. He's not one to gossip but he dropped a bombshell that's not common knowledge yet. Promise me you won't tell anyone."

"What? That Beaumont Estates has new owners? You know small towns love to talk and we do have some of the best gossipers around. So, what did Doc tell you?"

Kit couldn't believe Maggie already knew this. "Not much. They're ranchers from Montana, an older couple with an adult daughter who lives with them. They're bringing horses across the border, so the owner contacted Doc. He wants Doc to check them as soon as they arrive because he has a pregnant mare. Doc's been providing them with information like what documents are required and what needs to be done when they get here."

"When's that?"

"Doc said the owner would call him again when they know the day they are leaving. I think he said the last name is Rothwell. Or it might be Rodwell. It's something like that."

"What else did he say?"

"Their daughter is recently widowed, and she has a medical problem. That's all I know."

"That's rather vague, not to mention mysterious. I hope they're a nicer family than the Beaumonts were. We don't need another Olivia Beaumont back in the community. I haven't missed her for a second." Olivia Beaumont was calculating and malicious and her father was worse. Jackson had been ruthless and dangerous.

The mere mention of the Beaumonts caused Kit momentary bitterness. Kit hadn't thought about Olivia Beaumont for a long time. She remained one of Kit's least favorite memories and she was glad when they moved away. "I guess time will tell but they have to be better than the Beaumonts. I wonder what's wrong with the daughter."

"I'm sure we'll find out soon enough. I better get going. I've stayed much longer than I intended. Are you going to be okay?" Maggie wasn't overly concerned about Kit, just sad.

Kit nodded and hugged her best friend. She regretted her earlier rant and was grateful for Maggie and her friendship. Like usual, she was allowing emotion to impact her life. With determination she dismissed Rio from her thoughts, but she was unable to ignore the pain in her heart. More heartache caused by another annoying cowboy. She was even more depressed after Maggie left.

CHAPTER FOURTEEN

The Graysons had survived the harsh winter, but spring was here. With help from the Calhouns they were able to make it through the tough times, but it was getting busier. Finn continued to train in the arena but was looking forward to being back outdoors full-time. Last week's Chinook had melted the surrounding snow but there were still places in low areas where it remained.

Kit was sitting at the kitchen table when she heard the light knock as the door opened. Expecting it to be Lola, she looked over and smiled. Kit's heart stopped, and she averted her face to hide the sudden panic she was feeling when it was Rio who stood in the doorway. She didn't want him to know how much his unexpected appearance unnerved her. Her relief in seeing him was quickly replaced with anger. She held her breath for a moment before she turned her head back and glared at him.

It was pure pleasure seeing Kit until she turned to him. The frigid look she gave him was colder than an arctic wind. Not the welcome Rio was expecting.

"What the hell are you doing here?" Her voice was clipped and resentful and her icy gray eyes locked with his.

The coolness of her response didn't affect Rio. It wasn't like he hadn't experienced it before. He was just surprised. What had happened since he was gone? He was a little hesitant when he said, "I came to let you know I'm back."

Kit's eyes narrowed and she reacted with sarcasm, her go to when she was angry, "Really. We all thought you had moved on."

Her response and abrupt manner confused him, and his eyes darkened at her biting retort. He didn't understand Kit's behavior. He had no idea how much his absence had affected the Grayson family. "What are you talking about? Why wouldn't I come back?"

Kit was never one to hold back, "How the hell would we know since no one has heard from you since you left. I thought you were gone for good and had returned to your nomadic lifestyle with no commitments." All of her inner strength was needed to hold back her tears, but she could no longer hold back the hurt she was struggling with, "You said you would always be there for my kids, but you only care about yourself. Benny has been out of control ever since your brother and his family came back and you didn't. Kenzie is confused and Finn is angry, just like me." Their eyes locked and Kit's verbal attack continued, "I'm not the only one you hurt by staying away. You hurt my kids. That hurt ever more."

Kit's remarks affected Rio more than usual. He thought they had gotten beyond this a long time ago. "I told you my nomadic days are over. I left all that behind. I'm not going anywhere. I'm back with family." That family included the Graysons.

"Family cares about one another. They don't just disappear. I'm surprised you even came back." She knew she had hurt him when she saw the painful expression in his eyes. It had no effect on her. Kit wanted to hurt him back.

His penetrating look bore into Kit. "I'm surprised you didn't pack up my things."

"I thought about it more than once, but we were too busy to dedicate time to unnecessary activities that could wait."

Rio had seen that look before in her eyes and knew Kit's temper was winning and there would be no reasoning with her. This time his temper, which he had kept restrained, snapped, "You keep making assumptions about me. You did it when I first came here and you're doing it again. I thought you knew me better." He shrugged his shoulders, "I thought I knew you better."

When Kit heard him take a deep breath and expel it slowly, she knew he was trying hard to hold his temper. The thick silence between them couldn't be ignored. Trembling from the unpleasant exchange, Kit forced herself to keep eye contact. Her long lashes couldn't hide the anguish in her eyes. "Why did you stay away, Rio? Why didn't you phone?"

"I did call, and I did leave a message." His voice had that expressionless tone Kit had come to recognize when he was trying to keep his temper under control.

Temporarily taken aback, she glared at him in disbelief. Kit pushed her thick auburn hair from her forehead and looked at Rio with candid gray eyes and remained skeptical. "What the hell are you talking about? There was no message. I don't know if what you're saying is even true. You said you wouldn't be gone long. Why should I believe you now?"

Rio's own expression hardened. Kit still had the ability to get under his skin. His own temper surfaced, his eyes now dark and dangerous, "I don't lie. Ask the kids if they deleted my message since you won't take my word for it."

Her rising temper had brought a flush to Kit's cheeks. She held back another sarcastic remark, choosing to walk away instead. On impulse, Rio reached out and pulled her back. The man could be so infuriating because once again Rio had a disturbing effect on her. She slapped his hand away and quickly stepped back.

Rio released his hold and shook his head in frustration. He didn't want to get into a heated discussion, but he was compelled to defend himself, "You're always quick to judge and condemn. I don't want you to go on believing something that isn't so. You need to cool down and listen. This time I want you to let me finish, because you don't know what you're talking about."

Kit blinked first, failing to hide the hurt in her expressive eyes. "We are finished."

Rio's voice was clipped because Kit had put him on the defensive, "Believe what you want. Or you can ask the kids when they get home from school. They should be home soon." A groan escaped because he knew no matter what else he said it would be useless. She had made up her mind and there would be no changing it. Over the years, Rio had learned it was best to hold his temper.

"I'll just do that."

"What should I do in the meantime?"

"You can go to hell for all I care. We have nothing further to discuss so if you are intending to stay you can go find Finn and see what he wants you to do. He's been working his ass off for weeks." Looking at Rio's angry face, it was clear that Kit had struck a nerve.

Rio's expression turned resentful. Kit had insulted him like this before. It would be the last time. The door slammed on his way out.

Kit leaned forward and placed her throbbing head in her hands as her elbows rested on the table. The tears she had been holding back for weeks ran down her cheeks. At least she had kept them in check until he left. She hadn't given him the satisfaction of seeing her cry.

Rio walked away before he said something he'd later have cause to regret. Now that he was back he didn't know where he stood with her, but at least he still had his job. He swore under his breath as he headed back across the yard. He loved Kit Grayson and her children, but Kit was mad. A glint of anger remained in his eyes because she had been too stubborn to listen. Buddy, happy that Rio was back, followed faithfully at his heels. Rio knew it was best to keep his distance until Kit cooled down. He was nervous as he went to find Finn. Based on the reaction by Kit, he didn't know what to expect from Finn. Rio shifted uncomfortably when he found him getting ready to leave the arena. "What's up, Finn?" Rio didn't miss the hard glint in Finn's eyes, or the firm set of his jaw.

Finn's voice was raised in anger when he finally spoke, "I've been conditioned to all kinds of pain over the years. Living with the Graysons and being adopted changed that. Your deserting us brought the pain back," Finn accused. "You neglected your duty to us, Rio. We deserved better. I need to get over to the barn and clean the rest of the stalls I didn't get done this morning."

Rio heard real resentment in Finn's voice. "There was miscommunication, or should I say a lack of communication while I was away. I had to stay longer than I wanted to because duty called." When Finn's expression remained unchanged, Rio turned and walked away. He was tired of trying to explain everything. Hearing the bus coming down the road, Rio headed back to the house. There was the issue of his phone call that needed to be addressed.

Kit refused to acknowledge Rio when he walked back into the kitchen. The tension of the moment was broken by the arrival of the kids. Kenzie squealed with delight and ran into Rio's arms. Benny held back, confused, and angry like his mother. Kenzie quickly realized her mom wasn't as excited as she was. She wondered what was up.

Kit turned to Benny, "I'm going to ask you a question and I want the truth. Did you erase a phone message from Rio without telling me?"

Benny bit his lip and nodded, knowing he was in trouble.

Rio's harsh voice reflected his aggravation, "Do you remember what it said?"

Through tear-filled eyes, Benny confessed, "All I heard was the beginning." He glared at Rio and lashed out angrily, "You said you weren't coming back. That's all I heard because I was mad and deleted it. Then I got scared so I didn't tell anyone."

Benny's confession shocked Kit, "You need to think before you act out." Good advice even if she didn't always follow it herself.

Rio was quick to explain, "He didn't hear the rest of the message. I said I wasn't coming back right away because there were problems I had to deal with. I said it would take a while but I'd come home as soon as I could."

Feeling the sting of Rio's disappointing look, Benny started to cry. Knowing Benny was upset, Rio put his arm around the boy's shoulders and held him tight. Kit was surprised by the gentleness in his voice, "It's okay, Benny. I understand why you did what you did. Sometimes we act out in anger before taking a moment to think and we do things we wouldn't normally do when we're mad. Off you go, I still want to talk to your mother."

Benny knew saying sorry wouldn't be enough. Still upset, he ran to his room.

Kit was sure what Rio said to Benny was meant for her as well. She knew she had handled things badly because of her temper.

Kenzie felt sorry for her brother. She gave Rio a sideways glance. Seeing the look of concern on Kenzie's face he winked at her. She was elated that Rio was back but frowned as she went up to Benny's room to console him. She had missed Rio and hoped he and her mom would work this out.

Kit did not appreciate the fact that she could see triumph in Rio's dark piercing eyes. She had to struggle to swallow the lump of pride in her throat, "Fine, you were right."

"Pardon?"

"You were right."

"Oh, I heard you the first time. I just wanted to hear it again." Rio knew better but he couldn't resist teasing her. It didn't bother Rio at all that it had ticked her off, but her apology had surprised him. Rio knew he had to share more about his extended absence but now wasn't the time. "I'm back and I'm not going anywhere. I didn't know the doubts you were experiencing while I was away. I'm sorry."

The tug on her heart pulled harder but she resisted. "I'm glad you're back for Finn's sake."

He detected less anger in her voice "That's not the only reason I'm back."

Kit's senses stirred, a physical reaction she couldn't control. Their eyes met and Kit felt an intense sense of longing. This conversation had become too personal.

Rio's eyes never left Kit's face. "You know what's really sad about this? How you could believe I would do something like this?" With that said he walked out.

Kit knew he was hurt by the expression in his eyes. She went to the window and watched him cross the yard and head to his place. His comment had hurt her.

A few minutes later Lola walked in. "I see Rio's back."

"For now," Kit said sarcastically. Unable to ignore Lola's look of disappointment she managed more calmly, "You know Rio always brings out the worst in me. He has since the day I met him. I thought I was done with letting anger take over my life."

Lola refused to change the direction of the conversation and knew her next comment would only add fuel to the fire, "Maybe it happens more when love is involved."

"Don't go there, Lola." The fight went out of Kit. Her actions earlier were reflective of her ongoing struggle with her emotions. They were now under control. "When you're hurt it makes it easy to assume the worst. Benny's actions complicated things." Kit explained about the deleted message. "I understand why Benny did what he did, but there are consequences for such behavior. He will have to apologize to Rio."

"He's not the only one who has to apologize. I understand you laid into Rio pretty good."

"We all thought he wasn't coming back. Now that I know why Rio stayed away and what happened I'm less angry. Rio didn't deserve my anger, so I'll apologize." Kit knew it was the right thing to do but she still needed time to process what happened. "Benny has to learn accountability for his behavior. You're never too young to learn there are consequences."

"Or too old."

Kit let out a heavy sigh, "Are you suggesting I simply welcome Rio back with open arms and pretend everything is fine?"

"No, but I think you should take a little time and think about what happened today. You might also talk to your kids. Today impacted all of them, too." Lola didn't stay, knowing Kit needed time alone.

Today's events had been emotional, and Kit had to question her own reactions. What was it that fueled her anger? Kit sighed heavily because she knew. If she didn't love Rio, he couldn't hurt her like he did. She also knew Rio had feelings for her and their connection was more than physical attraction. Yes, he reminded her of Trace but that wasn't the reason she fell in love with him. Seeing Rio today, Kit decided she was willing to take a chance. It was time to admit her feelings to him. She wanted him in her life in every way, so it was time to find out how deep his feelings were. They were at a crossroads, and it was time to see what direction they were headed.

Rio was struggling as well. He had done a lot of thinking while he was gone, and Kit was always at the forefront of his mind. He thought about her every day. While he was away he had decided to propose to Kit as soon as he got back. So much for best laid plans. He'd been excited to get home and had so much to tell her but after today he didn't know what to do. Today's events had him confused and discouraged, but his feelings hadn't changed. Her love was worth fighting for. He just wondered how long the stubborn Kit Grayson was going to hang onto her anger. It could take days. He would never understand women or figure out why they had to make everything so complicated.

*****

It had been a couple of days since Rio's return. At least with Rio back some of the pressure was off. Finn had let go of his anger toward Rio as soon as he understood what had happened. Both kids had forgiven Rio right away. It was taking Kit longer to deal with her feelings, therefore, the atmosphere remained tense between them.

Rio was working on a saddle repair in the barn when Lola walked by on her way to the office. She needed to catch up on paperwork that had been put off and review the expenses for the last few months. "We fell behind while you were gone." She wasn't accusing, just stating a fact. "Kit said to tell you she wants you to go to town after lunch. She'll have a list of things we need by then."

Rio let out an exasperated sigh, and there was an edge of annoyance in his voice, "What, she couldn't tell me herself? Is she going to ignore me as if I didn't come home? I've explained until I'm blue in the face, but the woman never listens."

They were both aware of Kit's incredible stubbornness. "Not when she's mad and she wouldn't be mad if she didn't care about you."

Even knowing this, Rio told himself it was best to keep his distance and stay away from her. He'd been on the receiving end of one of her verbal attacks more than once. When she was like this there was no reasoning with her. Rio went on with his day.

Kit had spent days stewing despite admitting she was being unreasonable and resorting to avoidance. She was the reason there was still a feeling of unease hanging in the air. She had talked herself into apologizing a dozen times and postponed just as many. Her Grayson stubbornness kept winning but it was time to do the right thing and set things right. There was no time like the present. When she saw Finn she asked him if he knew where Rio was.

"He finished up in the barn and said he was going to his place." Kit changed direction and headed to Rio's before she could change her mind. She knocked softly but there was no answer. She turned to leave when the door opened. Rio's shirt was unbuttoned, and he was barefoot. He was just going to take a shower.

Kit was the last person he was expecting when he opened the door. He wondered if she was back on the warpath, and he was the target. He looked anxious, his manner uneasy as he buttoned his shirt. He didn't relish another confrontation, "I don't have another fight in me."

Kit stood hovering in the doorway, confused by his manner. The feeling of uncertainty hung in the air between them. "Aren't you going to ask me in? I need to talk to you."

A groan escaped him, and all the color drained from his face as he braced himself. He always knew his position here wasn't permanent. Was he going to be asked to leave? He remained apprehensive as he stepped aside to let her in. Maybe it was a good thing he hadn't unpacked his bags. Maybe this was the end of the road for him here.

One way or another Kit had to know where things stood with her and Rio. She shifted uncomfortably, knowing this wouldn't be an easy conversation. "I want a word with you, but I wanted to speak in private."

"Only one word? It takes two words to say, 'You're fired.'"

Kit took a deep breath. She wasn't happy with his attitude but knew she deserved it. "My bad behavior has been uncalled for. I overreacted. It does happen now and then. I could have handled this better, but my hurt and anger got in the way." Her flushed cheeks indicated inner turmoil as she waited for Rio to say something.

Rio had listened to her rehearsed speech, knowing how hard it was for her to apologize. His eyes lost their steely look, now replaced with a hint of amusement, "Did you miss me?"

This had taken a different turn. "The kids did," she stuttered.

Rio's expression changed, his eyes now dark and serious, "That's not what I asked, Kit. Did you miss me?"

As much as Rio could annoy her like Trace did, she had also fallen in love with him. However, she didn't appreciate his teasing, "You're enjoying this, aren't you?"

The corner of Rio's mouth curved slightly, "As a matter of fact, I am. So, did you miss me, Kit?"

Tears formed in Kit's eyes, "I really thought you weren't coming back."

He hated the look of despair he saw in her eyes. "I told you those days are over. I don't want a transient lifestyle and I'm not looking for something. I found what I was looking for when I came here."

Kit had one last unknown to clear up, "Why did you leave your cell phone behind?"

"I simply forgot it. I had other things on my mind like leaving all of you and not knowing what I'd find when I got to Mexico. I figured the sooner I left the sooner I'd be back. I didn't realize I had forgotten my phone until it was too late. I didn't expect to be gone long so I didn't bother getting another one. As you know, complications set in, and I had to stay longer. My life there is over. I have a new life." *Hopefully, it will be permanently with you and your kids.*

Now that the air had cleared between them, Rio went into more detail, stating the facts with little emotion. "As you know when our dad took Mom's remains back to Mexico he decided to stay. He met old friends and made new ones. The new ones liked to drink and gamble. Dad became a secret gambler and not a good one. I want to believe my dad was a man who would never renege on a debt, but he died suddenly. I had to stay and take care of things. There was no money, no investments, no life insurance. Nothing except debt. I didn't want our dad to have his name disgraced in any way. I didn't want to darken Cruz's memories of his grandfather. He idolized his abuelo. Nor did I want Dad's past following us." Rio remained guarded as he explained his extended absence, "Both Hector and I are honest and trustworthy. We found out our dad wasn't. It was easy enough to clear his debt, but it resulted in legal issues that took so much longer. It became complicated so it took longer than it should have. This has all been dealt with. I needed to protect myself and my life here. I didn't want anyone to have a reason to trace my life back to you and your family. My life is here, Kit. My ties to Mexico are gone. The first time I left Mexico was because I was running away. This time I left Mexico because I was coming home. I never meant to hurt you."

Kit didn't miss the shadow that crossed his eyes. "But you did." The tears came unexpectedly.

Rio raised her tear-stained face to him. He had so much to tell her. It took Rio a long time before he spoke again. He wanted there to be no doubt what his intentions were. "While I was away it hit me how much I love you. I could hardly wait to get back to Lola Grande." His arms tightened around her, "I love you so much it hurts. I couldn't stop thinking about all of you, wondering how Finn was coping. I knew you'd find a way to manage but it bothered me that you had to because of my absence. It all took so damn long. Every day away from you felt like an eternity. I missed you and I wished I were here with you."

Kit raised a surprised eyebrow. She certainly hadn't expected this, and she tried to hide her uneasiness by joking, "Why? Because I'm so irresistible?"

"You are a very complex woman. You're stubborn, frustrating, demanding, bossy and most definitely irresistible." A genuine smile curled Rio's lips, momentarily softening his features.

Kit didn't resist when Rio took a step closer and pulled her close. It felt like the most natural thing in the world to be in his arms. She tilted her head back and looked into his eyes. Kit felt an intense wave of longing. Her senses stirred, a physical reaction she couldn't control. She saw the yearning in his dark eyes. Her gaze was drawn to his mouth, now curled in a sexy smile. Kit closed her eyes, her lips parting and Rio's lips found hers as he kissed her with passion. Kit rested her head against his chest and clung to him, "Don't ever leave us again."

Kit still challenged him. He knew she always would. "What are you really saying, Kit?"

Kit was ready to reveal her true feelings, "There has always been chemistry between us but when the heart is involved it complicates things. While you were away it made me realize how deeply I love you. I've loved you for a long time but was too stubborn to admit it."

Rio needed to be sure, "I've had a hard time competing with Trace's memories and Doc's continued presence. You and the vet have a lot of history."

"Doc is a valued friend and that won't change. You aren't a facsimile of Trace. You are genuine, Rio Ortiz. It's you I love, and you will never have to doubt my love for you. Trace was a big part of my life until his death, but my life isn't over. You and I will make our own history together. I love you and my kids love you. I want you in my life."

Rio could see the truth in her eyes. "You're an exasperating woman, Kit Grayson. I could never stay away from you and your kids. You have become a huge part of my life, and I want all of you to be part of it forever. The land here draws you in and doesn't let go. I quickly became tied to the land and the people living here. This is where I belong. I'm back with family. I've travelled the world looking for something. I think I was looking for you." His voice was husky with emotion, "What do you want, Kit?"

"I want you to accept my apology and tell me you're staying."

Rio opened a drawer and pulled out a ring. It was simple but elegant. Rio spoke with calm deliberation and his eyes were serious, "My mom gave this to me years ago. She said when I found the right person to share my life with she would like the deserving woman to wear this ring. To my mom it symbolized love and commitment and hope for another generation to pass it on to with love." Rio dropped to one knee, "Will you marry me so I can become a permanent part of your family?"

It wasn't often Kit was speechless. This was the man she wanted to wake up beside every morning. This was the man who would fit in with her family because she knew he already loved them. He was the man who brought the unexpected into her life. Recovering her composure, she replied, "I would be honored to be your wife, but are you sure? You have seen me at my worst and I'm not likely to change."

Rio flashed his quick and cocky smile, "Yes. I want to share my life with you. We will definitely have an interesting life together." Rio opened the drawer again and pulled out another box, this one a little bigger. There was a purposeful expression on his face when he opened it. There were coins inside the ornate gold box. Struggling with his own emotions Rio continued, "These were my mother's and one of the things I wanted to bring back with me. It took several days for me to track them down, but it was very important to me knowing I intended to propose to you when I got back. The coins represent the apostles and show that a relationship to God is crucial to the success of a marriage and to share in all that they have together. At the same time, it reminds one to help those who have less than them."

"These are a family heirloom which are a part of a traditional Mexican wedding. The priest blesses the coins and places them in the groom's cupped hand at the beginning of the ceremony. The coins are then placed on a tray and set aside. Near the end of the ceremony, they are given back to the groom. I will pour the coins into your cupped hands and place the box on top. This act represents me giving you control of all my worldly goods. You know I don't come with much, but I will give you my undying love."

"That's beautiful and meaningful. What a lovely tradition." The tears came unexpectedly. "Rio Ortiz, I have shed a lot of tears over you. These are happy tears."

"As man of the house, will I have to ask Finn for your hand in marriage?"

"You will have to ask them all, but I would like to tell Lola first and on my own. I will gather the family, and you can join us. Give me half an hour, then come over to the house. I want you to hang onto the ring until we tell the kids together."

"Bossing me already. Good thing I'm used to it." Rio took Kit in his arms and sealed the deal with a kiss. Rio's lips were tender, his embrace gentle. It felt so right. "My life took on more meaning since I met you and your family. I hope your children will be happy with me as their stepfather. I promise to be a good dad to them."

Trace had adapted to the role of father, Kit knew Rio would as well. As for the children, she knew they already loved Rio. Trace had been a large part of her life, but she was ready to move on. Kit made a move to leave but Rio pulled her back and kissed her with an intensity that surprised both of them. Kit's cheeks were flushed when she left.

Kit was a little nervous heading upstairs to share her news with Lola. When Trace died, she had vowed she would never open that part of her life again. Well, that didn't work.

Lola was happy for Kit. "I know how much you loved my son. You and Trace had something special, but it is time to move on. Being with someone again on a commitment level requires a great deal of compromise and unselfishness. You and the kids will be welcoming Rio into a new role in all of your lives."

"I do love him, Lola, and so do the kids." Kit knew what she was doing was right. Rio was the man she wanted to share her life with and have him be part of the lives of her children.

"What do the kids think about this?"

"I haven't told them yet. I wanted to tell you first. He will be here soon so I better head home. I would like you to join us."

Lola embraced Kit. "Thank you for your empathy. I know you both love each other, and this is another case of life moving forward."

"Our family keeps getting more and more complex, doesn't it?"

"It does, but one thing remains true. We continue to share our lives with complete, and unconditional love."

The kids were a little nervous as they gathered in the living room. Kit stood by the fireplace and informed them Rio would be joining them just as Lola walked in.

Finn's first thought was they were going to fire Rio or had Rio just come back to say goodbye, this time for good?

The atmosphere was tense when Rio joined them and stood next to Kit. No one said a word. Rio took Kit's hand and placed the engagement ring on her finger. Kit blushed and Kenzie gasped. "I want permission from you to marry your mother and become part of your family."

Kenzie jumped up and hugged her mother and then Rio and gave them one of her sassy grins, "It took you two long enough. Can I be adopted more than once?" Benny slowly walked over to Rio, "Will I be able to call you Dad?" Rio nodded, too moved to speak. When Finn walked over and shook Rio's hand, Rio pulled him close and hugged him. Words weren't necessary between them.

Lola was the last to congratulate Rio, "A new branch will be added to our family tree, bringing your family together with ours. I am happy for all of us."

"I'm not sure what that makes me. I won't be your son-in-law."

Lola looked at Rio and smiled, "It makes you family, and you may call me Lola."

Rio had always shown her the respect she deserved due to her age and role as family matriarch, and he always called her Mrs. G. as requested. She refused to be called Senora or Mrs. Grayson but understood the respect expected by their culture. Rio's heart pounded as his voice became all tight and chocked, "I am more than thankful to be accepted by all of you. Thank you, Kit, for saying yes because now I will have this wonderful family."

Kenzie was beyond excited, "When's the wedding?"

Rio pulled Kit close, "I would like to get married on Thanksgiving. I have so much to be thankful for."

Kit's eyes warmed, "It's the perfect time. Thanksgiving it is, so mark your calendars."

That night, Rio joined them for supper, and it was like he had never left. The younger ones had a million questions, and he answered all of them, sometimes only sharing what was necessary to appease their curiosity. By the end of the evening, they were reassured that Rio was back to stay.

After Lola left and the kids had gone to bed, Kit and Rio sat together on the couch in front of the fire planning their future. Kit expressed her feelings about the wedding and hoped Rio would feel the same way, "I've already had a traditional wedding. Would you be okay if we have a small wedding with our family and close friends? I would like to honor both of the heritages of our families and I'm sure Lola and Anna would love to help with the planning of the wedding." Rio couldn't be happier with her idea and readily agreed. When she lifted her face his lips found hers and they sealed the deal with a promise of forever.

CHAPTER FIFTEEN

Once the Rodwells made their decision to move and the sales were finalized, everything moved forward quickly. They had been busy purging and packing for weeks. Laurel actually helped her mom. It was the least she could do under the circumstances, knowing she was the cause of the current upheaval in their lives. Genna hoped this was a sign of acceptance.

When it came time to do Gracie's room, Laurel disappeared. It was too difficult, like everything else she was unable to deal with. Laurel hadn't been inside her daughter's room since she got home so Genna knew it was up to her. Genna stepped inside. Nothing had changed since the accident. It was such a pretty little girl's room, light pink wall color with soft neutral accents. The wall behind her bed was wallpapered with a huge bunny sitting in a garden of flowers. The furniture was white, the bedding delicate, a ruffled valance across the bay window with the cushioned bench which was the perfect reading nook. The bookshelf was lined with Gracie's favorite books. Books that had been read over and over at bedtime. A scattering of toys remained on the floor; her favorite doll lay on her bed. For a moment, Genna's vision blurred. She missed her darling granddaughter.

Genna took time to treasure the memories, hearing Gracie's giggles, missing her snuggles. She packed up the toys that were still lying next to the toy box, emptied the closets and drawers. She gently placed the crocheted baby blanket in the packing box, memories tucked along with it. Genna cried when she placed the family picture of Sam, Gracie, and Laurel on top of the pile. It was taken just before Sam left. There were things that were set aside to be given away but everything else would be stored until Laurel was strong enough to deal with this part of her loss. When she was done, Genna walked by the closed door to Laurel's room. She had stayed there all morning knowing what her mother was doing. It broke Genna's heart, and she began to sob as she headed to her own room and closed the door. So many closed doors trying to shut out the painful past.

Genna had arranged for a moving company to come the day before they were to leave so they could pack up everything except what they would need that night. The movers would return early the next morning to finish packing the rest. A cleaning company would come in the day after they left. Neville's wife, Elsa, would let them in and inspect it when they were done. The Rodwells had decided to break up the long drive so it wouldn't be too much for them, especially for Laurel. They also didn't know how long it would take the men to clear Customs. Genna had booked rooms in Cranbrook, British Columbia. Darius had offered to sleep in the quarters in the horse trailer and stay with the horses. The motel had agreed to let them park the trailers at the far end of the parking lot.

Baxter had left most of the details for Genna to deal with. She was always organized, and Baxter was having a hard time with the move. It had become more emotional than he thought. He leaned back in his chair and analyzed the last few weeks. It was for Laurel's sake that Baxter had agreed, even though some doubts lingered. Were they ready for a big change like this? They had to be. They were leaving in a few days.

*****

A new day was unfolding, a new journey about to begin. The movers had been back and packed the rest of their belongings and left. The sky had lightened in the east as they loaded Genna's vehicle with personal things they didn't want in the moving van. Laurel had packed her journal at the bottom of her purse. It had all her feelings and deepest secrets. Everyone had their travel mugs with fresh coffee and Genna had packed a full lunch and snacks for all the vehicles. Genna's footsteps echoed through the empty house as she checked every room to make sure nothing was being left behind. She prayed they were doing the right thing as she closed the door. *The past is the past. Leave it here.* Genna sighed and blinked hard.

Faith would help carry her forward. She headed over to where the horse trailers were parked.

The two men worked silently while loading the horses. Baxter knew Neville and his hired hands would take good care of the remaining horses, but it was still difficult leaving them behind. It was an unsettling day. Baxter patted Darius on the back. Darius turned and headed over to his truck. Baxter's truck and trailer were parked in front of his, also ready to go.

Genna stood next to her husband. Today they were saying farewell to the place that had been home for years. They were all struggling with the reality of letting go. Genna knew this was more difficult for Baxter than it was for her. "None of us know what the future has in store. We are moving to our new home on faith. Drive safe."

"Darius and I will have to drive slower with the loaded trailers and I'm sure we'll have a delay at the border. I'll text you once we're across. We'll meet at the motel but don't worry about us. We'll get there as soon as we can. Go ahead and head out with Laurel, I just need a moment." A shadow clouded Baxter's eyes. There was no going back. Baxter looked around, taking in all that was being left behind. A lifetime of loving the ranch that had been in his family for generations. He swallowed hard as he climbed into his truck. He loved this ranch; he loved his family more.

Before Genna started the vehicle she said a quick prayer. *God, I trust in your plan and will follow the path you have for us. You have always guided our family through the challenges of life. Today we continue on the path you have chosen. Please guide and protect us through this next phase of our journey. Bring Laurel out of her darkness and back into the light. Bring back her joy.* She turned to her daughter and smiled. Laurel turned away. Genna added, *Give me the strength I need to move forward. Amen.* Genna gently touched her daughter's shoulder, "It's time. We have a long drive ahead of us. We may be leaving an important part of our lives behind, but you can leave the sorrow behind, too."

Laurel would love to leave the past behind, but she knew it would haunt her no matter where she lived. Her head started to ache. Laurel shifted and turned further into the window. She wanted to appreciate the efforts her parents were going through in the hope that a move would help her. Nothing could make her feel better about what she had done. Nothing would change the facts. *You can't escape reality. My sorrow is locked in my heart. My guilt is locked in my soul.*

Laurel was anxious, Genna optimistic. She pulled out of the yard with a renewed sense of hope. She knew it would be a long drive, but she would do her best to make the most of it. The time passed slowly as the miles stretched ahead of them. Laurel continued to stare absently out the window, preoccupied as she thought about what lay ahead. Her manner remained detached as they drove through unfamiliar terrain.

Genna was tired of driving. Mile after mile of silence added to her stress and her anxiety kicked in as they approached the border crossing. After answering a few general questions, they were waved through. She hoped it would go as smoothly for Baxter and Darius. It was a spectacular drive after they crossed into Canada, especially when the sky cleared, unveiling the majestic Rocky Mountains. It was more beautiful than she had imagined. Pictures could never do it justice.

Laurel finally relaxed and took in the beauty around her, captivated by the ever-changing scenery. The Rocky Mountains stood unyielding around them, undisturbed for centuries in their magnificence. Laurel loved the landscape, the rugged mountains with snow-covered peaks a spectacular backdrop to the west. Both were impressed with the unfolding beauty that seemed to grow right out of the rocks. Laurel couldn't help but be impressed. Genna turned into a pullout so they could stretch their legs and take in the stunning view. The silence around them was healing, different from the silence they left behind. Genna hoped Laurel felt the same sense of peace. God willing, they would all find peace and happiness at Willow Downs. Genna took a deep breath of the pure mountain air before telling Laurel it was time to go. The next stop would be their motel in Cranbrook.

Genna was glad to hear the trucks pull in an hour after their arrival at the motel. Once the horses were settled, they went for supper at the restaurant next door. They didn't linger, all of them were showing signs of fatigue and it would be another early morning. When Genna climbed into bed and the lights were turned off, she ended her day in prayer. She hadn't changed her belief that everything would work out and they had made the right decision.

The temperature dropped overnight but had warmed considerably by the time they had finished breakfast. They still had a long drive ahead of them. They pulled away together but had been separated before they got out of town. It didn't matter, Genna knew they would make better time than the men anyway.

Like yesterday, the landscape was ever-changing. Once they crossed the border into Alberta, Genna felt like Alberta was welcoming her home. She was filled with new hope. Not long after they turned north the highway led them through rolling hills of grass and sagebrush as far as the eye could see. Various shades of green once again bringing the countryside back to life. It felt more like home, the land now occupied by livestock on the open range. Genna was excited knowing it wouldn't be long now. The endless miles had counted down. Genna smiled to herself knowing she would have to get used to thinking kilometers. One more change.

Ten minutes later Genna saw the 'SOLD' sign she was looking for. The realtor had given excellent directions. Laurel had become more subdued by the time they arrived at the ranch. Genna entered the code at the entrance and drove up the paved drive. As they passed through the iron gates Laurel wondered if she had just moved from one prison to another. The driveway lead them up to the stately home. At one point, it veered off toward the outbuildings and fenced corrals. There was no activity on the property, but they could see the realtor's vehicle in the drive. Genna took an anxious breath wondering what Laurel was feeling. She had shown no sign of interest. Genna turned to Laurel, "Our future is here. It's up to you how you live yours."

Rows of tall Juniper trees along both sides of the long drive stood like sentinels protecting the new owners as they approached their home. A sense of calm enveloped Genna. The gardens were laid out beautifully but had been neglected. A little time and effort would change that. Once they were settled she would dress up the planters and revive the flower beds. She knew she would be checking out the local greenhouses as soon as she could. Genna loved to garden and had always been complimented on her landscaping at home.

It was the gazebo that caught Laurel's attention. The extended limbs of the willow trees would shelter the gazebo and yard from the intense heat on sunny days. For some it would be a place to rest and appreciate the view, for others a place to meditate or read while escaping the real world. Laurel immediately felt it would become her place of refuge, a backyard oasis. The house was grand with its wide circular drive welcoming the new owners home. Home. Would this ever feel like her home?

Genna entered the circular drive. When they pulled up to the front of the stately house, it was as exquisite as Genna imagined. They made their way up the wide wooden steps to the verandah where their realtor greeted them. Genna chatted with her as they made their way through the double doors into the spacious entryway. The house was refreshingly cool, but the kitchen was filled with sunlight. There was a beautiful basket on the island with a bottle of wine next to it. It was such a thoughtful and welcoming gesture.

The three of them explored the house together. The house had a feeling of being cold and lifeless and it wasn't due to it having been vacant. Genna was anxious to make it their home and bring it to life. When they were back in the kitchen, the realtor said, "I'll pick up my sign on the way out. I wish you and your family health and happiness in your new home." Genna and Laurel went out and unloaded the vehicle. They had stopped in town and purchased some groceries and a few basic necessities to get them through the first few days.

An hour later, the men arrived with the horse trailers. As soon as they were unloaded, Laurel went down to the stable to see Penny. Laurel had been impressed with the horse facilities when they drove past them on their way to the house. She waved at Darius who was unpacking equipment into the tack room. Laurel heard the moving van arrive. She would only be in the way until they left so she stayed away. Once they left, she knew there was a lot of work ahead for all of them before they'd be settled so she headed back to the house.

That evening, Genna took a break and sat alone on the steps of the verandah. To no one's surprise Laurel had escaped to her room right after a late supper. Genna chose not to be discouraged. Baxter and Darius were at the barn with the horses. Darius had his own place, a private dwelling away from the main house. It was much nicer than the bunkhouse at their old ranch.

Genna was surprised at how quickly the temperature dropped and knew it was due to the proximity to the mountains. As the quiet of the night settled over the land, the crisp night air was scented with the fragrance of the laurel leaves. Genna looked skyward and was at peace as she prayed. *Thank you for guiding us and bringing us safely to our new home. Heal our daughter and make her whole and healthy and let her find peace within.* She smiled when Baxter walked up the steps. "It's such a pleasant evening I think I'll have coffee out here on the verandah."

"Do you want to be alone, or would you like some company?"

Genna smiled at Baxter, "I'll pour two and be right back.". They sat side by side. It was their first night at their new home. Serenity surrounded them.

"Darius is worried about Penny so he's keeping an eye on her. I'm glad the vet will be here tomorrow morning."

The clouds continued to gather as they chatted, quickly turning into gentle rain. Genna headed indoors to do a little more puttering before bedtime. Baxter went back to the barns to check Penny before calling it a night.

Up in her room, Laurel had achieved a level of resignation. She had no choice but to keep on living despite the terrible emptiness inside her. She crossed the room to the welcoming window seat, one of the reasons she picked this room. She also appreciated the view from the window that offered an occasional glimpse of sparkling water. She remembered her mom telling her there was a stream flowing through the property. She pressed her forehead against the cool window pain and watched the rain slide down the window like tears. She could hear the wind crying through the night as if it shared her sadness. Laurel pulled out her journal.

Mother is already planning our future here. I feel sorry for her. Such a waste of time. Life attacks a person and destroys your plans. I've been watching the rain slide down my window all night. The angels are crying for me but there will never be enough tears. It's gotten so dark, the sky is like a cloak of doom. It feels like God's external force has entered my body and is raging inside. I don't want to feel this way.

As soon as breakfast was done, Laurel hustled across the yard to the barn where the horses were being kept. Everyone was waiting for the vet. Laurel loved the horses, grateful they couldn't pass judgement on her and her actions. She patted them in greeting, coming to rest at Penny's stall where she went in and sat down beside her. She loved her horse, but Penny was lethargic. Laurel was concerned. She wasn't due to deliver for a few more weeks, but she was listless. Laurel heard a vehicle drive in a few minutes later. Even though she didn't want to meet a stranger, she remained crouched beside Penny. She was anxious to hear what the vet had to say.

Baxter greeted the veterinarian when he pulled up next to the barn. "Welcome to Willow Downs. I'm Baxter Rodwell."

Doc reached out and shook the extended hand, "Welcome to Alberta. I'm Dr. Jim Parker but everyone calls me Doc. I like the name you've given to what was Beaumont Estates. Willow Downs sounds welcoming. This was always a beautiful ranch and the best hobby farm in the county. The previous owners had superb horses, but they seldom rode. Beaumont Estates was best known for its opulence and the Beaumonts enjoyed their social status but never fit in as part of the community."

"We only brought a few of our personal horses with us. The rest were included as part of the sale of our ranch. In time we will rebuild our stock, starting with Penny, our pregnant mare." Baxter waved Darius over and introduced him. "Darius is our friend and hired hand. He moved here with us and takes care of the horses." Darius stared at the vet with an intensity that made Doc uncomfortable. They all headed into the horse facility.

Darius moved away from them, but Doc felt his presence as he lingered in the shadows. Reserved by nature, Darius stood by silently and watched. He was very protective of the Rodwell family, especially Laurel. Darius remained guarded; trust had to be earned.

Laurel was very aware of the vet and studied him as he walked in, his stride long and slow as his feet crushed the fresh hay beneath the soles of his boots. He was quite tall but seemed to have a relaxed manner.

For a few seconds, Doc stood still, allowing his eyes to adjust to the dimness after the bright morning sun. Doc looked around and he noticed someone sitting next to the pregnant mare. The youth remained silent.

"This is my daughter, Laurel."

Laurel looked up when Baxter said her name. Despite her best efforts to remain composed, her heart was pounding. The pulled down cap couldn't hide the vacant look in Laurel's eyes as she remained distant and silent.

Doc found it hard to believe the youth was female. This had to be the daughter Baxter had told him about. Doc studied the fine planes of her face and realized his mistake. She was older than he thought and definitely female. Doc took in the pale, pinched features, and the dark circles under her eyes. She appeared to be docile and indifferent, which seemed odd. Looking closer he could see the tiny pulse beating in her throat. The poor thing was scared. She hadn't moved and was unaware of the disturbing effect she had on him. The enclosed area was charged with tension.

Doc wasn't sure what to make of the daughter. He expected her to greet him out of common courtesy, but she remained silent. Certainly not what he expected. At first he thought she was simply rude, but it didn't take long to realize there was something underlying causing her impolite behavior. Doc hadn't missed the anxiety in her intense blue eyes that had no life in them. Doc did pick up on her attentiveness to the mare beside her as she continued to stroke her neck to comfort her.

The vet had a quiet way about him that Laurel liked. The whole time he talked softly and stroked the horses as he checked them closely. His show of concern for the animals comforted Laurel and she began to relax. Doc was impressed with Baxter's magnificent horses. He had taken his time with each horse, and so far they were all strong and healthy. Doc had left Penny to the last. When he reached the stall, he knelt down beside the daughter, expecting her to leave. The feeling of anxiety gripped her, but Laurel didn't move. When Doc checked the mare with gentle hands. Penny snorted in discomfort. The vet's voice was soft as he tried to comfort her. The examination wasn't what he was hoping for. Her poor condition was more than due to the stress from travelling. He knew she would foal early, and it could be a difficult birth. He was concerned about complications and knew they would have to keep a close eye on her. He gave her a sedative to calm her. When he was done, he slowly unwound his lean frame from his crouched position, his hazel eyes sad. He pulled Baxter off to the side so he could express his concerns, "The other horses are fine, but your mare is in distress. I gave her a mild sedative that will calm her for now. You should move her to the birthing stall until she delivers. Keep her comfortable but I don't want to sedate her after today. She will need all her strength when she goes into labor. Her foal will likely come early, and it will be a difficult birth for both of them. It may come down to being able to only save one so that is something you must take into consideration."

"You're very direct," commented Baxter.

"It saves time when a decision has to be made. Call me if there is any change and I will come right out."

Baxter nodded in understanding, "I hope Penny will be all right. We've already lost so much."

Doc had to wonder what hardships the Rodwells had endured.

When they walked out together, Genna was on her way over to join them. Baxter placed his hand on Doc's arm to prevent him from leaving. He knew Laurel's manner had confused the vet. Baxter smiled at his wife and took her hand to draw her close. The time had come to explain their daughter's unusual condition. He gave a condensed version, feeling Doc deserved to know what he was getting involved with. The look of pain was evident as they told him about the accident and the reason for their move here. "Laurel's world, and ours, was shaken. Our move here wasn't a simple matter or made lightly. Laurel had locked herself away from everyone including us. She only left the house out of necessity. She had always been so confident and outgoing. Now she is a mere shadow of herself." Baxter's voice was bleak, "The sad truth is, Laurel is suffering from traumatic mutism and hasn't spoken since the accident. Her mind cannot accept what happened. She has resorted to avoidance in this unusual way." Both Genna and Baxter had tears in their eyes by the time they were done.

Doc's eyes widened in surprise. This was something Doc had never heard of before. He could see how much they were suffering and sensed their anxiety. He now understood the reason their daughter was reserved. "This can't have been easy for any of you. What do the doctors say? When will she get her voice back?"

Baxter responded to Doc's confused stare with a sad reply, "Maybe tomorrow, or the next day, or the day after that. It should have happened by now. We're all trying to deal with this the only way we can, one day at a time. Laurel is strong and healthy physically, but she remains emotionally traumatized. Laurel is hollow inside and lives without purpose. Since the accident, our lives have changed dramatically. We can work through these changes in our lives but we're afraid Laurel may never come back from this. We know she's still struggling with her grief, but her prolonged depression is unhealthy, and it's affecting all of us. It's been a difficult time for our family," admitted Baxter.

There was a hint of sadness in Genna's voice, "I pray every day for a miracle. Hopefully, moving here will be the answer to my prayers and Laurel will find her voice and we'll get our daughter back."

Seeing their tormented expression, Doc's heart clenched with compassion. He could see how much the family was suffering. Their daughter's accident had changed all of their lives. He understood better than they realized. The parents had to accept that no one understands another person's grief, but time would allow their daughter to heal. Everyone deals with grief in their own way and in their own time. Doc was grateful for what they had shared but a lot of questions ran through his mind because he had refrained from asking them, not wanting to appear too forward.

"Our daughter used to be so full of life. She lost her family, but we feel we have lost our daughter as well. She has locked herself away emotionally. We've struggled trying to deal with her condition. She has no idea how much her dad and I are suffering."

Doc couldn't ignore the tightness in his chest as he listened in sympathy.

With a torn heart, Baxter stated, "For now we just want to get settled. Willow Downs is now our home, and we will adjust."

Doc thought the Rodwells were the most incredible parents. He hoped this family would find the happiness they were looking for. Life could be cruel, and life could be unfair. Despite the uncomfortable circumstances, a strong feeling of pity for Laurel tore through Doc. Knowing what she'd been going through, he understood her behavior better. He couldn't get the image of Laurel out of his mind when he was driving to his office. She was an interesting little creature who could say a lot without saying a word. Her eyes had challenged him at first, but her expression softened once he was checking the horses. She almost smiled when he was checking Penny. He guessed it was her horse. Now that he knew more he wondered if time really would help Laurel. He had been more moved than he expected, feeling a powerful attraction and a need to protect her.

*****

By the end of the week, the Rodwells were down to unpacking the miscellaneous boxes. Baxter offered to clean up the kitchen when supper was done. During supper, Genna had told him they still needed a couple more hours before they were done unpacking, and Laurel was willing to help. Both of them worked away in silence. When Laurel opened another box her face paled. Inside were her family photos. The shock was more than she was able to cope with. Laurel left and headed to her room. Genna left to find Baxter.

"You look upset," Baxter said when Genna joined him in the kitchen.

"This has been more difficult than I thought. I know there's going to be a period of adjustment for all of us and I won't give up hope that this change will be good for Laurel."

Because he was struggling with the move, Baxter had to say, "Change is difficult even when it's by choice. This is a big change for everyone."

"Of course it is, but we chose to make this move."

"Laurel didn't have a say," he said with an undertone of regret.

"Laurel doesn't say anything," Genna said bitterly. She kept praying for a miracle. Instead, God seemed to be testing her patience, and she was failing miserably.

Baxter tried reassuring his wife, "We have seen a positive change. Laurel no longer confines herself to her room and spends more time outdoors. It's so beautiful and peaceful here. I can see she's more relaxed even though she still won't speak."

"Not yet, but we won't give up hope."

It had been another emotional day for everyone, one of too many. Baxter was concerned this was all too much for them. Leaning back in his recliner he analyzed the last few days. Even though some of his doubts lingered he understood the importance of their move. It was like Genna would always say, sometimes you have to take risks and believe in faith.

CHAPTER SIXTEEN

These days Doc was busier than usual, but he wanted to stop at Lola Grande before going to Willow Downs. Yesterday Coco had delivered, and her foal hadn't survived due to unforeseen complications. There were no complications with Coco, so she could be bred again. The Graysons understood things like this happen, so he was glad to see that even though Kit was sad she was okay. Over the last few days Doc had been spending more time at Willow Downs than he expected. He'd been dropping by their ranch on a regular basis due to his concern for their pregnant mare, knowing hers would be a difficult birth. But it was more than that. He was fascinated with Laurel and thought about her constantly.

As always, Kit greeted him warmly. She wasn't surprised to see him knowing he would want to check on Coco, but it was quite early. Kit was concerned about him, "Are you okay, Doc? You've been distracted lately. What's going on?"

Today was a professional call but he also wanted to talk to Kit about something else. "I'll go check on Coco first, but I could use a coffee if you have time, and we can talk then." He headed over to the birthing stall and wasn't surprised to see Rio with Coco. There was no longer a strained relationship between them and Doc was glad that Rio was back. Doc knew Rio's absence had upset Kit. She was back to her old self, and Doc knew Rio was the reason. This was one of the things he wanted to talk to her about before he left.

When Doc was done checking Coco he turned to Rio, "Keep Coco in here for a couple of days and then move her to the small, enclosed paddock. We have to keep her away from the other horses for now." The two men walked out together. Rio headed over to the main barn. Doc headed back to the house. Kit had two cups of coffee poured and was sitting at the kitchen table when he walked in.

Doc updated Kit on Coco and his instructions for Rio. He didn't miss the glow in Kit's eyes when he mentioned Rio. It reconfirmed what he knew, and he had accepted it. Doc knew it was time to explain his reason for staying to talk. It might be one of the most difficult conversations he would have. His deep friendship with Kit allowed both to share deep truths over the years.

Doc decided to get right to the point, "I have a confession to make, and I want you to allow me the time to hear me out. I've been doing a lot of soul-searching the last few weeks. I was caught up in my belief that I deserved to have you in my life because I always got everything I wanted. Professionally, I reached my goals and achieved success. I expected the same in my personal life. So, when I met you I expected to court you, win your heart, and marry you. I naturally expected you to pick me over Trace when you met both of us. I convinced myself you were exactly what I was looking for even when I knew your heart belonged to Trace." Their marriage was a constant reminder of his failure to succeed at something that was important to him. "When Trace died I thought my plans that had been on hold for so many years were back in play. I thought I had a chance when Trace died, but then Rio was a challenge because he was so much like Trace. Trace had been replaced by another damn cowboy. I couldn't compete but I couldn't let go. I wasn't used to failing at anything. I thought if I kept coming around I could win you over." Doc's voice became deadly serious, "It's okay, Kit, I came to the realization I was never the man for you, and you always knew that." Looking back, he realized his feelings for Kit had been more infatuation and disappointment at losing her to Trace. Deep down he knew Kit had strong feelings for Rio, even if she hadn't admitted it to him or herself.

Kit was astonished by Doc's confession. This was a side of Doc she hadn't seen before.

"I faced my truth about your feelings for me. I've known it for a long time, but I continued to come by out of habit and friendship."

Kit appreciated the comfortable relationship she had with Doc. "I never want that to change. It would break my heart to lose you as a friend."

Great sorrow was evident in Doc's eyes. "I have another confession to make. I wanted what Trace had, and I was envious of your family life." There was such sadness in his voice.

His unexpected confession was painful to hear. It was such an honest and revealing conversation.

"I know you love Rio. You should tell him how you feel before it's too late. I think Trace would have rooted for Rio."

It was Kit's turn to divulge, "I finally admitted my feelings for Rio when he was gone. As soon as he returned we confessed our feelings for each other. We're engaged and planning a Thanksgiving wedding."

"The rumor mill must be down. I'm not surprised by the news, just that I hadn't heard it yet."

"Only the family knows. I haven't even told Maggie. I wanted to tell you myself and I didn't want you to hear it from others but there's never been the right time. You've been so busy and rather preoccupied. The kids were sworn to secrecy, but I know Kenzie is bursting to tell Lucy Rose. Now that you know, I'll invite Maggie for coffee. I've been bursting inside as well." She took Doc's hand in hers, "You can love more than one person at the same time. We just love in different ways. I have always loved you, Doc, but I loved my husbands to the depth of my soul. I love Rio the same way."

"You and Trace had something special. I hope you will have that again with Rio." They looked at each other and smiled. Nothing had changed between them.

The last few days had been more stressful than he realized and not only because of the conversation they just had. He still wanted to talk to Kit about the Rodwells. The story Baxter and Genna had shared about their daughter had shaken him. It was an odd situation for sure. Doc had come to the realization he was experiencing a draw to Laurel that was unfamiliar. He continued to be curious about her and couldn't get her out of his mind. "I'm on my way over to Willow Downs before I go to the clinic. I met with the Rodwell family when I went to check on the horses they brought across the border. They have a pregnant mare I'm concerned about."

This was one of the things Kit admired about Doc. He was dedicated to the animals he treated. He also extended his caring to the people who owned them.

"The parents, Baxter and Genna, are a lovely couple, but their widowed daughter is suffering from traumatic mutism due to a vehicle accident several months ago." Doc filled Kit in on a few details based on his own observation, "When I met their daughter she looked like a forsaken fawn who needs nurturing to get stronger. Then we made eye contact. Laurel Easton is a lot like you. Not because you both lost your husbands, but that girl can say so much without uttering a word. Her eyes can read you like a book and shoot daggers at you at the same time." Doc's eyes had softened as soon as he mentioned Laurel. Things changed for him when the Rodwells moved into the area. He just didn't realize how much.

"Have you met your match?" Kit teased lightly.

Doc had to laugh in spite of the heavy conversation. "You could be right, she's definitely a complex young lady. She appears to be fragile but I'm guessing she was completely different before her accident. She's gentle and confident when dealing with the horses. I need time to figure her out. She's definitely not like anyone else." He found the young woman intriguing, and it wasn't due to her circumstances. "Her parents hope their move here will be the miracle needed for her recovery. Laurel hasn't spoken a word since the accident. Her condition has been hard on them. They're struggling with their own grief."

"Did they tell you what happened?"

"The accident was due to bad weather and Laurel was driving. I'm sure she's caring a lot of guilt because her husband and daughter were killed along with the driver of the other vehicle. Laurel was the only one who survived, but mentally and emotionally, she died too."

This conversation touched Kit deeply. It hadn't been that long since she had experienced her own heartache and grief. Kit could understand the deep feeling of guilt. It was understandable why Laurel hadn't come to terms with everything.

"I sense such sadness in her. You were so strong after Trace died."

"Not really. I had to lean on my friends a lot. You and Maggie were always there for me. Maggie was a little tough at times, especially in the beginning, but that's Maggie. I can't repay you for the support you've given our family over the years and especially since Trace died. You've always been there for us."

"I always will be. That won't change even after you and Rio are married. I really am happy for both of you. For years, I wanted you to see me for the man I thought I was. Now I hope you'll see me for the man I really am."

"You are such a good, kind, honest man and that is enough for any woman. I love everything about you. Your loyalty as a friend, your compassion and empathy for others, your respect for people, your dedication to your clients."

"Thanks for coffee and your time. I better run."

"Any time, Doc. I hope everything will be okay at Willow Downs."

Laurel woke early and listened for any sounds of activity. All was quiet so she went and sat on the familiar window seat, now familiar with the view of the gazebo and the stables beyond. Shafts of early morning light filtered through the window as she gazed out. She was slowly coming back to life, even though she still didn't speak. At least now she was able to escape the confines of her bedroom, slowly emerging from the self-imposed exile she'd been living in before the move. She had managed to dull the sharp pain, but it didn't ease her guilt. It was hard to imagine ever feeling whole again. She dressed quickly, grabbed a banana, and left the house. She listened to the birds chirping in the nearby trees as she ate her banana on the front steps. For a moment in time, she was as carefree as the birds. The gentle breeze bringing cool air was refreshing. A Chinook arch had formed to the west promising warmer days to come. Spring had always been Laurel's favorite time of the year. Taking a deep breath, Laurel drew in the perfume of the flowering laurel bushes next to the house. Maybe the combination of a new home and new life would bring healing and the answer to her mother's endless prayers. She wandered down to the gazebo.

Genna looked out the kitchen window and saw Laurel in the gazebo, a forlorn figure whose shoulders sagged as she sat hunched over. Genna was grateful for the small changes she was seeing in Laurel. Her daughter was spending time outdoors and was again helping Darius with the horses.

She even seemed to have a little more interest in life in general, especially since meeting the veterinarian. She was always with him when he was checking on Penny and his presence seemed to comfort her and offer her a sense of security. But Laurel still wouldn't leave the property. Genna had to wonder if she would ever return to normal. She looked upward. *Forgive me for my moments of weakness. I am grateful to have our daughter. I trust in your plan for her and if it is your will she will return to normal. If not, help me to understand and accept. Your will be done.*

The morning air was crisp, but Laurel could feel the warm rays of the morning sun. The sense of stillness was broken by the wind in the tress. She let the gentle breeze caress her cheeks as she breathed in the fresh mountain air. She knew she was waiting for Doc but for some reason he was later than usual. Laurel wasn't prepared for her initial reaction to the vet. She felt at ease with him within minutes of meeting him. She headed over to the barn when she saw him coming up the drive, anxious to see what he would have to say about Penny. They had all been concerned about her since the move, but the last few days Penny had just been lying in the birthing stall.

Doc greeted Laurel warmly when she joined him at his truck, "Morning, Laurel. How's Penny today?" *How stupid are you? You know she doesn't speak.* Doc had been flustered ever since he left Lola Grande. "Let's see how Penny's doing this morning." Penny was lying next to the railing. He wasn't prepared for the state he found her in. He immediately called the office to cancel his appointments. Laurel instinctively knew what was happening; Penny was in labor.

As anxious as Doc was about the mare he remained calm. He dropped down beside Penny and in a soothing voice he examined her as she struggled to deliver. The mare's swollen stomach clenched beneath his hands. He was unable to settle her, but he couldn't give her a sedative. The exhausted mare would have no energy to push. Penny continued to pant heavily, and sweat was streaming down her sides. Another contraction caused Penny to flinch and whinny louder. Doc knew she was fighting to survive as contractions racked her body.

Even though this was distressing Laurel because she had enough pain in her life, she made no move to leave. She looked at the vet with pleading eyes. He nodded, understanding her wordless request to let her stay. Genna, who had come in to see what was happening, went to get Baxter.

Doc was challenged by the situation because he was as stressed as they were. Penny had no strength to push. Timing was now critical if he was going to save either one of them.

Doc turned to Baxter when he walked in with Darius. "Your mare is too exhausted to do this on her own. I have to do something now or we will lose them both." Those were the facts. Doc knew he needed an extra pair of hands. As if Darius knew, he was at his side prepared to help. Doc guessed he had helped with births before so knew he would be both strong and capable. He looked at Laurel with sad eyes before asking Baxter, "If I can only save one, which one do you want me to save?" He knew it would be a tough decision for the owners. He was glad he didn't have to make it.

"Save the foal." Shocking everyone, it was Laurel who spoke. Her words were barely audible, "Every newborn deserves the chance to live. You have to save this baby for both of us."

Everyone stared at Laurel in disbelief.

The despondency in her voice pained Doc. "Are you sure?" Doc watched as Laurel struggled. A spasm of pain washed over Laurel's face as it drained of color, "I'm sure."

Doc turned back to Baxter who nodded. There were tears in his eyes.

Laurel sat beside Penny as the exhausted mare closed her eyes and exhaled her last breath while Doc worked on the newborn foal. Laurel began taking deep breaths as if she was breathing for the newborn foal that was fighting to take her first breath. *Please don't let her die like Sam and Gracie,* Laurel pleaded silently. A moment later the filly was breathing on her own.

Doc was grateful to have safely delivered the foal. The miracle of new life. He turned to the others, "You have a beautiful filly." His eyes rested on Laurel, "I'm sorry I couldn't save your mare, but the foal is healthy."

"Can we call her Bella?" Laurel whispered, as held back tears fell without warning. A foal's birth had allowed her to emerge from the darkness that had engulfed her for so long. Genna took her daughter in her arms to comfort her.

Tears leaked out of the corners of Baxter's eyes, "Bella it is." He turned to his wife, "We have our daughter back." The family had experienced a monumental moment. Two miracles sharing a moment in time. Just then Bella stood and teetered on her wobbly legs.

For some reason, the vet's heart twisted. Doc didn't realize just how significant today was, but he felt the emotions from everyone. Doc's compassion drew him in. "Lola Grande, your neighbouring ranch, runs a first-rate operation breeding and training horses. One of their mares lost her foal yesterday. I can call and see if they would be open to a foster transaction, and we can use their mare as a foster mother. Mares that have lost their own foal are the most likely candidates for fostering. The Graysons breed a strong line of horses, but her foal had complications. If you and the Graysons are willing we can see if they will bring Coco here. She is a healthy candidate so maybe Bella will take to her and Coco can foster feed her."

"Before I make the call I'll milk your mare and feed her foal through a tube. This will give her the immune protection needed for now. Foals should nurse within two hours. If the Graysons agree they can have Coco here before that. We have to keep Bella fed and hydrated until they get here. If Coco and Bella accept each other your foal will get the nutrition naturally. If that doesn't work, you'll have to manually feed the foal."

"Please go call them," pleaded Laurel.

Darius appeared out of the shadows. Doc was sure there was an interesting story behind the man's employment. "I'll take care of removing Penny when you're done with her so the new foal can meet her foster mother."

Doc went out and leaned against his truck. His face was solemn as he gained control before making his call. Kit answered right away knowing it must be important. It hadn't been that long since he left the ranch. "I have an emergency at Willow Downs and as a result I have an unusual request."

Kit listened in sympathy as he explained his idea about fostering and readily agreed, "I'll be there as quickly as I can." She strolled across the yard and found Rio in the tack room. "Can you hook up the horse trailer so I can load Coco and take her over to the old Beaumont ranch?" After a quick explanation they were both on the move.

"Well, Coco, we need to take a drive. There's a new baby down the road who needs a mama. I was devastated when you lost your baby but there's a little filly that needs you now. Let's go help her." Kit continued to talk soothingly to Coco as she led her to the horse trailer.

The mere thought of the Beaumont ranch brought momentary bitterness for Kit. Jackson Beaumont was instrumental in the fire at Lola Grande that took Trace's life. Even though Kit had her closure when she confronted the Beaumonts in their home she was a little nervous about going there. None of the Beaumonts were around anymore. Jackson Beaumont had died and his wife, Evelyn, had moved to Florida right afterwards. The daughter, Olivia, who was always a pain in Kit's life, had moved to Calgary and was running the family business. Their paths no longer crossed but it was still hard to leave the past behind. She hoped the new owners were better than the Beaumonts.

Doc went back in and shared the good news. Time dragged for everyone while they waited. It was only when they heard the truck and trailer drive in that Laurel allowed herself to feel hope. She followed Doc outside. For some reason she was expecting a man. Instead, Laurel watched a tall, willowy woman slowly lead a beautiful mare down the trailer ramp. She was greeted with a friendly embrace by the vet, handed him the reins and followed him into the barn. Kit remained at Doc's side as he walked Coco into the birthing stall and led Coco to the orphaned foal. Bella took that moment and rose. She gingerly walked over and nestled up to Coco. They all held their breath as something beautiful happened. Kit's mare stood still allowing the foal to move closer and begin to suckle. The bond was immediate as Coco whinnied and accepted the foal. Everyone had tears. Even Darius had to swallow hard. Doc turned to Laurel and smiled. Both horses had accepted each other. It was a divine moment.

So many miracles in one day. What were the chances there would be a nurse mare so close? Genna's faith had been restored.

Doc was as excited as everyone, but he had to keep it real, "It may still take time for the fostering mare to fully accept the foal. I'll stay and monitor both of them. I want to make sure the foal is fine and continues to bond with Coco." He was prepared to stay through the night. They would know for sure by morning.

This had been emotional for Kit as well. "I'll head home. I hope it all works out." Doc pulled Kit close and kissed her on the forehead. He understood what Kit was feeling. This had not been easy for her. Kit's voice remained husky with emotion, "Go tend to the horses. We'll talk later." Kit had difficulty keeping her voice steady as she bid farewell to Coco.

Baxter walked Kit to her truck, "Our family will be forever grateful to you for your generous actions. We can't thank you enough."

"I hope it continues to work out for Coco and Bella." As Kit climbed in she heard Baxter say to himself, "Two miracles in one day." and wondered what else had happened. The Rodwells had already brought drama to the ranch. She hoped this wasn't a sign of bad things coming.

The next few hours were tense for everyone but both horses seemed to be doing well. It was now long past the supper hour. Genna knew her time was better spent elsewhere, "I'll go make something to eat. You can all come in when it's ready."

"I'll stay here and watch over the horses." It had been a long exhausting day, but Doc wanted to stay with Coco and Bella. They appeared to be doing fine but he wanted to be sure. He understood the significance of today's events and he didn't want anything to happen to set Laurel back.

Laurel also chose to stay. Her words came slowly, her voice still a little shakey, "I need to stay here. I couldn't do anything for Gracie. I need to be here for Bella."

Genna knew how important it was for Laurel to stay. "I'll bring you both something when it's ready." When she returned with their food and a thermos of coffee, Doc and Laurel were sitting silently on the bale watching the horses continue to bond.

Doc was feeling confident that Coco and Bella had accepted each other but he'd stay through the night to make sure. It had been a stressful day for everyone, and it was going to be a long night, but it was no surprise to him that Laurel continued to stay.

Laurel felt at ease with the vet, so she was comfortable asking, "Tell me about the lady who brought Coco. You seem to be close."

They would be spending hours together, so Doc decided to go into more detail than answering with a simple yes. Besides, it would help her understand more about the community their family moved into. "Kit Grayson and her mother-in-law, Lola Grayson, are the owners of Lola Grande. The ranch operates a horse cutting business. Caballo Stables has a good reputation and breeding horses is another successful part of the business. Coco is only one of the fine stock of Grayson horses. Kit's father and his family own the neighboring ranch, Valley View. The two families are very close, and I've been friends with all of them for years. Kit's husband, Trace, was a very close friend of mine, even before he married Kit. I've been there for the Grayson family ever since Trace died. It was a tragedy that didn't have to happen. Trace was a good man. His death affected the whole community and it's in times of crisis that the community pulls together and helps those in need." Doc took the time to share the unconventional ties between the Calhoun family and the Graysons. "We are all exceptionally close."

Laurel was surprised he shared what he had but it made her more curious. When he remained silent, she confessed, "I'll miss Penny. She was a gentle horse and would have been a good mom."

"You have a nice touch with horses."

Laurel appreciated the compliment. Doc was caught off guard when she smiled at him, causing his heart to beat faster. It was the first time he'd seen her smile. As curious as Doc was about Laurel, he held back from prying. He didn't want to open up the painful part of her past her parents had shared with him and now she had the additional pain of losing her beloved horse. She had revealed so much of her caring nature while handling Bella's birth. He guessed she was a good mom herself. He knew it was time to change the subject. "I know your family moved here from Montana. I haven't spent time in that state. Was your ranch similar to this one?"

Laurel was grateful for the vet's empathy. It was hard losing Penny so close to losing her family and she didn't want to go back down that dark path. She was positive her parents had filled him in with the details of their move here and her unusual behavior. For some reason she was uninhibited with this stranger. "Our ranch was nestled in Bitterroot Valley along the border of Montana and Idaho. The picturesque valley lies between the Bitterroot Mountains and the Sapphire Mountains. The river was named after the pink flowering plant that has bitter tasting roots, and it's actually the state flower of Montana. Our horse facilities were comparable to these, but our house wasn't as elaborate. I'm glad we moved here. It's so picturesque with the magnificent Rocky Mountains and it exudes a feeling of peace, and you begin to believe everything will be right again."

From that point on, their conversation flowed easily despite both of them remaining somewhat guarded. Laurel appreciated the fact that Doc didn't ask personal questions. Therefore, she was able to remain at ease with him.

Baxter came in to say goodnight and brought blankets, a fresh thermos of coffee and a plate of Genna's homemade cookies. He was reassured the two horses were doing fine. "We can't thank your friend enough for what she did. See you in the morning. Come get me if something happens."

"I'm sure they are going to be fine. Good night, Baxter."

Doc and Laurel continued to talk, keeping it casual and time passed until fatigue took over. Doc stretched out against the bail and placed his hat in his lap. Laurel curled up beside him, fast asleep in minutes. Doc covered her with one of the blankets and pulled his own up to his chest and nodded off. He was exhausted; it had been a stressful day for him too.

It was the early morning rays shining through the cracks that woke him. He had checked on the horses several times during the night while dozing in between. He nudged Laurel and she woke, blinking her eyes in confusion. "It's morning. Both Coco and Bella are doing fine but I want them to stay in the stall for now."

They both looked over when Genna came in. "Darius offered to watch the horses. Come in and have breakfast with us. I'm sure you both need a substantial meal." They smiled at each other as Doc pulled Laurel to her feet. They were famished and in need of coffee.

It was a more relaxing day than yesterday as they sat around the table, all grateful for how yesterday turned out.

"Thanks for everything you've done for us over the last few weeks. We're forever grateful to both you and your friend." Genna had already thanked God in morning prayer for answering their prayers. They had their daughter back and hopefully on the road to a full recovery. She smiled as she watched her daughter. Laurel hardly took her eyes off the vet. Right now, the whole family looked at him as their hero.

"It's always nice when things work out. I need to get to my office, but I'll stop on my way home and check them again."

Laurel's heart quickened knowing he'd make sure the horses were fine. Or was it because she would be seeing him again? She was happier than she'd been in a long time. She left to go shower. For the first time since the accident, she took a little more time with her appearance. Yesterday had been an emotional day on many levels. Mixed emotions had overwhelmed her as she emerged from the darkness. Peace surrounded her and seeped into her soul. Laurel grabbed her journal. *I thought I was done mourning the loss of loved ones, but miracles also happen. New life replaces lost ones. Prayers were answered yesterday. Maybe God is listening.*

*****

Since the birth of Bella, Laurel was spending less time in her room. Bella gave Laurel a reason to get up early every morning and a purpose in her life. She gave Laurel something else to think about and occupy her days. Laurel hurried to get herself ready and head downstairs. Her heartbeat quickened at the sound of Doc's truck pulling into the yard. She knew she'd been waiting for him. Pleasure washed over her as she headed over to the barn.

Her good mood faded a little when Doc gave both horses a positive bill of health because she knew it would be the end of his daily visits. She felt better when he said, "We can take Coco and Bella over to the small paddock. Would you like to lead one while I lead the other? Let's see how they adapt to being together in a bigger space where Bella can romp."

Once unleashed, Coco began to graze while the young foal pranced. A few minutes later Bella went over to her new mom and began to suckle. The fostering had been a success. Doc turned and smiled at Laurel. Laurel was elated and smiled back. Suddenly, the tears came. Without a second thought, Doc took her in his arms and held her tight.

Laurel pushed away. "Sorry, that had to have been awkward. Emotions got the better of me." She turned and left.

Doc was captivated by the young woman who left abruptly and knew he wanted to know her better. He would enjoy learning more about her. Doc returned to his truck and left.

Laurel headed to the gazebo. She watched the horses and thought of her loss, now angry at the ugly twist of fate that followed her here. It seemed unfair that her beloved Penny was gone, just like Sam and Gracie. She was unable to empty her mind as she wondered if her pain would ever end. She remained distracted until she heard another vehicle coming up the drive.

Kit couldn't wait another day to see how the fostering was going so had headed over to Willow Downs. Her eyes teared when she pulled up to the small paddock where Coca and Bella were now being kept. Darius was at the rail watching but wandered over to the barn as soon as she pulled up. *What an odd man,* thought Kit.

Laurel watched from her vantage point as Kit wandered over to the rail. Coco was grazing, Bella by her side. Kit let out a heavy sigh as she leaned forward and put her arms on the top rail. Coco nickered softly when she heard Kit's voice and wandered over, the young foal right behind her. Kit scratched Coco's nose knowing how much she loved it. Kit put her arms around Coco's neck and started to cry, emotional over what had transpired in the last few days. Another strong tie to Trace had been cut. Life continued to throw her curves. With gentle fingers Kit stroked the mare's forehead. Coco flicked her tail and welcomed the gentle petting. Kit's voice was thick with emotion, "Hey Coco, how's your new baby doing? Adoption seems to run in our family, even with our horses." She missed Coco but she knew she had done what was right. Bella took off frolicking, tossing her head and flicking her tail. It was nice to have a few minutes to herself with Coco.

Laurel's heart ached seeing how sad Kit was. She could tell Kit was crying. After giving Kit a few minutes, she crossed the yard and greeted Kit casually. "Mind if I join you?"

Kit felt like an Amazon standing next to Laurel for the young woman was very petite. She was cute with her frost-tipped hair. "I'm sorry you lost your mare. I'm glad to see Coco and Bella have accepted each other and Coco has adjusted to her temporary home. I hope you don't mind the unannounced visit. Your dad said it would be fine to stop by anytime. I miss Coco. She's very special to me." There was more than a hint of sadness as she shared the night of Coco's birth and the bond that had formed between Coco and Kit. "Because Coco was born during a miserable spring snow storm and was the color of hot chocolate, we called her Coco. She has a calm nature and has delivered several of our finest horses."

Laurel smiled sadly, "Penny was the color of a bright shiny penny. She was skittish in nature, and this was her first foal." *She was probably traumatized by the move and couldn't recover. More guilt.* "Our family can't thank you enough. Your kindness helped save our beautiful filly."

"That was thanks to Doc's quick thinking. I'm so glad it worked. Doc says they've both adjusted well to each other."

Laurel turned her attention back to Kit, "You and the vet seem to have a special bond." Her voice was tight with new emotion. Laurel knew she was fishing.

Kit understood the unspoken question behind the comment. She had seen the lingering looks and exchanged glances between the two of them when she brought Coco here. She also picked up on the fact that every time she and Doc were together, Laurel's name kept coming up. "Our paths cross professionally and socially but we've been good friends for years. I trusted Doc when he said your family needed Coco."

The sky continued to darken as they talked. It was completely overcast by the time Kit was ready to leave. Baxter came to join them, and Laurel made an excuse so she could escape.

"I want to thank you again for your generous deed. I hope I'm not out of line asking this, but would you consider selling Coco since Laurel lost her horse?"

Kit hadn't expected this. "I'll have to get back to you. I feel I should talk to my family about this." Kit knew she had made up the last part as an excuse. His request had caught her off guard. She would talk to the family but in her heart she knew what the right thing to do was.

Kit appeared to be composed but Baxter heard the stiffness in Kit's voice. "I understand."

She wanted to watch them longer, but she didn't want to overstay.

That night Kit called Baxter Rodwell. Sometimes you have to let the good go as well as the bad. As difficult as her decision was she agreed to sell Coco. "We all have a purpose in life, even horses. Willow Downs is where Coco needs to be now." Baxter immediately agreed to her price. He would have paid anything to make his daughter happy. Kit thought it would be easier over the phone. She was wrong but at least he didn't see her tears.

CHAPTER SEVENTEEN

Laurel continued to be on Doc's mind. On his next visit with Kit, he brought up the Rodwells. "I have a favor to ask you. Would you and Lola do one of your "welcome to the neighborhood" visits with the Rodwells? I'm sure Genna and Laurel could both use a friend. It's been quite hectic since they arrived, so they haven't had time to meet anyone. You and Lola both know what it's like to be new to a community." He was trying to keep his tone casual hoping to conceal his feelings. Laurel Easton had captivated him from the moment they met.

This was one of the many things Kit loved about Doc. His kind nature and gentle heart was who this man was. His compassion for others was genuine and he was always extending his kindness to others. "Lola and I are actually going tomorrow. We were giving them time to recover from their traumatic events over the last few days." Kit watched him with a thoughtful expression on her face, "You've been spending a lot of time at Willow Downs." Maybe it wasn't all business. He seemed to be awfully concerned about a young lady he had just met.

"Besides monitoring the horses, I've been helping them get settled."

"It's your nature to want to help. That's one of the reasons you're a wonderful vet. I stopped by yesterday to see Coco and had a brief conversation with Laurel. The fostering seems to have worked."

Doc nodded, "Bella's a beauty."

"Laurel isn't bad either," teased Kit.

Doc ignored Kit's teasing but couldn't refrain from grinning, "I think the Rodwells would like to buy Coco." Doc waited for Kit's response.

"They already have. It was the right thing to do."

*****

Laurel had planned her escape and wandered over to the gazebo. She knew Kit and Lola Grayson were visiting today. They were doing the neighborly thing by coming over to officially welcome them to the rural community. Laurel wanted no part of it. She wished everyone would leave her alone. Kit seemed nice enough when she met her, but Laurel wasn't ready for the grand gesture. She was still numb from the emotional tailspin she'd been through. First with the accident, then the move, and most recently with the horses. She remained where she was as she watched the Graysons drive up to the house.

Today, Kit paid more attention to the ranch's transformation as they approached the house. Both of her previous visits were under stressful circumstances. Signs of spring were everywhere but it was the added touches with the planters and manicured flowerbeds that made you feel welcome. She took a deep breath to ease her built up tension. Kit noticed Laurel in the gazebo and wondered if she would be joining them. Doc had commented that she continued to be withdrawn due to the accident and loss of her family.

"Somebody has a green thumb," commented Lola, as they walked to the front door.

Genna opened the door before they even knocked. "Welcome ladies. I've had the pleasure of meeting Kit, but I've been looking forward to meeting you ever since you called. Those homemade cinnamon buns are a lovely surprise."

Genna was everything Lola expected. Her hazel eyes were accented by laugh lines that enhanced the character of her friendly face. Her voice was warm, and her smile was welcoming. Lola liked her immediately. "When I moved here with my young family, we were welcomed warmly by the wife of my husband's boss. Sadie Calhoun is Kit's grandmother and became my best friend, one that I desperately needed. I had no friends due to the transient lifestyle we'd been living. I was so lonely and apprehensive because I didn't know how long we'd be staying. Sadie showed up at our door with homemade cinnamon buns and over the years we have shared many pots of tea. Tea makes everything better, doesn't it?" Lola handed

Genna the cinnamon buns and smiled, "Please call me Lola and may I call you Genna?"

Genna nodded. "Kit, you're welcome to join us, or you can join Laurel. I believe she has escaped to the gazebo." There was a pleading look in Genna's eyes that Kit understood.

"I'll go see if I can find her. Enjoy your tea." Kit knew the two ladies hit it off when she heard Lola compliment Genna on the beautifully landscaped gardens before entering the house.

Sitting on the island was a vase of freshly cut flowers adding warmth to the spacious kitchen. Genna was excited to give Lola a tour of the house. Lola could see they were settling in, but as beautifully decorated as the house was, there were no photos anywhere. Lola thought it was odd. Maybe they were still unpacking. By the time tea was ready both ladies felt comfortable with each other.

Lola expanded on what brought her family to Alberta and what kept them here. "Years ago, God guided us here. At the time I was terrified because I didn't understand his plan but in the end it was the best thing that happened to me and my sons. It allowed for a new beginning for us. Life reshapes our lives in unexpected ways. I hope this move is as good for your family."

"Thank you. Life constantly changes direction, and we adapt. I've learned over the years to rely on my faith. I prayed to find a way to help Laurel. One day I came across the listing for this ranch. When I saw all the willow trees and that laurel bushes were part of the landscaping I knew God was guiding me. The spiritual meaning of laurels is to encourage one to continue believing in themselves and reminds us of our strengths."

Genna's eyes were sad, "Laurel's accident was not only tragic but traumatic. We waited for days for her to wake up. When she finally did it was worse than we expected. We knew she was fine physically, so we weren't prepared for her mutism. Baxter and I were devastated when we were told there was nothing medical that could be done for her. She would talk when she was ready. One day of silence drifted into the next and days became months." Genna opened up to Lola knowing she'd understand in a way that Baxter couldn't, "I was afraid we'd lost our daughter. I grew tired of being strong for everyone due to the unexpected events that changed our lives. I had to rely on my faith that God would not forsake me."

Lola understood. "Sometimes we have to be strong for others and we have more strength than we realize and by the grace of God we get through each day." It had taken continued strength for Lola to help her family over the years.

"We had the courage to move here on faith, hoping for a miracle and God answered my prayers. Laurel has finally emerged from her imprisoned silence but she's still dealing with her emotional trauma. She has her voice but refuses to speak about her husband and daughter or about the accident. There's still something deep inside that is bothering her. Mothers know these things. For now, I'll continue to respect her privacy, but I want her to be happy again."

Lola wanted to comfort Genna, "We deal with a lot in our lives, don't we. You and I have lived long enough to accept there is loss in everyone's life, but you can't let heartache consume you. Everyone has their history with sadness and we both know it never goes away. In time we find the strength to get through the tough times. This will pass and all of you will get through this dark time."

Genna's faith was strong, "Out of darkness comes the light. I've experienced sad things in my life, and I've struggled like everyone else. We all do, but I've been blessed despite the hardships. We don't know what tomorrow brings or if there will be another tomorrow. Now that we're settled here we will move forward. I know it was especially difficult for Baxter to leave but he seems to be adjusting. This is such a beautiful ranch and the scenery surrounding us is spectacular."

Lola decided to share a few details about the ranch, "We all have history and so do places. Locals say our ranch has always been overshadowed by bad luck. Your ranch has history as well. The Beaumonts left due to unpleasant circumstances. People seem to like to dwell on the bad, so they overlook the good. Some even enhance and change the facts to make it more tantalizing. Ignore the gossip. I know your family will make Willow Downs your own and bring back the good like we did."

Both women were wise to the fact that life could change quickly, and it wasn't always what you expected. Age helped them to accept unexpected changes quicker. "There is heartache and pain in everyone's life. We've learned a lot about death and the meaning of life. Dealing with death is just one of life's hardest lessons."

Genna agreed with Lola, "We've learned to cope better, but we continue to hurt for our children as we watch them struggle. Laurel's still mad at God for his cruelty."

Lola's eyes darkened with sorrow as her own memories surfaced. "Kit was the same way when my son died but time is a wonderful healer. It takes understanding on our part to give them the time they need. Laurel will be fine."

Genna declared without a doubt, "Fate can be such a powerful force, but faith is stronger. You and I put our trust in God, and he guided both our families here. Laurel is like a changed person since we moved. She still spends too many hours alone but now they aren't always in her room. Her spirits are improving. A large part of that is due to Doc Parker."

Lola understood how a move could change lives in a positive way. It also brings others into our lives and changes everything. There was a quick flicker of amusement in Lola's eyes. She had noticed that Doc wasn't dropping by as often at Lola Grande and Kit had told her he was spending more time at Willow Downs. She had already guessed the reason why. God works in mysterious ways.

"I can tell Doc is a nice man who is kind and thoughtful. He quickly became more than just our vet. His wife must be a gem considering all the extra hours he's been spending here."

Lola didn't know if Genna was fishing for information, but she answered anyway. "Doc isn't married. Someday, some woman is going to be blessed to have this fine man as a husband. Our family has known Doc for many years. He's an honorable man who has strong values and firm beliefs."

Genna was surprised to hear he was still a bachelor at his age. "Laurel is doing so much better since we moved here, and Baxter has adjusted to the move as well. He sacrificed a lot, but he would do anything for his daughter. We both would. We don't always understand God's plan, but we let him lead us because of our faith."

While the older women chatted inside, Kit wandered over to the gazebo. She knew from experience that Laurel had stayed away on purpose, but she decided to invade her privacy hoping a conversation with the young widow would help her through her grief. She knew how a sudden tragedy could change a person's life. Kit had experienced more tragedy in her young life than any person should have to.

Laurel appeared cool and distant when Kit approached, and Kit sensed her displeasure. Unlike her mother, Laurel's look was unwelcoming; she would rather be by herself. Kit only needed a moment before deciding on the direct approach as she sat down next to Laurel. Because Kit had been knocked to her knees more than once, she was filled with empathy and would be there for this young widow so she could again appreciate what she still had in her life. Even though Doc had told her a great deal about Laurel, she had no idea what he shared with Laurel about her. "I know a lot of your story and I'm sincerely sorry for your loss. Doc wouldn't have shared if he didn't care. He respects people's privacy, but he thinks maybe I can help you because of my own past. He's a very compassionate man, and he thought it might help you if we talked. Death is difficult, especially when it comes too soon." Kit was only a few years older than Laurel, but she had dealt with a lot of tragedy in her life.

"Life can be cruel for no reason," Laurel said bitterly. Her eyes darkened with guilt, *It's worse when it's your fault. I should have died that day because I was driving.*

Some things were still hard for Kit to talk about but if it would help Laurel she could do it. A reflective look clouded Kit's large gray eyes, "When I say I understand it's because I do. I don't know if Doc shared my past with you and that I've been widowed twice." By the look on Laurel's face, Kit knew Doc had not shared this. Kit briefly shared her tragic story and could see Laurel's guard come down.

"You wake up every morning and expect your day to be like every other day. In a heartbeat it changes. Your life crumbles around you and you have to struggle through so many emotions. It's such a shock that at first you don't believe it. You think if you lock yourself away it can't be real. I was self-indulgent and wrapped myself in self-pity and struggled through all the emotions. I even resented Trace for dying." Kit's voice cracked with remembered pain, "Trace died because of the vindictive act of a sick man. I really struggled because it didn't have to happen. The dreams we had were unfulfilled. I was consumed by bitterness, drowning in sorrow and angry at life. I was living each day looking through my grief. It clouded my vision, and I was stuck in a negative place caused by a traumatic event.

I didn't know how to cope. Our husbands may have died due to different circumstances, but our reality is the same. There's a phase you go through, the one where you can't believe anything is ever going to be right again. For a while you lose part of yourself. You don't know who you are anymore. Then when you think you've gotten through it and you start to heal, you find it still hurts. Don't let it consume you. Let life back in and in time it takes over the hurt. I promise you, the pain you're feeling right now isn't forever." Kit knew in time Laurel would understand.

Laurel hadn't missed the slight tremor in Kit's voice. It moved her but conflicting thoughts continued to torment Laurel. She decided to be as direct as Kit, "I'm adjusting because I have to, but I can't help it that I'm struggling. Life isn't always fair, is it?" She felt she hadn't been able to grieve her loss due to the guilt.

Kit tried to explain, "Grief can take away your life if you allow it to because you feel you lost control over your life. Change is more difficult when it isn't by choice. When you're really low you feel like you're on an out-of-control roller coaster ride and you can't stop it to get off."

"And it's taking you straight to hell," Laurel said bitterly.

"Everyone copes with heartache differently. It's more difficult when someone young dies or it's unexpected. I know your grief is still new. The invisible wounds are the ones that last the longest, but they do heal in time. Everyone has their history with loss. Your whole world was turned upside down months ago and your life changed in an instant. I was dealing with anger. You're dealing with guilt. You can't go back and change things. You lose more than those who died. For a while you lose a part of yourself. Once I accepted Trace's death, life got easier. Acceptance allows you to move forward. Allow yourself to grieve. That is also part of the healing process. Before you realize it you slowly open yourself to live and love again."

Laurel continued to listen without comment. This was the first time someone had taken the time to talk honestly about the feelings she was experiencing. Kit was someone who understood because she had lived through her own loss.

Kit's gaze remained understanding, "Even when time dulled the sharp pain I continued to allow my grief to consume me, so I handled things badly for a long time. We can get caught in a very dark place. You don't want to stay there. In time I realized I could only heal if I let go of my anger. You have to let go of your guilt. We have more strength than we realize to get through tough times and in time we do."

"How did you get through it?"

"Life doesn't allow one to remain locked away in self-pity. My family needed me. They were struggling too. You do realize this is very hard on your parents. They are also suffering."

Laurel's eyes darkened with sorrow. She could no longer hide the additional guilt that continued to haunt her. "I know my withdrawing has made it difficult for them."

"I had to let the past go and move on. I know that's easier said than done and it takes time. It doesn't mean you forget the past. Just don't let it keep you from moving forward. I won't lie; it wasn't easy in the beginning, and I still struggle like everyone else. Three children creates continuous challenges. On a good day, I handle it. On a bad day, I go to my room and scream."

Laurel appreciated Kit's honesty, "Does it help."

"I think it frightens the children enough that they're on their best behavior for a few days. It sure makes me feel better. On sane days, I go for a walk, usually down to the corrals. Or I sit outside on the verandah and gaze at the mountains. They help put everything in perspective by the sheer magnificence of them. They make my problems seem small and I know when I get up in the morning the mountains will still be there, but my problems don't have to be. I'm not saying life will be easy, but it wouldn't be even if we didn't have to deal with the unexpected changes life deals us."

"I have trouble believing this is real. I can't believe Sam and Gracie are gone. I don't even remember their funeral. How can life be so cruel?"

Kit could relate because she had felt the same way. Trace's funeral had been a nightmare to live through. "I know from experience how one tires of the well-wishers who pat your hand and tell you how sorry they are, and it will get better. That's not what you want to hear, but they mean well, and they are right. I promise not to pat your hand, but it will get better."

Laurel actually laughed. Were certain events in life actually scripted and people just acted out the role? It was comforting to talk to someone who actually understood. "It's getting easier since we moved here."

Kit's looked over to the main house, "Sadly, death leaves a heartache that only time can heal but the loved ones we still have make it happen sooner. Lola, Trace's mother, told me nothing is forever. Nothing good and nothing bad. That's life. Lola gave me many lectures along with good advice. You get on with your life and move forward because if you don't you lose a little of yourself every day. Don't stay locked in the past. I had to learn to accept life under all circumstances and accept that I couldn't change anything. There's loss in everyone's life and you and I know it can happen at any time. You can't let the heartache consume you. Time will help you with that too. You've survived the hardest part."

The frantic despair in Laurel's voice was evident, "If I let go of the pain I let go of them. In time they will be gone."

"You'll find a way to keep your husband and daughter in your life while at the same time letting go."

"I miss Sam and Gracie every day. My biggest regret was not being able to say goodbye," Laurel confessed, once she was able to swallow the lump in her throat.

Kit said knowingly, "People we lose are still with us in our hearts and in our memories. Talking about them becomes part of the healing process. It keeps them with us. It's hard moving forward knowing you will be spending the rest of your life without them, but your life isn't over. It's just different. Our whole family experienced major changes that were out of our control, but we moved forward. Unexpected events change our lives. Change is good and bad, but you learn to accept it either way. You will be okay, Laurel. It doesn't mean you won't get hurt again, but you don't want to stop living."

Understanding Laurel's unhappiness as well as her fears about moving forward, Kit continued, "The past doesn't go away but life does get better. We all adjust to the changes in our lives. We have no choice. Certain days will be harder than others as you learn to cope. Father's Day is always difficult because my kids miss their dad. My youngest keeps saying he would like another daddy. Sometimes you have to dig deep to find your inner strength. We do have the strength to get through the tough times and are again able to cope better. Even now, I have challenges. It's not always easy being a single mom. I want you to know difficulties continue no matter what your life is like." Kit flashed Laurel a compassionate smile, but kept it real, "When someone loses all that is familiar, nothing else matters. You feel all alone even when you're surrounded by the people who love you. It will never be the way it was. Once you accept that, you can finally move forward. When you let life back in it takes away the hurt and fills the void you're experiencing right now. You don't stay in the darkness when you move forward."

Despite her involvement in the accident, Laurel wanted to keep on living, even though it was difficult. She realized Kit had more than her share of grief in her life. This was something they had in common.

"This traumatic experience has affected more than just you. I'm sure you realize how much this affected your parents. Because your parents love you, they have made major changes in their lives to help you to move forward."

Laurel nodded, thinking about the deep love her parents had shown her and the sacrifices they made moving here.

"We have more strength than we realize to get through the tough times. You manage to pick up the shattered pieces of your heart and thanks to the love of friends and family you slowly begin to put your life back together. We still have loved ones around us, and we can depend on them until we can once again stand on our own. Like me, you have a loving family for support as well as someone who understands. I would like to be your friend."

"That would be nice." A bond was formed by shared grief. A friendship was beginning based on that bond.

"You also have a friend in Doc."

Laurel smiled freely for the first time, "Doc said you've been here before you brought us Coco. He said you were here when the Beaumonts owned it."

Kit didn't go into the reason why. "The interior of the home was immaculate and grand. The splendor of it didn't make it a home. Driving up today, it already presents a feeling of welcome. You and your parents have done a wonderful job bringing it to life."

"That's all because of Mom," confessed Laurel.

"Our home at Lola Grande is much more rustic, an original farmhouse with that good old country charm. You have to come over and visit one day."

Laurel appreciated the invitation but doubted if she would. "I never tire of the view around me as I breathe in the pure mountain air. It grabs hold and draws you in and peace takes over." They both inhaled deeply, taking a moment to reflect on their losses.

An old ache gripped Kit as she confessed her ongoing struggle, "Life isn't always easy, but it is real. Death is a hard lesson to escape from. Even though time has passed it still hurts and there are times you wonder "what if". I'm grateful for the life I have but it's still difficult at times," Kit said honestly.

Laurel had to ask, "How do you move forward when it's so difficult? Do you stop wondering 'what if'?"

Kit had learned to live with her loss. She chose her words carefully, "I allow myself to do that sometimes and I go back in time and remember. I'll never forget either of my husbands. They are part of my past, but I keep the good memories alive. I let the bad go a long time ago. Even though our loved ones aren't here with us, they are always in our hearts. The bad memories fade in time. Hold onto the happy memories, those precious moments that made up your life together. Remember them with joy rather than sorrow. Everyone has their history with sadness, but life still goes on. You can't let the heartache consume you. When I come back to the present I count my blessings for what I do have, and I focus on the good in my life. I welcome every new day and deal with whatever it brings."

Tears of self-pity stung Laurel's eyes. Laurel sat there, childless and a widow. This conversation was opening fresh wounds, but time with Kit allowed Laurel to admit, "There's this huge void in my life, not to mention the hole in my heart. I'm still trying to come to terms with my loss, but I have accepted what happened."

Their conversation had brought back a lot of painful memories for both of them. "No one understands another person's grief, but you and I have experienced a common loss. I hope I haven't offended you by anything I've said. I hope I've helped instead."

Laurel's eyes expressed her appreciation, "You've helped me a lot." Laurel felt like she had spent time with an older sister whose life was as traumatic as her own.

"Feel free to call my anytime and please consider me a friend."

Genna and Lola stood on the verandah and saw that Laurel and Kit were still together in the gazebo. Genna called out and waved. Kit got up and left and waited by the truck. She didn't realize how long she had been talking with Laurel. It had been an intense conversation for both of them. "I hope Laurel and Kit had a good visit. It must have gone okay since Kit didn't come back. As I said, we are all adjusting to the move here, but Willow Downs is beginning to feel like home. Lovely people like your family and Doc Parker have made our transition here easier."

Lola smiled encouragingly, "We have to keep having faith. This too will pass, and your daughter will be fine. It's time for you to start living for you now. I have a friend I'd like you to meet. Her name is Anna Ortiz. She and her husband moved here a few years ago. She invited me for a visit tomorrow afternoon and said to bring you along. You have no excuses, so I won't take no for an answer."

"I would love to meet your friend. Thanks again for the cinnamon buns and I really enjoyed our visit. I'm looking forward to tomorrow." Genna welcomed her new friendship with Lola Grayson. It felt natural and comforting.

Lola gave Genna a hug, "See you tomorrow."

After the Graysons left, Laurel remained in the gazebo. Kit had given her a lot to think about. She needed time to collect herself and process so much of what Kit said. She appreciated Kit's openness and honesty. Their conversation had a powerful effect on her because Kit was someone who truly understood.

That evening, Laurel was thinking about Doc knowing he had helped instigate the visit. Laurel had to admit she looked forward to seeing him. She had hoped he'd stop by on his way home. When he didn't she wondered if he was at Lola Grande instead. It seemed like he and Kit were very close. It was evident the first time she saw them together. She wondered what their relationship really was.

CHAPTER EIGHTEEN

Willow Downs felt like home. Now that their lives had settled the Rodwells had fallen into the routine they had before moving here. Genna and Baxter were again attending Sunday morning church services and were being welcomed into the community. Today, they had been invited to stay after church and join the minister and his wife at their home for lunch. Another couple they met had also been included. Laurel was glad her parents were making friends. She was also invited but wasn't ready to leave the ranch.

The old Laurel was slowly emerging, having worked her way out of her silent world. She was no longer as fragile as she was when they arrived. Her body was stronger, healthier. The flashbacks had ceased, and the nightmares were less frequent. Laurel knew she was doing better. She was still healing emotionally but she'd made great progress here in the quiet country. Time outdoors had given her more color. Back was the sparkle in her eyes that had been vacant for too long. Having found acceptance, she was beginning to let go of the guilt that had smothered her in Montana, but it was being replaced with grief. In time she would work through that too. Time had dulled the sharp pain, but she knew it would have been harder to cope if they hadn't moved here. Thanks to her parents she had come a long way in a short time. Her family had been her salvation, along with Doc Parker. She had welcomed him into her life, glad to have a friend who accepted her situation. She also had to acknowledge the role Kit had played. Her visit had helped her more than anything else.

The afternoon sun, hot and high, beat down from a clear blue sky. The gentle breeze stirred the leaves on the willow trees. Laurel sat taking in the smells of summer surrounding her, the fresh-cut grass, the fragrance of the flowers planted around the yard. The wind often carried the scent of the laurels. She enjoyed the warmth on her skin as she tipped her face to the sun and let herself become absorbed into the silence. This was a different silence, not the self-imposed silence she had inflicted on herself. The sense of stillness was only broken by the wind in the trees. She had to admit she loved it here at Willow Downs and was learning to adjust to her new life. The wall she'd built before she came here was slowly coming down. The hollow look in her eyes was gone but sadness lingered. Laurel emptied her head of negative thoughts, unwilling to allow herself to dwell on the unhappy memories that would invade. Time passed unnoticed as she sat caught up in happy memories.

Laurel was excited when she saw Doc's truck coming up the drive. Her automatic reaction was pleasure mixed with surprise. The horses were doing fine, and it was Sunday. She flushed because she'd been so deep in thought, and it was Doc who kept taking over her thoughts. Truth was, she was drawn to Doc. It was rather disturbing because it was a pleasant sensation. Thanks to him, she had come alive and the world around her was beginning to brighten. She smiled at Doc as he ambled up the walk. Having spent the morning alone, she was restless, "I'll show you my favorite spot if you're staying."

"I have no other plans today."

Laurel's eyes brightened, "There's a stream that flows through the back of our property."

His smile was tender, "It's a bit muggy today so a stroll along the stream sounds refreshing. We might get a thunderstorm later."

They crossed to the back of the house and followed the worn path down to the water's edge. "I often escape down here. There's something special that happens when I'm here. I like the silence. It's different than the silence I inflicted on myself," and she giggled.

Doc hadn't picked up on Laurel's sense of humor yet.

Laurel led them along the meandering stream flowing within the narrow banks. The willows along the bank were well established and their shallow roots clung to the earth along the edge of the stream, offering shade as they watched the stream flow along the eroding bank. Sunbeams filtered through the willow trees, and signs of summer surrounded them, especially the fragrance of wild flowers. They walked in silence, both enjoying nature at its finest. The cooler air was invigorating. Maybe it was the company. Either way, Laurel was happy.

It was enjoyable being with Doc. Laurel found pleasure in his company. There was a natural ease between them. It felt like they had known each other for a long time instead of just weeks. A comfortable silence fell between them as they sat side by side on a fallen log listening to the stream ripple over the polished rocks, unaware of the clouds hanging low over the mountains and drifting their way. When thunder clapped and lightning flashed across the darkening sky, they decided to head back to the house. When thunder cracked again, they knew it might be a good idea to hurry. When Laurel slipped climbing the bank, Doc kept a firm grip on her hand until they got to the top. To his surprise she smiled and continued to hold his hand as they returned to the house. By the time they got there the gray clouds had passed without rain and the sky was clearing.

Genna and Baxter were sitting side by side on the swing. No one was around when they got back from town. Seeing Doc's truck, they guessed he and Laurel were off somewhere. As usual, Darius was nowhere to be seen. Both turned in surprise when they heard voices and saw Laurel and Doc coming around the corner of the house holding hands. Seeing the Rodwells, he quickly let go.

Baxter exchanged an amused glance with Genna and squeezed her hand. Words weren't necessary. They had noticed a positive change in Laurel since they moved. Even more so since their daughter started spending time with the vet. Laurel was on the road to recovery, often with Doc at her side. Genna detected another positive change in Laurel since the visit from the Graysons. Laurel hadn't shared anything about her conversation with Kit, but she seemed more involved in life. Her smiles came easier and there was a lightness in her daughter's voice she hadn't heard in a long time.

Doc and Laurel joined her parents on the verandah. Laurel was glad to see her parents as happy and relaxed as she was. She knew the last few months had been difficult for them.

Genna brought out cold drinks and cookies. Their conversation flowed easily until Doc casually said, "I have an easy day at the clinic on Friday. Why don't you drive into Diamond Valley. You would enjoy walking around town and popping into the quaint shops and we could meet for lunch." Doc paused when he saw the color drain from Laurel's face.

For a moment Laurel's eyes clouded over. A hush fell before Laurel confessed, "I haven't driven since the accident." She questioned if she ever would. She hadn't even left the ranch. What happened had shaken her confidence, and she was still traumatized.

Doc could see Laurel was dismayed by the idea. Maybe it was because of his relationship with Kit for so many years that he spoke without thinking, "We all have times when we need to find the courage to move forward and there's no time like the present. You can do this if you want to. All you have to do is try."

Laurel felt the condescending tone in his voice was unacceptable. She actually turned on him, "Don't talk to me like a child."

Doc understood her reaction, but he continued to push. He didn't walk on eggshells like everyone else, "Don't behave like a child. Besides, I'm used to talking to my patients and they don't talk back."

What right did he have to talk to her like this? Beyond annoyed, she snapped, "They obey because they have to. I'm not one of the horses."

He wanted to laugh but managed to control himself, "No, you're sitting there like a stubborn mule. It's time to break out of your comfort zone. Besides, my patients love me."

Laurel was not amused by Doc's humor. "Only because they don't know better. You could be a little more sensitive to my fears," she accused.

Baxter and Genna didn't know what to make of the exchange between them. They sat back and continued to watch, not sure how this would end.

Knowing how important it was for Laurel to do this, and he knew she could, Doc ignored the reluctance in her voice. "I'll come with you, and we can take this as slow as you want. I have all day. You can drive around the circular drive to start. After that, if you feel comfortable we can drive out to the road." Doc had already witnessed her underlying strength. Was he about to experience the stubbornness he'd witnessed when he first met her? He held his breath. No one spoke, waiting to see what was going to happen next. Everyone knew it was the only way to move forward. The question remained, would she?

Laurel knew there was no point in putting it off, so she agreed with great reluctance. They would need to use her mom's car since they hadn't replaced Laurel's vehicle that was written off after the accident. Doc had offered his, but she knew she would be more comfortable driving a vehicle she was used to. Laurel didn't miss the look of concern in her mom's eyes as she handed her the keys. Laurel's eyes challenged back. "You can't continue to protect me. I need to do this." *I can do this*, she told herself despite the fact that she was experiencing a sudden wave of panic.

Despite her fears Laurel forced herself to take the next step and climbed into the driver's seat. She swallowed hard, her heart was pounding, and her mouth had gone dry. Was she ready for this? She took a deep breath to control her nerves. It helped; or maybe it was Doc's smile of assurance as he climbed into the passenger seat beside her.

Doc spoke softly, "I understand you're nervous."

Laurel sat motionless, her face now drained of color. Panic rose in her throat, "Nervous! I'm scared as hell." She still hesitated as anxiety grabbed hold. *Relax*, she ordered herself. She took a deep breath as she grabbed the wheel with shaking hands.

Doc watched as Laurel struggled, "Don't worry, Laurel you can do this."

His confident words helped. Her heart rate settled, and the shaking ceased. Once her legs stopped trembling she started the car and eased away from the house.

Baxter watched them go. "She's in good hands with Doc."

After the third time around the circle Laurel was more relaxed and headed down the drive. By the time they reached the main road Laurel felt liberated. More and more of the old Laurel was coming back. She was ready to continue further. A hint of amusement pulled up the corners of her mouth, "Left or right?'

"Are you sure?"

Not waiting for his response, she turned right. "Let's hit the road, partner," and pressed down on the acceleration.

Doc gasped, "Slow down, Laurel, this is a gravel road."

Laurel gave him a sassy grin, her eyes twinkling as she slowed down, "I'm messing with you. I wanted to make you uncomfortable. Not exactly fun, is it." Amused by his reaction she laughed. It was the first time he had heard her laugh. It was music to his ears.

Doc laughed too, He was beginning to see a new side of Laurel. She was full of spunk and had a unique sense of humor. She was fun when she let her guard down.

Laurel actually felt a thrill as they took off. It was the first time she'd been away from the ranch. It was exhilarating as they continued down the country road before returning to the ranch. Both Genna and Baxter were on the verandah waiting. It had been a long hour for them. To their relief, both Doc and Laurel were smiling when they got out of the car.

Genna decided to invite Doc to stay for supper.

Doc readily agreed. He was far from ready to call it a day. He enjoyed spending time with the family. He wasn't surprised that Darius joined them. Conversation remained easy around the table. Genna was curious, "You must live around here, or you wouldn't be able to stop by as often as you do. Not that we mind."

"Our family ranch is about a half hour south of here. My parents moved to High River when Dad finally retired. The town has everything they need including a hospital which they felt was important at their age. They didn't want to live with their kids."

Laurel smiled at her parents, "I didn't expect to still be living with my parents but I'm so grateful for their support." Her words were sincere, and she showed no sign of resentment.

"My older brother, Bryce, and his family live in the main house, and I have a log cabin tucked into a secluded clearing, so I have my privacy. Bryce and I are equal owners, but he runs the ranch and draws a foreman's wage while I run my practice. I help when I can, but my practice keeps me busy. I also have living quarters at the back of my clinic. As you know, I can get called anytime, night and day. Sometimes it's easier to stay in town rather than driving back to the ranch, especially in winter. Be warned, the winters here can be extreme."

Baxter was curious, "Do you have cattle or is it more farming that you do? I saw both as we were driving here when we moved."

"We do both. Our ranch is an average sized family ranch. Times are changing and so is ranching. The younger generation doesn't want to take over the family farm so they're being bought up. Now we're seeing large cattle ranches and fewer original homesteads."

"Did you always want to be a vet?" Darius asked. "You were wonderful with Penny. I know how difficult it was to let her go so the foal could live." Darius didn't take to strangers, but he liked this young man, and he trusted him.

"Growing up Bryce helped Dad with the farming, and I helped Dad with the animals. Even as a kid, I knew how to help them when they were sick or if a cow was in trouble. I often saved a calf that might have died. I felt so bad about losing Penny. Loss never gets easier." He changed the subject, knowing it was still a sensitive one, even for him. He shared some local history. "I'm blessed to have grown up here. The country is real; the people are trustworthy."

Genna couldn't be happier. Tonight, it felt like life as they knew it before the accident. They had their daughter back. Driving again was such a positive step for her. Genna knew a large part of Laurel's progress was due to the vet. Genna recognized it as a good sign that she was showing interest in others.

Laurel walked Doc out. The warmth in her eyes took his breath. She smiled in gratitude and hugged him in appreciation for being her encouragement and her strength.

"I'm impressed with your courage. I know it wasn't easy, but you did it."

Laurel gave him a smug look, "I'll see you Friday. You owe me lunch."

Doc was aware of the significance of her remark. "My pleasure. Drop by the clinic at noon."

Laurel didn't go back inside. The gentle coolness of the night was refreshing as she watched the fleeting sunset drop behind the clouds. Today had been another monumental day in her life.

CHAPTER NINETEEN

Thin white clouds drifted like ribbons across a sapphire blue sky. Nature could be incredibly healing for the mind and spirit. Laurel's eyes were as clear and bright as the sky above. Gone were the shadows beneath her eyes that had looked so sad. The world around her was alive and so was she. Laurel wandered over to the gazebo, her safe place, her sanctuary. The wind whispering through the willows promised the return of serenity to her life while the Alberta Chinook wind warded off the demons. A light breeze gently caressed her. Laurel lifted her face, enjoying the warmth. The healing power of nature was her therapy. The beautiful sounds of nature surrounding her replaced the screaming accusations of guilt. When she breathed in the pure mountain air, a feeling of peace surrounded her. She took another deep breath, taking in the aroma of the flowering laurel bushes around the gazebo while watching the butterflies flitting over the blossoms. Laurel knew her mother would say Mother Nature was working her magic, and the butterflies were a reminder that our loved ones are near. Maybe her mother was right.

Time here had allowed her release from the living darkness, and Laurel had finally come to terms with her loss even though heartache still remained her constant companion. Thanks to Doc, she had overcome her fear of driving and ventured off the ranch to have lunch with him in Diamond Valley. Laurel's thoughts shifted, no longer on the beauty surrounding her. The look on her face was one of profound sorrow knowing the hurt she had caused her parents. Laurel was ready to let it all go, but she needed to address one other area of guilt. She felt her heart clutch in a moment of nervousness as she called her mom over.

"I love sitting here in the gazebo. For some reason it gives me peace. I think it was both easier and quicker for me to recover because we moved here. Thank you for your patience and understanding. I haven't been fair to you and Dad. I was detached those first days, and I remained stuck in a negative place for a long time due to the accident. It was a life-changing event, and I struggled to cope. I can't imagine how difficult it was for you and Dad." Laurel remained introspective. "I locked myself away, mentally, emotionally, and physically. I thought it would help but it didn't. The guilt and pain were overwhelming." At the time Laurel felt it was deserving, but her behavior had to have been extremely hard on her parents. Speaking slowly, Laurel chose her words carefully, "I believe this was more difficult for you and Dad than it was for me. I made my escape, but you couldn't. You had to stand by and watch me mourn in silence. I'm sorry. Can you forgive me?"

Genna broke in when her daughter faltered, "You have to forgive yourself first. None of us handled this very well. We were all confused and scared. Your dad and I put our trust in God like we always do, and he answered our prayers."

"I believe the hard part is over. I have found acceptance. Gratefully, the passing of time has helped me through my misery, but nothing takes away the emptiness."

"Things like this happen; that's life. We don't always understand God's plan."

"Living here has helped me deal with my loss, but I miss Sam and Gracie every day." Their deaths weighed heavily on Laurel.

"We all do," Genna said, her voice revealing her own heartache.

Laurel was ready to share her journal with her mother, the last step before leaving the darkness behind. "I have to let the past go and move forward. That's what I want to do today so there is one important thing I have to do. I need to share my journal with you. Words I couldn't say are written there. The tears I couldn't release spilled as words on blank pages." There was a moment of regret in her eyes, "I was filled with guilt. I couldn't deal with it. It was such a dark time for me in the beginning. Writing in my journal started as a penance. As time passed, it became my salvation."

Their conversation had been intense. Genna wondered if she was prepared for what was going to happen next? While Laurel went to get her journal from the house, Genna took a moment to pray. *Thank you for healing Laurel and giving her the courage to share her journal. I'm about to face things I wasn't prepared for. Grant me the gift of courage to accept and understand. Give me the wisdom to know what to say, and how to encourage Laurel as she moves forward, as we all move forward together.*

When Laurel returned with her journal she handed it to her mother. She knew there would be passages that would hurt her, but Laurel hoped it would help her mother understand what she had been dealing with. Laurel left her mom to allow her the privacy she would need and went inside and headed to the spare room where her mother had put the box of family photos. Next to it was a box she hadn't seen before. Curious, Laurel took it down first. Inside were all the newspaper articles, doctors reports, and legal documents relating to the accident. Her hands shook when she held the death certificates of Samuel Wyatt Easton and Gracie Dionne Easton. This was reality at its cruelest. It was all in there, the part of the traumatic event she hadn't dealt with. It confirmed what her mother always told her. The accident was not her fault. When she was done she placed the box back on the shelf and took the box she wanted and went to her room. Inside were her family photos. It was time to welcome them back. They were still apart of her life. Laurel spent the next couple of hours lost in happy memories while wandering down memory lane, embracing her life with Sam and Gracie. There were pictures of happier times: their wedding photo, the day in the hospital when they became a family, Gracie's first birthday, pictures of them as a family, pictures of her and Gracie without Sam because he was away. When her thoughts turned inward, the memories of the accident returned. This time she had total recall. She relived the moment of impact, and it jarred her memory, allowing the final release of her guilt. The accident wasn't her fault. For too long, the fog in her head had distorted the reality. Her mind was now clear, the guilt around the accident gone along with the foggy memories.

Alone in the gazebo, Genna's hands shook as she held the journal. It was her turn to find the courage to accept what her daughter was now willing to share. Her eyes darkened with sadness once she began reading. The handwritten entries were heart-wrenching. Laurel hadn't journaled daily, but her entries were reflective of her mental state due to ongoing guilt. Time passed unnoticed as Genna turned page after page. Unbearable pain caused Genna to pause when her eyes blurred. She forced herself to continue, even though every word was raw and revealing. She hadn't realized how much Laurel was suffering, unable to believe her parents when they told her it wasn't her fault. She didn't believe them because she thought they were wanting to protect her. Genna felt her own guilt overtake her, saddened by the fact she had trusted the doctors and remained quiet when they said to allow Laurel to recover in her own time. Maybe if they had shown her the newspaper articles describing the traumatic event it would have helped her daughter sooner. Lost in a haze of scrambled thoughts, Genna chose not to go down that road. The past was the past. Decisions were made on trust and love, and they would move forward the same way.

Genna put the journal down. It was too much to take in all at once. Until now, she had no idea what their daughter had endured. She began to cry, understanding how guilt could overtake a person and not let go. She took a few minutes to compose herself, then picked up the journal, and continued to read. She knew Laurel's words would continue to hurt her, but she had to read all of them. The more she read, the more she realized where the traumatic mutism came from and by the end, Genna could see the healing progress from one stage to another. When she reached the end, Genna read Laurel's final entry again. *My life is back, along with my voice. My tears have washed away my guilt and helped me to heal.* Genna closed the diary. There were no more secrets between them.

Laurel went back outside. Her mom was still sitting in the gazebo, the journal lying in her lap. Laurel sat down and took her mom's hands. Neither spoke. Finally, it was Laurel who broke the silence, "I found the box you had hidden away. The details were all there." Her voice dropped to an agonizing whisper, "I really thought the accident was my fault."

"I know that now. The doctors told us not to go into details. You had to find your own way out of your silence. We were giving you time to heal emotionally. It has been a very difficult period for all of us. You have no idea how many tears I shed for you."

"I thought you were trying to make me feel better by saying it wasn't my fault because of the fog. I was driving and I thought I hit the other car.

Now that I know everything I can truly move forward. I lived too long in a void of nothingness."

Genna needed some clarification of her own, "I realize why the accident resulted in mutism. What I don't understand is why it took so long for you to finally talk."

"I couldn't," Laurel stated simply. "I was able to journal, but I couldn't force the words out verbally until Bella's birth. It was the release trigger I needed. I couldn't save Sam or my Gracie. I had to let you know how important it was to save Penny's foal. Every mother, human or not, would chose to save her baby. I couldn't let an innocent baby die."

"I do wish you could have talked sooner," Genna cried out in despair. "We knew you needed time, but it was difficult on your dad and me. We didn't know how to help you. In desperation we moved here."

Laurel was humbled. "I know the sacrifice you and Dad made for me and I'm grateful for the unconditional love our family has. I'm glad we moved here. I don't know what would have happened if we stayed in Montanta." For a brief moment the haunted look was back in Laurel's eyes, "I can't believe Sam and Gracie are gone. I miss them so much."

"You'll find a way to keep them in your life. I know how hard this has been for you because I felt like I lost my daughter, too."

"While you read my journal I went through the pictures you packed away when we moved here. I miss Sam and Gracie every day. I do have happy memories. They were just locked away. Today they found their release. My new life is here. It's time to welcome Sam and Gracie to Willow Downs. They will always be part of our lives, but I can move forward without them. I don't know what I'm going to do moving forward so, for now, I'm just going to take it one day at a time. The writing helped but it didn't heal. That will still take time, but I have accepted what happened. Mom, I'm going to be okay."

"Thank you for sharing your journal. I could have handled this better." In fact, Genna felt she had failed in many ways. "We have all endured the struggles but as a family we have come to embrace the change. We now have a clearer vision of how to move forward."

Laurel smiled at her mom, but her smile was sad, "I would like some time to myself." Genna got up and left and Laurel watched her mom walk away. She knew she hadn't been the only one suffering. She had heard her mom's guilt, such a hard thing to live with. Laurel wouldn't carry that guilt, but she felt bad. It was time for forgiveness, starting with herself. It would allow her to move forward in every way. Suddenly the tears came, all the tears that hadn't found their release.

Darius, who was walking by, heard her sobbing. Blinded by tears of his own, he headed to the barn. He hadn't cried since he left home. Darius had been truly affected by this family's trauma. He loved this family who had become his family.

Laurel had taken the time alone to sort out her tangled emotions and the events of the past few months. Dry-eyed and completely spent, Laurel returned to the house and asked her parents for forgiveness. Genna hugged Laurel. There was no need for forgiveness. Instead, she thanked God in gratitude for helping their daughter heal.

Laurel went up to her room, opened her journal and wrote, *"It's time to live in the real world without lingering in the past. Tomorrow is a new day. I choose to move forward.* She knew she had written her last entry. She returned to get the box with all the details relating to the accident and placed her journal inside. She placed the box back on the top shelf and closed the closet door, a conscious move to close the door to her past. She had fought her inner battle for months and won. She was able to exercise the last of the demons that had haunted her. Laurel returned to her room and walked to the window. She looked beyond the ranch, beyond the mountains to her future. She looked up and began to pray.

After supper Laurel returned to the gazebo. Within minutes she was lost in thought. It had taken her a long time to deal with her guilt and today she was able to let it go. There were still times she was overtaken by dark thoughts. Her face took on a haunted look due to the return of ghosts from the past. She was still finding it hard to accept losing Sam and Gracie. Their deaths left such a void in her life, a reminder of her unfulfilled dreams. She sat lost in thought, unaware of the passing of time. Laurel was startled when Doc's voice pulled her from her memories.

"You were so deep in thought you didn't hear me drive in. Maybe you would prefer to be alone?" Sensing the agony she was in, he sat quietly waiting for her to respond. This behavior wasn't new to him. He recognized the grieving process because he'd seen Kit struggle the same way. He could see Laurel was trying to deal with the familiar sorrow. Doc hated to see the pain in Laurel's eyes. For months he had seen it in Kit's eyes when Trace died. Grief was hard and some days were harder than others. He hoped he could help Laurel like he had helped Kit. Doc remained silent, hoping Laurel would open up. He would welcome anything she shared knowing it would help him to understand her better, and he would learn more about her as a person. That included the life she had before she moved here.

A shadow crossed Laurel's face, reflective of her ongoing struggle. She had spent an emotional morning with her mother. Was she strong enough to take another step forward? She was quiet for a long time. Maybe it was time to confide in Doc, so he understood who she was and what she had been dealing with. Knowing she could trust him, she turned to him and began, "I was thinking about Sam and Gracie. It was an agonizing loss in many ways. Sam was a gifted doctor who was kind, intelligent, confident and had the ability to listen to others and my sweet innocent Gracie had the biggest smile you've ever seen. I'm sure she's lighting up heaven every day. Some nights I pretend the brightest star in the sky is Gracie smiling down at me."

There was a hint of sadness in Laurel's smile, but her voice was calm, "I met Sam at Urgent Care where he was a resident. I had an abdominal attack that required an emergency appendectomy. Sam was the attending resident. I was young and infatuated by his charm and good looks. He was tall, dark, and handsome with a killer smile and he flirted with me in a subtle way. Needless to say, the attraction was there but it was more than that. As soon as I was no longer his patient we began dating. There was no whirlwind courtship. We simply fell into a relationship with plans to marry right away but something seemed to always come up so our plans would get delayed. I began to feel his relationship with me was one of convenience rather than me becoming a part of his life. I had graduated with a degree in Business but because we were getting married and he said he didn't want a working wife, I continued to live at home. I began to feel ashamed of spending all my time doing nothing after working so hard to graduate. I felt I had so much to offer. I began to feel remorseful for doing nothing while I kept waiting to get married. I had all the time in the world to plan the perfect wedding. All I needed was a date. One night Sam came home all excited and said he had a big surprise. I was foolish enough to think he was finally going to commit to a date so we could get married. Instead, his big surprise was a huge shock. It was the last thing I was expecting. He had accepted a short assignment with Doctors Without Borders. A short assignment meant six months instead of a year. I didn't have any say. It didn't matter to him that my dreams were being put on hold. Our shared goals seemed to have changed. It was like they didn't matter anymore. I was devastated. I began to question his commitment to us. He knew I was upset so he turned on the charm. He told me everything I needed to hear to remain in our relationship, including a promise of a wedding as soon as he returned."

"Mom and Dad suggested I take a vacation and go visit Cameron and his family in Florida, so I spent a couple of months with them. It was a special time for me. I got to see my brother as an adult in his own environment. He's a loving husband and a wonderful father. I missed Sam even more and could hardly wait until he returned, and we could start our married life together. When Sam returned home, I continued to live at home with my parents. I began planning our wedding again, but Sam would still not commit to a date. Months kept passing by. I tried to keep busy, so I did a lot of volunteer work. It was rewarding and filled a void, but this wasn't the life I'd been dreaming of. I wanted to get married so I could be Sam's wife and we could start our life together. One night we had a big fight, and I think he realized I was tired of waiting so at his suggestion we eloped and got married in front of a Justice of the Peace. It was nothing more than a weekend away without family or friends to share our special day. I was excited to become Sam's wife because now we would be making new dreams together. I thought the Sam I first met was back and we would have this wonderful life together."

Laurel paused for a moment, "Sam was always very methodical and logical. It made sense to continue to live with my parents after we were married. My parents agreed since it was only going to be until we found our own place and that depended on where Sam would establish his practice. I told you Sam was very charismatic, and once again, I bought into his vision. I thought he was being considerate but in time I realized it was convenient. It made it easy for him. He had no responsibility in our marriage. My parents converted a portion of their home into a suite for us. It was nice but it wasn't our home. Once you're married you soon realize what your spouse is really like. The luster of wonder gets washed away by your tears. He was like someone I didn't know. I told him before we got married that I had become interested in the area of fundraising. I wanted to apply my leadership and communication skills toward a worthy cause. I was confident I had the ability to analyze what was important to potential donors. I knew I was more than capable of organizing events so I had all the confidence knowing I would be able to do this on a large scale. I had so much enthusiasm and potential. Sam snuffed out that enthusiasm with his wants and erased my dreams for our future, again reiterating he didn't want me to work because of his unpredictable schedule. He wanted me home when he was home. Sam continued to concentrate on his career and commitment to Doctors Without Borders. Looking back, I realized how many things began to change as soon as we were married. The only thing that didn't change was how everything was all about Sam and what he wanted."

Laurel was now caught up in remembering. Doc was so easy to talk to, so she continued, "I told you he was a good listener. His ability to listen didn't apply when I would tell him something he didn't want to hear. He hated any kind of confrontation. He was competent and assertive. It may work well in the work force but at home his assertiveness began to feel controlling." Doc heard the anguish in Laurel's voice.

"We weren't moving forward together in our relationship. I willingly supported my husband in his career choice, but I needed more out of our marriage. When I told Sam I wanted a baby, he wasn't excited by the idea. He didn't say no, but we were married over a year before he finally gave in and agreed to starting a family. Sam changed with the arrival of Gracie. I knew there would be a time of adjustment, but he was becoming irritable more often. I thought part of the reason was due to having a new baby. He wasn't getting the rest he needed. I even thought maybe I was the problem. Being a new mother, I was often too tired. He started taking more shifts and spending nights at the apartment he had kept in the city. You start to question the little things that change. I actually began to believe he was having an affair. No amount of reasoning could erase my fears. Was there a part of my husband I didn't know about? There were times he'd trip up on a lie or use an excuse he had used before as to why he had to stay overnight in the apartment. Lies are hard to keep straight. During one of our fights, I accused him. He immediately became defensive and angry and kept asking if I didn't trust him, but he never once denied it. It's heartbreaking when your beliefs are changed by reality. I felt like I didn't know him anymore. I couldn't understand why he didn't want to talk about our plans and commitments to each other? Too many factors weren't in my control, the biggest one being Sam." Laurel took a deep breath to collect herself. When she turned back to Doc, with candor she stated, "You are the only person I've shared this with. For some reason I couldn't tell my parents. Maybe I was afraid if I said it out loud it would be true. I didn't want it to be true and if it were true they would be disappointed in me."

A shadow crossed Doc's eyes as he heard the despair in her voice. It was hard to see her struggling with self-doubt.

"Life moved forward but nothing changed. Sam kept avoiding the subject whenever I mentioned having another baby. Before I knew it, Gracie was three. I longed for another child, but Sam wasn't interested. He said he was an only child and Gracie could be too."

Laurel's look changed, "Then came the phone call. It was like I knew before he even answered it. The organization desperately needed a replacement doctor in Columbia. One of their doctors had to leave due to health reasons, so Sam agreed to go. Despite his promise, he justified his decision. He said it was only until they could find a replacement. I think once Sam agreed they quit looking. I told him how lonely it was when he was gone but again it was all about Sam. He didn't understand how I could be lonely with my family around every day, and I had Gracie to keep me busy. He didn't get it. I could keep busy and fill my days, but I still spent my nights alone in my room. He kept saying he'd be back soon. I was grateful we were still living with my parents. They were such a strong support system for me with Sam gone. I will never understand how Sam could ignore his responsibilities here without a second thought. I would do things with his family so they could spend time with Gracie, but it wasn't the same without Sam. His absence was harder this time, especially for Gracie. He was away for Gracie's fourth birthday. Another special occasion without her daddy. It hurt knowing Gracie missed him. Evening prayers always ended with, 'Bring my daddy home'."

Laurel wasn't done. It was like a valve had been opened, and to her surprise things she had never shared before poured out. "Doctors Without Borders often work in a remote environment with limited resources and amenities. I seldom heard from Sam and when I did it was always brief. Doubts surfaced. I wondered if he had agreed to stay by choice. I even wondered if there was someone there he loved more and that's why it was so easy for him to stay. If he truly loved me why would he have gone away and why didn't he come home? When you're alone you get lonely. When your loneliness takes over, your thoughts get darker. I would find myself wondering what Sam was doing, and with who. I would see occasional posts on social media and there was a pretty young doctor who was often in the same pictures as Sam. I found it odd that they were always next to each other. She was one of the doctors who was also on his last tour, and they often attended the same medical conventions. I began to wonder if it was more than a coincidence. It's easy for your mind to jump to conclusions."

Laurel paused, how much more was she willing to share with Doc? "Once I worked my way through my self-pity, I decided to take my life back. It would no longer be controlled by Sam's life choices. I knew our marriage was going to take work to survive. Now it was up to Sam to do what was best for our family. He needed to be present as a husband and as a father. It mattered to the future of our marriage. I also wanted another child but only if Sam agreed to take on a full-time position in town. My trust in him had been shaken but I was willing to give him a chance. I wanted the family I always dreamed of. Sam had to decide if he wanted to remain in our marriage and commit to our family. I was prepared to divorce Sam if he took another assignment with Doctors Without Borders. You've witnessed my stubbornness; I don't back down. I was ready to move forward with or without Sam based on what happened when he returned home. The last time we talked he told me he had an interview set up with one of the medical clinics in town. We would have another baby and once he got his practice established we would find a place of our own. I wanted to believe he meant what he promised but I had been led down that road more than once. I struggled with that truth all the time. Sam swore this assignment was his last." *I guess it was.* "I need to hang onto the belief he would have kept his word and never leave us again. I'll never know for sure and now it doesn't matter." There was nothing more to say but she couldn't stop the tears that fell.

Because Laurel had shared her deepest grief, Doc knew they had developed a new level of trust. He wanted to take her in his arms and hold her and promise her that everything would be okay. Instead, he reached out and wiped her tears away.

A faraway look darkened her eyes before she turned away. Laurel hated seeing the pity in Doc's eyes. She knew she was the only one who could erase it, just not today. "I know Sam's parents blamed me for the accident. I think they also blamed me for his absence when he'd choose to work away. It's always easy to place blame to cover your own guilt. Maybe the Eastons had failed as parents and that's why Sam made the choices he made. I can sit here and excuse Sam for who he was by blaming myself and his parents, but the truth is Sam was who he was by choice. His life decisions were his choice and based on what he wanted out of life with no consideration for others or the effect his actions had on us." Laurel felt somewhat disloyal since Sam wasn't here to defend himself.

Laurel had shared everything with Doc, the good and the bad. She smiled but managed to look twice as sad. "I believed we would be happy again. We had a beautiful daughter and new plans for our future together. Then it was all taken away. My heart is heavy, and I'm filled with sadness when I think of them. I'm still working my way through my grief. I have put the tragedy behind me but there are days like today when it sneaks up on me. I'm beginning to let the past go and focus on good memories and the happiness life brings. I'm again seeing the beauty around me. I don't know what I would have done without my parents and you."

Compliments made Doc uncomfortable but pleased him too. His words were gentle when he spoke, "Thank you for trusting me enough to share everything." He knew Laurel had opened her soul to him.

Laurel's voice became reflective, "Sometimes I find myself dreaming about what might have been, but I am learning to accept what is. Yet you wonder if you had made other choices would it have been different?"

"You can't play the what-if-game, Laurel. It does none of us any good." He was speaking from experience.

"The old Laurel is back despite the changes. I was strong before and I'm strong again. Strong enough to move forward." She could close the door to that part of her past.

Doc didn't want to read too much into her last words, but they gave him hope.

"My parents made a good life for me and doted on me. I expected that from Sam. Gracie's father really had nothing to do with raising our daughter. I am so grateful to have such loving parents who want the best for me. They moved here because of me, because of my accident. As you know, I wasn't doing very well." She smiled at Doc through misty eyes, "I'm glad we moved here. I think they are, too. I am putting the pieces of my life back together. There are pieces missing but I can move forward without them. Thanks for listening. You keep seeing me at my worst. You're a brave man to keep coming back."

Their conversation had been intense. Laurel now needed time alone. So, did Doc. He was solemn when he left. He had some soul-searching of his own to do. What he felt for Laurel was a new experience. He had to evaluate the depth of his feelings for her and decide how to move forward. He knew his feelings were stronger than simple attraction.

CHAPTER TWENTY

Laurel was on her way to the barns to help Darius. Her heart quickened when she saw Doc pulling in because she wasn't expecting him. When he did drop by it was usually on his way home, but they had just finished breakfast.

Doc pulled into the drive and joined her, "I'm on my way into Calgary so I can't stay. I've been putting off errands for the last few weeks and I can't put them off any longer, but I have something to ask you. If you have no plans this Sunday, I'd like to give you a tour of my place. Unless there's an emergency, we'll have all day. My brother and his wife, Amber, would like us to join them for supper. Amber is a lovely gal, but I have to warn you she talks a lot. Bryce, on the other hand, is the silent type. Heads up, they have three young kids."

Laurel had mixed feelings. It pleased her that Doc had mentioned her to his family, but she was still nervous about meeting new people. She hadn't been out socially since the accident.

Doc understood her hesitation. He waited, not wanting to push her like he did with the driving.

Laurel knew she needed to get on with her life. Her initial sense of apprehension was giving way and a faint tremor of excitement flowed through her. She knew she'd enjoy the day Doc had planned. Time spent with him was easy and if she found the day overwhelming, he would understand her need to leave. In spite of her initial fear, curiosity got the better of her. Her face took on a look he had come to recognize. With a sassy grin she teased, "I have to check my social calendar. Good news, I happen to have that day free." *Just like all my other days.*

Doc laughed, "Well book me in for Sunday."

The excitement at having said yes was quickly followed by reservation, "Thank you for the invite. I want to fit into my life here, so I know it's time to venture beyond the ranch." This was a step forward that needed to be taken. In truth, she'd welcome the change.

"I better run, or I won't get anything done. See you Sunday, I'm looking forward to it." Doc was glad Laurel was making an effort. It showed she was emerging from her grief.

"I'm looking forward to it, too." Laurel was surprised because she meant it.

"Oh, by the way, the Calhoun Labor Day barbeque at Valley View is coming up. It's more than a barbeque. It's a festive event that is enjoyed by every age group and is considered to be one of the social events of the year in the community. Your family will be invited and it's important to attend. It will help all of you to fit in sooner and will be the perfect opportunity to meet others in a casual setting. The Calhoun family are admirable people and welcome everyone warmly."

The thought of meeting a bunch of strangers terrified Laurel. Hopefully, meeting Doc's family would be less stressful, and she knew she had shut herself away from others for too long. *One step at a time.* Doc's invitation couldn't be considered a date. It was just Doc being friendly and introducing her to more people.

Darius usually joined the family for the evening meal. Laurel thought of Darius as an honorary uncle. He had been part of their family longer than she had. It was once again feeling like real family time. There were still times when Genna couldn't believe the positive change in Laurel. Baxter was just happy considering he was against the move in the beginning, and it turned out to be the best thing for his family. "Darius told me Doc dropped by but didn't stay long. He's been dropping by a lot since Bella was born. I hope there's nothing wrong."

"Bella is fine. I think it's another filly Doc is coming to see." Everyone was shocked because it was Darius who spoke. He gave Laurel one of his slow smiles.

Laurel blushed right up to her roots as she explained Doc's quick visit, "I'm spending time with a friend who is kind enough to show me around."

"It was a date back in my day," teased her dad, which was followed by a low chuckle from Darius.

"I like Doc. He's easy to have around. I never feel uneasy when I'm with him." She dated Sam for months before she met his family. Her heart began to pound in her chest. Was this a date? Was she starting something she wasn't ready for? She quickly changed the subject. After supper Laurel decided to address something else that was concerning her. She stayed to help her mom in the kitchen while her dad left to watch television. Darius had gone back to his place. "Do you have time to talk?"

"I'll make us a pot of tea and you can tell me what's bothering you. Are you sorry about agreeing to go out with Doc to see his place? Your dad and Darius were only teasing."

"No, I'm excited about Doc's invitation. My life has been in limbo for months. I know I needed time to recover but lately I've been feeling a combination of loneliness and boredom. I need something to occupy my time now that we're settled." She regretted the many days she had locked herself in her room. "I'm ready to face new challenges. I'm going to update my resume and look for a job." She had been a strong, independent woman before the accident.

Genna was glad she was sitting down because this was a complete surprise. "Don't rush into this, Laurel. It can be stressful, and it could trigger more anxiety."

That possibility was a shared concern, but it wasn't going to stop Laurel. "It would be new anxiety, and I know I'll be able to cope. I'm stronger than you think."

"I've seen it for myself."

Laurel smiled at her mom, "A new day is full of unknowns, and it's also full of possibilities."

Genna also smiled. Her daughter was throwing her own words back at her.

"I miss the spontaneity I had before meeting Sam, when I was independent and able to follow my dreams. I've put a lot of thought into this. I'm ready to face new challenges and this time it's my choice. Of course, I'll have new job nerves, but I know how capable I am with change." They both laughed; they'd been dealing with change for months. "There will be the normal fears that go along with starting any new job due to unfamiliarity and performance pressure. They disappear when you settle in and start feeling comfortable. A new job can be exhilarating." Laurel's eyes had that special light in them that had been missing.

"So can a new relationship," teased her mother.

"I'm only looking for a new job, not a new husband."

"I don't think you have to look far if you are."

Laurel's heart fluttered wildly, "You're worse than Dad and Darius. Besides, Doc is seven years older than I am."

"Age is only a number so don't let that be a concern. You probably never knew this because it had never been an issue in their lives, but my dad was ten years older than my mom. Their age difference didn't matter because the age gap was filled with their love for each other." Laurel had to appreciate how her mom could always present a positive slant on things.

*****

Laurel had been anxious all week, especially since Doc hadn't dropped by during the week and now it was Sunday. She spent the whole morning in her room deciding what to wear and getting ready. Hearing Doc's truck pull into the driveway, she took a deep breath to calm her nerves as she left her bedroom.

Laurel walked into the kitchen wearing a flowing maxi dress the color of newly bloomed lilacs. Her summer-streaked hair had grown and now curled loosely, framing her face instead of being hidden beneath the baseball cap she always wore. Time in the sun had warmed her skin a honey gold. She looked like a healthy young lady.

Doc was mesmerized and his heart skipped a beat. It was as if an angel had floated into the room, "You look lovely," he stuttered. His face turned crimson. He had never stuttered in his life. He was the one who was suddenly nervous. He hadn't felt like this since he was a teenager. Doc was dressed casually, dark denim jeans with an Eagles t-shirt under an unbuttoned shirt. It amazed Laurel how he could still look proper when he was dressed so casually. Laurel knew her own cheeks had colored. She was still nervous as they walked out together but felt better knowing Doc was also nervous.

Doc drove with relaxed ease, sharing basic information about Alberta, the neighbouring ranches and more about his own ranch and family. Their conversation remained casual, and Laurel was soon engrossed in the scenery surrounding her. A sunny glow spread across the land. The Chinook arch had already formed to the west and would soon come down from the mountains and howl across the land. The dry hot days of summer were counting down. "I wouldn't be surprised if we have an early fall. The crops are high and full. If the weather cooperates it will be a better than average yield for the farmers around here and we'll have bumper crops."

Laurel had to ask about his taste in music. "Are you really an Eagles fan? I pegged you as the Garth Brooks type."

There was a light-hearted expression in his eyes, "Well, there you go judging on appearance. I do like singers like Garth, Tim McGraw, old-timers like George Jones and Conway Twitty. You can't escape country music in these parts, but I also like listening to Queen and The Beatles. Meat Loaf is one of my favorites. I even go to jazz concerts occasionally. I like all kinds of music, depending on the mood I'm in. What do you like? If I had to guess based on when I met you I would say, Simon and Garfunkel."

Laurel started to laugh knowing the implication behind his teasing. "I don't know which is my favorite, 'Bridge Over Troubled Water' or 'Sounds of Silence'." When she laughed her eyes sparkled. She hadn't realized the sense of humor Doc had which made her like him even more.

"What else should I know about you, Laurel?"

"As you know, I also have an older brother who is a brilliant business man and a good family man. His wife has always been a stay-at-home mom by choice. Cameron travels a lot, and their kids are active in extracurricular activities so she's always busy. They're planning on coming here for Christmas. You'll get to meet them then. It won't make much difference for them to fly here instead of where we used to live."

"Was it hard leaving your other home?"

Laurel was honest, "I was too numb at the time, and I felt even more guilt knowing we were moving because of me. My parents sacrificed a lot to move here hoping it would help me. I am beyond grateful for their love and support. I'm doing okay most of the time and I'm adjusting and learning to fit into my life here. Now that we've been here for a while I'm glad we moved. I love it here. Mom and Dad, and even Darius, are happy and have settled in, but I need to do something to move on with my life. I think it's time for me to start looking for a job."

"Maybe I can help you with that." Laurel raised a questioning eyebrow, doubt evident in her eyes. "I got you driving, didn't I?"

"That you, did. I know you said you have cattle, but do you have horses as well?"

"We do and we all ride. When I have time I like to ride in the country. Nature helps bring balance into my hectic life."

Laurel understood the power of nature, good and bad. She had experienced both. "What's your horse's name?"

"Scout. He's a painted pony that I acquired from one of my clients when they moved into town. I assume you ride."

"Since I could walk. I've missed riding and I really miss Penny but thanks to you I have Coco and Bella." Laurel wanted to know more about him. "Have you been married?"

Doc took a deep breath. The conversation had taken an unexpected turn. "No."

"Why haven't you married?"

He wasn't sure he wanted to answer questions like this. How could he tell her he loved his best friend's wife since the day he met her and had been patiently courting her since she became a widow. Not knowing how to respond, Doc left the question unanswered. He pointed to the drive on the left, "We're here." Bedlam erupted when they pulled into the well-established yard. Two dogs started barking and three kids burst out of the house, the parents right behind them. They were all anxious to meet the new friend.

Bryce Parker was exactly like Laurel imagined, another good-looking cowboy. He was a little taller than Doc, lean and fit with broad shoulders, muscled chest, and big hands. Amber was dressed as casually as the men, wearing jeans and a loose fitting bright pink top that clashed with her copper red hair. Her hair was pulled up in a loose knot but whisps had managed to escape. Her blue eyes sparkled, and her smile was warm in greeting.

Laurel felt a little overdressed, but Amber was quick to put her at ease. "I love your dress, it looks so comfy and cool. Living on a ranch and having three kids, I find it easier to dress like the rest of them. We all dress up for church which I look forward to and the kids hate." Her comment released a groan from one of the twins.

The larger of the two dogs went over to check out the newcomer. "You don't have to be afraid of Remo. He's a rescue dog Bryce got a few years ago and he's Bryce's loyal companion. The friendly one that might lick you to death is Dory. Bryce found her lying in the ditch when he was mowing the grass along the road. She was pregnant so somebody just dropped her off and left her."

"Nobody told me Uncle Jimmy was bringing a girl." This disgruntled remark came from the same twin who groaned.

"Laurel, meet the outspoken Hudson and his twin brother, Hunter." The identical six-year-olds stared at her with intense blue eyes in round freckled faces. Red hair hung out from beneath their baseball caps. "And this is Harry, our four-year-old."

My God, three boys. "It's nice to meet you boys."

The youngest went and stood in front of Laurel, "I'm a girl." It was hard to tell. Like the boys, she wore jeans, gum boots and a ball cap. To prove it she pulled off her cap and a mass of strawberry curls were released.

Doc picked her up and ruffled her hair, "Yes, you are and the cutest one in the county. Even with dirt on your chin." He set the imp down and turned to Laurel, "Her brothers called her Harry to bug her, and it stuck but her given name is Harlow. This is my friend, Laurel. I brought her here to meet all of you because she doesn't know many people here because her family is new to the area." He bend down and whispered in the other twin's ear, "Be nice to her. She's kinda shy like you." Hunter nodded and smiled. It was the first smile from the solemn boy.

Doc's tender actions touched Laurel's heart.

"Dory has new puppies," declared the excited little girl.

"How many?" asked Laurel.

"Too many," answered Bryce.

"Five," said the twins in unison.

Harlow glared at her brother. She felt it was her news to share. "We don't get to keep them. Daddy says two farm dogs are enough. Wanna go see them?"

"I would love to. I bet they're cute and cuddly." Laurel had always had a dog growing up. Her last dog was put down about a year ago, but they were planning on getting their own rescue dog when Sam got home, and they had their own place. Another dead dream.

Doc looked down at her summer sandals. Laurel shrugged off his practical observation because there was no way she was going to disappoint the little girl. She allowed Harlow to pull her forward and they headed to the barn. Dory, the proud mother, lead the way. The more time Doc spent with Laurel, the more interesting she became. She was down to earth and was adapting to new situations with ease.

Harlow and Laurel both fell to their knees and giggled as the puppies began climbing all over them. Laurel wouldn't have missed this moment for anything. "How old are they?" Laurel asked as she picked up the one closest to her. She laughed freely when it started licking her face as she snuggled the puppy closer.

Harlow responded like a typical farm girl, "They're over a month old and are already weaned, but we need to start finding them homes in a couple of weeks."

"Do you think I could have this one?" Laurel's face revealed more than her words. Having a puppy would allow her to dream again and would give her life purpose.

"I know it will be okay, one less to get rid of. Don't tell anyone but I named her Holly. Mom says we shouldn't name the puppies because their owners would like to name them."

"I promise not to tell, and Holly is the perfect name for her. Did you name the others?"

The little girls eyes danced with mischief, "No, the rest are boys. Holly is like my sister."

"Are you sure you don't mind if she comes and lives with me?"

"I know you'll love her, and Holly already likes you, so it will be okay for you to take her home when she's ready. Maybe I can come visit her?"

"That's okay with me if it's okay with your parents. I think Mama Dory would like her babies back. Let's go see what the guys are up to." Harlow took Laurel's hand, and they headed back to the house. They were drawn to the sound of laughter coming from behind the house.

Uncle Jimmy was lying on the ground while two rough and tumble boys were wrestling with him. As soon as Harlow saw the guys wrestling she broke into a run and jumped on a surprised uncle. Doc's laughter deepened. Instead of walking by Laurel took a moment and watched. Doc looked up and grinned, "I think they've got me beat."

Laurel was acutely aware of his muscled arms as he wrestled with the kids, and she experienced an unexpected moment of physical attraction. He was fun and outgoing, not at all the serious, all business vet she first met. It was a moment of insight into his sensitivity with children instead of animals. She felt her heart warm knowing he'd make a good dad. "I'm going to go in and visit with Amber and see if I can help her get supper ready."

Laurel knocked gently on the door before entering. Amber smiled when Laurel joined her. She had just finished unloading the dishwasher.

"I love your enormous kitchen. It's bright and sunny and like most country kitchens it has a warm, homey feel."

"We've been spending the last few years fixing up the house. We finished the kitchen renovation last year and I love it. To me, the kitchen is the heart of the home. As you know it tends to be the gathering place and it's where we spend most of our time."

"Is there something I can help you with?"

"You can help me later when it's time to set the table. Why don't we sit and have a visit. I don't get many girl talks in around here."

Laurel smiled and accepted the glass of iced tea Amber handed her. "I bet you're a very busy mom. Your kids are adorable and energetic."

Amber laughed, "And exhausting. Having the twins in school full-time next year will make life a lot easier even though Harlow is quite the handful on her own."

"I see boys are much more physical than girls. They were wrestling with their uncle when I came in. Mind you, Harlow joined right in."

"The kids love watching Wrestle Mania. I think the boys hit the nail on the head calling it Wrestle Maniac."

Laurel knew she was moving forward and more accepting of her loss when she found herself talking about Gracie and sharing a few of her antics.

Amber thought Laurel might be uncomfortable talking about kids knowing she had lost her daughter, but it was hard to talk about anything else when they are your whole life. Amber tried to keep the conversation light, but curiosity got the better of her, "I hear you've met Kit Grayson. Now there's a family that has had more than their share of tragedy. I'm sorry, Laurel, that was an insensitive comment considering your tragedy. I know you experienced a significant loss that resulted in you and your family moving here." Doc had talked often about the Rodwells and Willow Downs, so Amber knew Laurel's story. "Doc is generous with his time and will come to a friend's or a neighbor's aid without being asked."

Laurel knew this to be true since her family had already experienced this more than once. Thanks to Doc, she had both Bella and Coco. "Life can take such strange twists, and we don't know why. He's been a great friend since our family moved here."

Laurel might as well not have spoken. Amber kept right on talking, "My brother-in-law is considered a prize catch. He's handsome, established, and a really nice guy. Jim's a hard-working man, both here at the ranch helping Bryce and at the clinic. A sensible woman would grab onto a man like him, but the single gals around here don't have a chance. He's attracted to his best friend's widow. Has been even before she was married to Trace. I don't know what's going on with them now but there's a hired hand that lives at Lola Grande that could be the problem. Rio Ortiz was hired to help out when Trace died in the fire that burned the barn down. It was a horrendous loss for the Grayson family. They had a real hard time when Trace died because it didn't have to happen, but they seem to have recovered and adjusted. After the rebuild was completed, Rio was hired full-time at Lola Grande. Interesting, very interesting. Rio is as handsome as the devil in a very rugged way. He's Mexican like Trace's mother who is a stunning woman even at her age."

Laurel had seen the connection between Doc and Kit the day Kit brought Coco to Willow Downs. A rush of color now warmed her cheeks. Did Amber think there was something personal going on between her and Doc? The last thing she needed right now was a man in her life romantically. Doc was her much needed friend.

"Doc has been infatuated with Kit Grayson for years. I thought for sure he and Kit would get married, but I think her hired hand has something to do with that not happening. Knowing Jim, he's probably being respectful, but he better not wait too long."

"Anyone tell you that you talk too much, Amber?" Doc said as he stood in the doorway.

"All the time," she responded, unconcerned that he was annoyed.

Laurel guessed Amber often spoke without thinking. She was glad they were interrupted but wasn't sure why Doc's angry reaction made her uncomfortable. Was it jealousy? As soon as he smiled at her, her spirits lifted.

"Bryce said to let you know the barbeque is hot and he's putting the steaks on."

"Everything's ready in here except for setting the table."

Doc turned and walked back out without saying another word.

"Laurel, if you like you can grab the place mats out of the drawer over there. I'd love to fancy it up with a pretty tablecloth but with three young kids I've learned to keep it simple. The plates are in the cupboard next to the stove and the silverware is in the drawer right below. I'll start getting the rest of the food on the table."

As soon as the meat was done, the noisy troop came traipsing in. Doc led the way with a giggling Harlow on his back. "Special delivery. Did someone order a sack of potatoes? Where should I drop it?"

"Take Harry back outside and drop her in the trough," teased Hunter. He had gotten more comfortable with having Laurel around.

Harlow squealed, "Don't you dare, Uncle Jimmy."

It was challenging trying to get the kids to go get washed up until Bryce took a step forward. As soon as they returned, Harlow pushed past her brothers so she could sit next to Laurel.

The meal was hectic but pleasant, conversation was light, and they were kept entertained by the kids. Laurel soon learned Hudson liked to talk as much as his mother. Laurel was enjoying herself and laughed along with the others.

"Who left room for dessert? Rhubarb crisp, ice cream, or both." The adults had both while the kids settled for ice cream. Both Bryce and Doc enjoyed seconds. Doc teased Harlow by stealing a spoonful of her ice cream. Laurel knew it wasn't the first time he'd done this. Laurel found him even more appealing when he was relaxed and in his own environment.

The boys had grown fidgety so were excused from the table. Amber grabbed for the wet wipes that sat permanently on the counter and handed one to Hudson, "Here, wipe the ice cream off your chin before you take off." Hudson grabbed it, gave his chin a quick swipe, threw it on the table and took off after his brother who had already made his escape. Amber grabbed another one and swiped it over Harlow's mouth.

"Mommy, can I show Laurel my room?"

Mommy. Laurel's heart stopped momentarily. Would she ever hear a child call her that again? Unexpected moments like this tormented her. She had to swallow hard wondering if the pain ever went away. Laurel knew it would hurt Harlow if she refused so she accepted. A look of pure joy lit up Harlow's face and erased Laurel's discomfort. How easy it was to make a little girl happy.

Amber couldn't contain herself once they were out of earshot, "Laurel is perfect for you."

"Don't go planning the wedding yet," groaned Bryce, while Doc sat quietly accepting the truth. He was falling in love with Laurel. The right woman had finally come into his life.

When Laurel returned, Doc suggested they take their leave. They went outside and gathered on the front walk to say goodbye. "I won't be back, I'll go to the office and stay there tonight."

"See you tomorrow," replied Bryce. Amber just smiled, drawing her own conclusion.

Laurel was sorry to see the visit come to an end. She enjoyed feeling alive again. It had been such a normal day away from the ranch. "Thank you for inviting me. I enjoyed the day, and it was a lovely supper."

"Come back anytime. You're always welcome."

A rush of pleasure spread through Laurel, and she hoped there would be another time. She liked the Parker family.

"Okay, kids, inside. It's bathtime."

"We just had one," grumbled Hudson.

"I don't want my hair washed," whined Harlow.

"Tonight, it's just a quick bath since it's later than usual."

"Good night guys, be good or run fast."

Bryce punched his brother gently in the arm. "Don't encourage them."

Harlow pulled at Laurel's hand and pleaded, "Will you come back and see us?"

"I have to come back to get my puppy." Laurel bent down and whispered in the child's ear, "You take good care of Holly until then." To Laurel's surprise, the little girl threw her arms around her neck and hugged her tight. The warmth of the smile Laurel gave Harlow was dazzling. She was so beautiful now that she was coming back to life.

Doc held the door for Laurel as she climbed into his truck. They pulled away waving until they couldn't see them anymore. "I hope it wasn't overwhelming? Harry sure took to you."

Laurel had been surprisingly comfortable with Doc's family. The day was fun and relaxing. "I really enjoyed myself. Your family was warm and welcoming, and the kids are adorable. I'm glad you warned me about Amber. The woman can certainly talk. Why are you looking at me funny?"

Doc grinned, "I'm just checking to see if you still have both your ears. Amber can talk the ear off an elephant if she's given the chance."

Laurel giggled, enjoying his innocent teasing. It wasn't the first time she enjoyed his humor today. "You're right, but I like her. I learned more about you. I hear you're the number one bachelor in the district and a prize catch. How come you never married?"

"I run fast," Doc said and left it at that. He wondered how much Amber told her.

Laurel let his evasive comment go. "You're good with the kids." Once again she thought he would make a good dad.

"They're good kids. Harry is a sassy little thing and is as much trouble as the twins are together. She may look like the picture of innocence, but she's the trouble maker."

Laurel had picked up on the mischievous glint in the little girl's eyes. Harlow reminded her of Gracie. It made her wonder what her own daughter would have grown up to be like. Laurel's voice was heavy with emotion, "I was really anxious about today because of the children. I haven't been around any since Gracie died. I thought it would be harder, but it was the best thing for me. I missed my hugs from Gracie and our special moments. I found that again with Harlow. Moving forward, this will all get easier."

"Are you really going to take one of the puppies?"

"I'm used to having a dog. They're wonderful companions."

"Do you have a doghouse?"

"It stayed behind when we moved, but Darius will love to help me build one. I can hardly wait to bring my puppy home. I know Mom and Dad will be surprised but they will enjoy her as much as I will."

"Do you have a name picked out?"

"Harlow named her Holly so Holly it is. Speaking of names, I was surprised how often Kit Grayson's name came up. Amber talked about her non-stop while we were chatting."

"Kit's a longtime family friend. My path crosses professionally and socially with families around here all the time but especially with the Calhouns and the Graysons. Kit had a hard time when her husband was killed, and we were all there to support her."

Especially you by the sounds of it. Laurel immediately felt like she was being catty. Doc had been there for her as well.

Daylight was fading by the time they reached Willow Downs. Doc remained the perfect gentleman and walked Laurel to the door. She invited him to join her on the patio swing. It had been a long time since she sat beside a man on a moonlit night gazing up at the stars. She was surprised at how natural it felt with Doc. There was a light breeze blowing off the mountains and the stunning summer sunset highlighted the sky. They sat quietly and watched until the crimson lights faded away. When the darkness of the night closed in around them, Doc knew it was time to take his leave. They both stood, a little hesitant about what would happen next. Recognizing the stirring interest in his eyes, Laurel's desire was awakened. She felt alive inside, her heart raced, and her body warmed. It was an intimate moment. Doc wanted to kiss her, but she quickly looked away. He warned himself to go slow knowing she was still vulnerable. He was a patient man and would give her the time she needed. Laurel's heartbeat slowed when he moved away. Doc strolled down the walk grinning. For him, it had been a perfect day.

Laurel sat back down, cheeks still flushed and watched the vet's truck disappear down the road. Doc had drawn her away from her world of grief and back into the everyday world she had to live in. She had needed this day to forget about her troubles and once again experience the joy of everyday life with others. It was a pleasant change from the sorrow that had held her in its grip for so long. After today, she knew she would no longer isolate herself at the ranch. Laurel had begun to come alive. Doc was a nice man, and she enjoyed being with him. They were developing a comfortable relationship. Spending the day with his family drew him closer. Now she had to work through new emotions. She knew today meant something special to both of them.

Laurel continued to enjoy the quiet of a perfect summer night. It felt like God was letting her know that sometimes silence was okay. She smiled to herself. Her mother's strong beliefs were beginning to have an influence on her. By the time she headed indoors the stars sparkled bright and the silvery moon hung high in the velvet sky. She knew her mom would be waiting to hear all about her day with Doc. Laurel felt like a teenager.

CHAPTER TWENTY-ONE

Doc's last appointment cancelled so it was earlier than usual when he headed home. Instead of going straight home, Doc pulled into the drive at Lola Grande. He wanted to talk to Kit about Laurel. He had spent the last few days thinking about offering Laurel a job at the clinic. He felt sorry for Laurel but that wasn't the only reason he was considering hiring her. He'd seen how well she related to animals and had observed her with the horses under very stressful circumstances. Now that Laurel's protective layers were being slowly stripped away, he was getting to know her better. He quickly realized she was intelligent and caring.

Kit went out and greeted him, wondering what brought him by at this time of day.

"I know it's close to suppertime, but do you have a few minutes to talk?"

"Why don't you stay and have supper with us, and we can talk afterwards without being interrupted. Rio's helping Matt build his new Quonset and he won't be home until dark and Lola's in the city visiting a friend and they're going out for supper. The kids never stick around once the dishes are done so we can talk then. Come in while I finish getting supper ready. It's not much but you are more than welcome to join us."

"Thanks, I'd like that."

As predicted, the kids scattered right after supper. Kit started the dishwasher, poured two coffees, and joined Doc on the verandah.

"I want to talk to you about Shelby's job at the clinic. She's given notice. With this being her and Riley's third child, she says she wants

215

to stay at home and raise her family, and they're even considering home schooling the kids. I have to find a replacement." Shelby was Kit's sister-in-law and half-sister. Everyone was confused by the complex relationship between the Calhouns and the Graysons, but the two families were very close. Shelby had worked for Doc since she graduated from college. She had been such a smart-ass when she was young but had always been good with the animals and their owners. It would be hard to replace her, but Doc understood her wanting to be at home. Shelby had matured and become a loving and devoted wife to Trace's younger brother. "Laurel mentioned she's bored and would like to find a job. I thought I'd mention the position to her. It would help her to feel like she's fit in and become part of the community. What do you think?"

Knowing Laurel's past and what brought the Rodwells here, Kit felt she had to ask, "Is she ready?"

"It was Laurel who brought it up. It was a casual comment, but she was serious. She says having a job will give her purpose now that they're settled. It would be an ideal solution for both of us."

This conversation wasn't at all what Kit had expected but it might be a good idea. "What do you know about her work history? I feel I'm at a disadvantage to state an opinion because I hardly know her."

"Laurel actually has a degree in Business. When she married her husband he didn't want her to work but Laurel kept busy. She had so much free time before she had her family and again when her husband worked away. She filled her time volunteering for different organizations, and she believes strongly in social responsibilities that act in the best interests of society as a whole and is committed to caring for others. She worked with organizations for the benefit of the community and the people in it. It was her way of filling a void due to her husband's absence. It gave her purpose and provided her with a connection to others."

Kit was impressed; volunteering was a noble deed.

"Laurel would have learned valuable skills by volunteering. Skills like leadership, organization and planning, communication, and interpersonal skills, all of which are important to have when working for me. She offers valuable experience. She's also intelligent so I believe she would quickly learn the office skills required. I know she'd be more comfortable working for someone she already knows. From what I've seen I'm confident she would be a good replacement for Shelby."

Kit sat back and smiled as Doc went on about all the qualities the young lady had. When he was done, she gave him what she hoped was good advice, "I guess you have to talk to Laurel and determine how serious she really is. Maybe lead into it like you did with me and see if she expresses an interest."

"I knew you'd know what I should do." Now that this topic was out of the way, there was something more personal he wanted to talk to Kit about. Doc realized there were quite a few things about Laurel that he liked, and it was getting more difficult for him to hide his feelings. "I invited Laurel out to my place to show her around and we stayed and had supper. I was a little surprised when she said yes right away. You don't think she said yes just to be polite do you?"

"I don't think Laurel does anything she doesn't want to. You've made quite an impression on her."

"She enjoyed being away from the ranch and meeting my family. Harlow adores her. It's been, 'Laurel this and Laurel that' ever since." His look changed and became more serious, "I really like Laurel and enjoy spending time with her and getting to know her better. She's not as shy as she was but she's still vulnerable."

Kit's face had taken on a familiar look and Doc guessed she was thinking about Trace. She smiled reflectively, that's how it had started with Trace. "Laurel may be vulnerable but don't be afraid to pursue her. You two have a connection that is stronger than friendship. I've seen the sparks between you."

Doc chuckled, knowing it would be silly to deny it, "Thanks for dinner and the advice. It's time to head home."

"Are the Rodwells coming to Dad's barbecue?"

"I'm sure your dad invited them, and I mentioned it as well."

"I'll try to make time to visit with Laurel if they come. I still remember my first time meeting everyone. I had just arrived at the ranch and was still getting to know my new family. I was scared to death."

*****

It was still early as the welcoming rays of the morning sun drew Laurel to the window. Today was the barbeque at Valley View and the Rodwells were going. If Laurel was being honest, she was more excited than nervous. She knew she'd be meeting a lot of new people but if they were like those she'd already met, she knew there would be nothing to worry about. For Laurel, it helped knowing Doc would be there. Hopefully, they would spend time together.

Valley View was a bustle of activity by the time they arrived. The informal setting was welcoming, laughter and music filled the air. Genna tucked her arm into Laurel's for support as they strolled around back. Genna could tell her daughter was nervous, even though Laurel presented a happy face for her parents. There were a lot of people milling around, way more than they expected. With a sense of anticipation, Laurel looked around for Doc but couldn't find him. When she didn't see him, she realized she wasn't as emotionally prepared for today as she thought. She took a deep breath as anxiety set in. Maybe it was too much too soon. She hoped Doc would show up but maybe work was keeping him away. She knew what it was like to be a doctor. It didn't matter that Doc Parker's patients were animals. They were important to him. She was actually glad when she saw Kit approaching.

Kit saw Laurel scanning the crowd and knew she was looking for Doc. Kit also wondered where he was. She had seen the Rodwells arrive and was making her way over. "Welcome to Valley View. I'm happy you came. Come with me and I'll introduce you to my dad and his wife." Kit told them a bit about the ranch as they crossed the yard. By the time introduction had been made, Lola had also joined them. Lola and Genna greeted each other with a hug and left together when they saw Anna. Laurel watched her dad leave with Kit's dad. A few minutes later Baxter was standing next to Rio at the bar. Laurel couldn't help but wonder who the ruggedly handsome man was. He looked like he didn't fit in, but he was definitely comfortable in his environment. Kit could see positive changes in Laurel from the first time she met her. Of course, her anxiety showed but she looked stronger and healthier. "I hear you have a new puppy. Has she adapted to her new home?"

Without Kit's kindness, Laurel would have felt isolated. "I ended up taking one of her brothers as well. The other pups found homes, and I thought Holly might be lonely, so Dax came home with us. They have definitely livened up the place. Darius has a new buddy, Dax follows him everywhere." By the time Kit spotted Doc she had already introduced Laurel to the rest of her family and they were now chatting with Maggie. As soon as Laurel saw Doc she smiled. Kit was also pleased to see her friend making his way over. She knew Laurel had been waiting for him.

Doc was anxious to get to Laurel but his progress was slow. Everyone knew the local vet, so Doc continued to be drawn into conversation. Normally, it was one of the things he liked about the Calhoun barbeque but today he was wanting to get to his intended destination. "I'm glad to see you here with your family. I wasn't sure if you would come." Doc appreciated Kit's thoughtfulness towards Laurel, who unconsciously took a step toward him. She drew comfort having him close.

They chatted for a while but it was Doc who took Laurel's arm so he could take her around to meet people. As soon as Doc and Laurel excused themselves Maggie expressed her amusement, "So that's Laurel Rodwell. She's a pretty little thing but still a bit fragile looking. I hear Beaumont Estates has been transformed and brought back to life. I'm glad to see that it has had a positive effect on the daughter as well. Or is that Doc's doing? Let me guess, Doc feels sorry for her."

Kit was sure Laurel had captured Doc's heart the day he met her. "It's more than that. I do believe our dear friend is enamored. They aren't a couple, not yet anyway."

"Maybe history will repeat itself and they will be blessed by Valley View's magic love dust. That's what happened to you and Trace."

"You have always been a romantic fool, Maggie," but her eyes immediately found Rio in the crowd of people.

Laurel's hand rested on Doc's arm for emotional support as they moved about meeting people. In a community like this Laurel knew everyone knew her story, but history had proven that gossipers never get all the facts right. Who knew what they were thinking. Doc was always greeted warmly, and everyone was making Laurel feel welcome. With Doc by her side, she began to relax and enjoy herself. In between greetings Laurel couldn't help but allow her gaze to drift and it always seemed to rest on Kit. Doc noticed and commented, "People gravitate to Kit because of her friendliness to everyone."

"Kit came over as soon as we arrived. I've already met all of her family. Her dad took mine with him and has been introducing him to local ranchers. Dad's probably in his glory." Unexpectedly, Laurel was bumped into, and she looked down to see a child looking up at her. Laurel gasped, for the little girl looked so much like Gracie. She struggled to even her breathing as the color drained from her face and she felt faint. She had to close her eyes as the urge to cry swept over her due to mixed emotions. In the moment, she felt cheated.

Doc sensed her panic when she gripped his arm. "Let's take a walk down to the creek behind the main house. I'm sure by now you're overwhelmed by meeting so many people."

When Doc took her hand, Laurel smiled gratefully. He was always so thoughtful. "I would appreciate a break away from everyone. There are a lot more people here than I was expecting." She was relieved to have endured the initial meeting of so many strangers, but it had been too much to take in all at once.

They wandered down to the creek and found a shaded area. Their conversation flowed as freely as the rippling water in front of them. Laurel was thankful for the reprieve from the continuous hum everywhere. She had enjoyed the day at the Parker ranch, but this was more than she had expected. Hearing the ring of the bell announcing it was time to eat, they returned to the others. The time away had helped to make Laurel feel better.

After the meal, the tables were cleared away, games were set up, the bar reopened, and the festivities continued.

Kit was enjoying time to herself in the shade, allowing herself a moment to reminisce. Despite all the changes over the years and the passing of time some things remained the same. Today was one of those days. It was a day all about community and the gathering of friends and family. She smiled when Maggie joined her. They both watched as Doc walked by with Laurel, hand in hand.

"Doc hasn't left her side since he got here. Did you notice he joined the Rodwells at their table at mealtime? Do you think Doc's in love with Laurel and doesn't know it? Has the fish been hooked, and she just needs to reel him in. You've seen for yourself the way they look at each other. It's time our vet gets married and settles down. Even though I'm sure Laurel's younger than him by a few years, they appear to be a perfect match."

Kit had been watching her dear friend throughout the day, seeing the chemistry between him and Laurel. Kit knew more than she could share. Doc had put his trust in her to keep his private feelings a secret. Their trust in each other was a strong bond. She watched in silence wondering if Laurel's feelings were as deep for the vet. She knew from experience how easy it was to remain behind a protective shield after you lose your spouse, so it was hard to tell.

Maggie's eyes twinkled, "There's something magical about Calhoun barbeques. I think someone sprinkles love dust before we get here so love is in the air. Maybe Valley View's love dust will work its magic again today."

"Always the matchmaker, Maggie." Maybe Maggie was right. Kit recalled the early sparks that had ignited the relationship between her and Trace. She smiled recalling how her feelings changed for Trace by the end of her first barbeque. She looked over at Rio who ignited the same sparks.

Laurel sought out her mother who was across the yard chatting with Lola. The two women had become friends. She joined them and while the two women chatted away, Laurel looked around for Doc. He had been totally attentive to her all day, but he seemed to have disappeared. When her gaze drifted, she spotted him in a secluded area talking with Kit. Despite the fact they appeared to be deep in conversation she meandered over. As she got closer she stopped, suddenly concerned she would be intruding. She could hear them talking quietly but couldn't make out what they were saying and found herself moving closer. Not wanting to draw attention to herself she stood in the background behind them, listening to two friends engrossed in a private and honest conversation. Laurel nearly gasped out loud hearing Doc tell Kit he loved her. What she overheard upset her more than she expected and she was overtaken by a surge of jealousy, When she heard Kit say she loved him too, she turned and fled. She was miserable and wanted to go home. For Laurel, the joy of the day was gone.

Unaware of what just happened, Kit and Doc remained in deep conversation. Their love for each other did go beyond friendship because their relationship had been a special one for years. Kit would always love Doc, but it was the kind of love she had for her family and her dear friends.

She wanted the best for him, and she would never have been that person for him.

Doc's face was grave, his voice almost inaudible. This was a moment for total honesty. "I accepted a long time ago that you love Rio, but I want what you have. I have everything a man could want, except my own family. My life is good, but I don't want to be a bachelor forever."

Kit was touched and smiled at him in understanding, "I believe that might soon change. We both know your life took a new direction since the Rodwells moved here. It seems you and Laurel already have a special connection. Maybe you found the right person. You've never looked at me the way you look at Laurel."

Doc grinned sheepishly as he agreed, "I don't know what it is, but there is something special about Laurel."

"I like, Laurel. She's a nice young lady."

Doc nodded his head, "Laurel is much more than that. She's a strong woman, one with grit and sass. She's a lot like you, but in a calmer way. She's like a small whirlwind while you can be like the Tasmanian Devil."

"No wonder you like her," teased Kit.

"She has captured my heart," Doc admitted softly. "I've waited a long time for that special person. I really like her."

Kt started to laugh, "Come on, Doc, it's me you're talking to."

Doc gave a sigh of resignation, "Fine. I've fallen in love with Laurel Easton. It wasn't the instant chemistry like there was between you and Trace. Even between you and Rio. With me and Laurel, it's like a quiet calm with hidden whispers of what is yet to come. I'm comfortable with the calm because it's who I am." Doc's voice was thick with emotion when he confessed, "I feel something different with Laurel. It's like I want to be with her all the time, my day is brighter when I see her. I always wondered if I would find someone special to share my life with. I will always have feelings for you but I'm beginning to understand what true love really feels like. Laurel has captured my heart and opened my heart to new dreams."

Kit couldn't be happier for her friend. Laurel would suit Doc's tender nature and kind heart. Kit's response was sincere and just as honest, "I believe you have finally found your soul mate. I will always love you as one of my dearest friends. It pained me knowing I couldn't share the same feelings you hung onto for me after Trace died. You're such a good, kind, honest man, and that's enough for any women." Kit placed a hand on Doc's arm. Her words were gentle when she spoke, "I can see you married, with a family and you may have found the lady to fill that role. I think your life can be complete if you follow your heart. Love is definitely worth the risk. Look at the risks I've taken since you met me. I came here looking for my dad not knowing if he would reject me like my mother did. I ended up marrying a cocky cowboy who annoyed the hell out of me when we first met. Now I'm getting married to Rio and putting my trust in our future together. I'm doing that because I love him, and I know my life wouldn't be complete without him in it. If what you feel for Laurel is real take the time to see how she feels about you. It might take a while for her to completely open up because she's still grieving but I can see she has feelings for you. Laurel likes you. It might even be more than that. Don't let her get away."

Doc agreed and got up to go find Laurel. He didn't intend to let that happen. It wasn't very long, and he was back. "The Rodwells left suddenly, and I can't understand why Laurel wouldn't have said goodbye. I asked your dad if he knew why they left, and he said Baxter said something upset their daughter. I overheard Maggie talking with Lola and she said she saw Laurel walking away from us when you and I were deep in conversation. Do you think she overheard us talking?" Doc didn't wait for Kit to respond, "It's not too late. I think I'll head over to Willow Downs and talk to Laurel."

Kit grabbed his arm, "I think it's best if I talk to her first. I won't reveal your true feelings, but I do believe she's in need of a woman-to-woman conversation. This isn't just about you. It's about feelings coming back to life and being confused by them. As you know, I've been there. I'll go first thing in the morning."

"That's probably a good idea. I'd probably say or do something stupid."

Kit flashed him a compassionate smile, "I'm sure everything will be okay."

CHAPTER TWENTY-TWO

The next morning, Laurel headed down to the stream. The arrival of fall had changed the landscape, coloring it with the rustic colors of autumn. Laurel's life had been changing as rapidly as the colors of the trees around her. Within weeks the leaves would fall to the ground and be blown away by the strong westerly winds Alberta was known for. Yesterday had upset her, having overheard words that were carried through the air like a shared secret. What she heard confirmed the strong feelings she had developed for Doc. If she didn't have feelings for him it wouldn't have mattered what she heard. A shadow crossed her face. She wasn't strong enough to lose someone else she cared about. Over the summer, he had become an important part of her life. Doc had helped erase the darkness she had been living in and colored it with subtle shades of hope and brighter colors of joy. The conversation she overheard had played in her mind many times. As a result, she had lost her faith in Doc, a man she had come to trust. Laurel was heartbroken. Would what she shared with Doc die just as quickly as the fallen leaves underfoot?

The air was still crisp as she headed back to her sanctuary. Laurel refused to admit she was waiting for Doc, hoping he would come over to see why their family had made an early departure from Valley View. Maybe he hadn't even noticed, or he didn't care. She looked out when she heard a vehicle approaching. To her surprise and disappointment, it was Kit Grayson. Kit waved as she pulled over and parked. It was too late for Laurel to get up and leave. *Maybe Kit is here to see Coco. Not likely, or she would have parked alongside the corral.*

Genna also heard the vehicle. She was glad to see Laurel had made a friend. She was unaware of the sudden displeasure her daughter had developed toward Kit. Laurel had been struggling in silence with her feelings.

Laurel looked solemn, even sad, when Kit walked over to the gazebo. She wasn't greeted warmly, confirming Kit's belief that Laurel had drawn her own conclusion on a conversation she obviously overheard.

"I'm not in the mood for company." Laurel's voice had a definite edge.

Kit ignored the dismissal, "This isn't a social visit."

Laurel was taken aback by Kit's directness.

"We need to talk. Something happened yesterday that upset you, and I think there's a misunderstanding that needs to be cleared up."

If Kit was going to be direct, Laurel decided to be just as direct, but she wasn't able to hide the hurt in her voice, "When you and Doc were together yesterday I overheard you say you love each other. Doc's sister-in-law, Amber, said he has loved you for years so the attention he's been giving me has confused me."

The anguish on Laurel's face tugged at Kit's heart. "That's why I had to come today. You only heard part of the conversation and drew the wrong conclusion. You need to know the relationship Doc and I have. I do love him, but I'm not in love with him. There are different kinds of love. I love Doc in a special way, but he has only been just my friend. There's nothing romantic between us. We have been friends since I moved here. I met him the same time I met Trace. The two of them were already friends. I didn't know either one of them, but my first impression of Trace was that he was one arrogant cowboy. Doc, on the other hand, was everything he is now. I want you to know everything. Doc and I actually went out briefly, but Trace and I couldn't deny the sparks between us. Doc was too much of a gentleman to try and come between us. Sadly, for years he thought he loved me in a deeper way, but he always respected my marriage."

Laurel didn't know they had dated. How could Amber fail to share a detail as important as this? She remained unconvinced.

Kit smiled knowingly and took Laurel's hand, "I have always been honest with you since the day we met so there is no reason not to believe what I tell you today. Doc and I have a long history, and we will always have a love for each other. For me, Doc is the best friend I've ever had. I can never repay him for all the support he has given our family over the years, especially since Trace died. He's a good man. The other thing you need to know is that Rio Ortiz and I are getting married at Thanksgiving. When you find that special love, you know. I have that kind of love with Rio. I still miss Trace every day, but there is no longer a void in my life. Rio filled that void once I was able to pick up the broken pieces of my shattered heart. Doc also played an important role in my life. He was the strength I needed when Trace died, the stability based on a true friendship, and a love for both me and Trace."

Their conversation was slowly taking away Laurel's hurt. Her voice caught, "I'm sorry, Kit. I thought it was more than that."

"Your changed life is still difficult now that you are living every day in the real world. It becomes more complicated, especially when everything and everyone is still new to you, Even more so when your heart becomes involved, and you don't know how to cope. Your life was deeply shaken but you put the tragic event behind you, and you've proven that you are strong enough to move forward. Life is too short not to live it to the fullest every day. It's okay to get on with your life. None of us know what the future has in store. All we need is the courage to move forward as we embrace change."

Laurel's expressive eyes were troubled. "I don't know if I want to fall in love again."

Kit understood Laurel's fears about moving forward in this direction, "Yet you have feelings for Doc, or you wouldn't have gotten upset when Doc was talking to me at the barbeque. You're still young. Hopefully, you'll give love another chance."

Laurel shook her head in denial, but she was only fooling herself, "Did you ever feel you were betraying your husband by having feelings for another man?"

"I think it's a female curse to torment ourselves with reasons to feel guilty until we have analyzed everything from here to the moon before we decide it's okay to let it go. I know both of my husbands would have wanted me to move on and I did when I was ready. First, with Trace and now with Rio." Kit smiled reflectively, "I love Rio but that doesn't change the love I had for Mike and Trace. You don't have to forget how much your husband meant to you in order to move on. I've learned to remember the love and cherish the memories."

"These new feelings have me conflicted. I'm confused and scared but excited at the same time. When did you know you were ready?"

Suddenly it was like all of Lola's words of wisdom popped into Kit's head, "You just know. The right man entered my life a long time ago, but I was too cautious because of circumstances. So, even when you find the right man it may take time but in the end it's worth it. Time allowed me to heal. Time will help you too, Laurel."

For a brief moment they were both lost in the past. Even though Kit missed both Mike and Trace, she chose to remember the happiness they shared, rather than the emptiness left behind. Kit shared her deepest feelings, and her words were deliberate, "I know this is still a difficult time for you because your loss is still new and painful. It was no different for me when my husbands died. I vowed never to open that part of my heart again, but things continue to change as life moves forward. That's life; good and bad. To be honest, my heart still hurts at times when I think of them. Maybe it always will. Despite being complicated with unexpected twists and turns, life is wonderful. We never know who or when someone new enters our lives and it's okay to get on with life in every way."

The unspoken message caused Laurel's cheeks to flush. She smiled, but there was something sad in her smile and her eyes glistened with unshed tears. It would mean another step of letting go.

"Even though our loved ones aren't here with us, they're always in our hearts. You hold onto the good thoughts, the happy memories. Those precious memories that made up your life together. You continue your healing process by letting go. It will take time, and that time is different for everyone. I really struggled in the beginning when Trace died. Doc was a strong supporter, and I know he has been there for you. The Graysons and the Calhouns have always considered him a true friend. Your family can as well. Doc is an honorable man. Our friend is honest to the core and a real gentleman. You can't stop love when the right person enters your life. Falling in love with another man takes nothing away from what you had with your husband."

The look on Laurel's face changed and Kit was rewarded with a brief smile. Laurel had to admit she liked the vet's mentioned qualities. She could add a few of her own. She also had to admit she had developed strong feelings for Doc.

When Laurel became quiet Kit continued to pry, "What else is bothering you?"

Laurel wasn't sure how to answer. She didn't know what Doc's feelings were.

Kit took her hand, "Doc is rather adept at hiding his feelings until he knows someone well. You aren't the only one guarded. Because I've known Doc for years, I can tell he's in love with you. Doc has a special look in his eyes when he looks at you. He has never looked at me that way. It's obvious you feel something for him, so give him a chance. Doc asked me if I thought it was too soon to start courting you. He's waiting for you to decide if that's what you want. He's not only a good man, he's also a patient man. He will give you the time you need. I've learned a lot by experiencing death and the meaning of life. We live, we love, we lose loved ones, we let go, we love again. Nothing can protect us from bad things. I believe love is what makes the bad bearable."

Laurel nodded, thinking about the deep love her parents had shown her and the sacrifices they made moving here.

"Fate works in mysterious ways. There may be more than one reason you moved here."

"Not very subtle, Kit." They both laughed.

A friendship had grown stronger between the two women. What Laurel needed now was time to sort out her tangled thoughts and mixed emotions. She no longer questioned Kit's sincerity, but Kit had given her a lot to think about. She was glad when Kit said she had to leave. After Kit left, Laurel processed the intense and honest conversation they had. Laurel was grateful she had survived the accident, and knew it was time to make the most of her life. Her life wasn't over. It was natural that part of her still wanted what she had, and she knew she could have that again with someone else. She didn't have to feel like she was cheating on Sam. She longed for a man to love and trust enough to marry and who would give her the family she so desperately wanted. She could easily envision Doc being that man.

Genna saw Kit leave and it didn't take her long to seek Laurel out. "I was surprised to see Kit today."

"No more surprised than I was."

"She didn't stay long. Is everything okay?"

"It is now." Laurel told her mom what happened yesterday and most of their conversation today. "You know I've been dealing with a lot since the accident. Grief no longer consumes me. I was feeling sad because I was missing what I had and lost and what could have been. I felt my hopes and dreams had been taken away. I have worked through my guilt and found acceptance. I've healed mentally and emotionally since moving here. Today, I choose to let the unknown fears go and remember what was good in my marriage and move on. I'm open to love again, and I can move forward with hope and new dreams." To do that there was one more confession she had to share with her mother.

Laurel decided to share the dark side of her marriage. She could no longer pretend her marriage to Sam was all good but none of what she was feeling about her marriage now mattered one way or another. She needed to start moving forward with honesty and openness. This was something she hadn't shared with her parents. It was time to release the last of her secrets. She knew her mom wouldn't judge. That was one of the things she liked about her mother. She always saw the good in everyone and she would remind her of Sam's good qualities. The fact that Laurel felt she could share was another positive step forward.

When Laurel was finished, Genna was dismayed but not surprised. Mothers know more than their children often give them credit for. "You had such an independent spirit before you married Sam. Sometimes I think you got married before you were ready."

"What are you talking about. Sam and I were together for a couple of years before we finally got married."

"You were a couple, but you weren't together. Sam was always working or away. You were caught up in being in love and it got overshadowed by who Sam really was. I could tell you regretted not pursuing your studies. It's not too late."

"I'm not that person anymore."

"No, you're not, but you are still a strong, independent woman. You can still have what you lost. I don't think you have to look far if you decide to get married again."

Her mom's comment surprised. Laurel. She thought she had kept her feelings for Doc secret. Truth was, she really like Doc. Maybe he was that special someone. She knew she could make a commitment to another man but was it too soon. "I should be scared to death to enter into a relationship, but I feel so comfortable every time I'm with Doc. We have many things in common, it's like we fit as a couple. He's a valued friend."

Genna hadn't missed the look of new hope in her daughter. "I think Doc would like to be more than a friend. He's a nice young man, darling, and I think you've already fallen in love with the tender vet. Give him a chance."

"What if it doesn't work out?" Laurel couldn't chance adding more heartache to her list.

"What if it does? I see you looking at him only to find him looking at you. Dad and I used to do that."

"You still do, Mom. I never thought something like this would happen to me again, especially this soon. I've been trying to ignore what's been building between us, but I can't pretend anymore."

"None of us can control what happens to our hearts. Life has a way of helping us discover ourselves. If this is God's plan he will give you all the guidance you need. It's time to live for the future and you don't want to move forward alone. If you listen to your heart, you can have the life you once had as a wife and a mother."

Kit had basically said the same thing. It was a relief to admit her feelings, "I think Doc and I are falling in love with each other. I just think it's too soon. What will people think?"

"You can start a new life guilt free. You are the only two people who matter. Feelings cannot be measured by time. We have no control over what happens, but we have learned that we can't waste the life we have. There's no guarantee of a tomorrow for any of us and we don't know what tomorrow will bring. What we have is today and we don't want to waste it. Your dad and I are creating a permanent life here. You have your whole life ahead of you and you're starting to make a new life for yourself. New memories are being made, happy memories. It's okay to move forward in every way."

Laurel looked over at her mom and smiled. That might even include a new love as well as a new family.

"There are wonderful times ahead for you. Let the past go. We all have regrets, make mistakes, have failures. We can't change what was, but we have learned lessons along the way. You can move forward with a chance for a new start, a new opportunity to love. Faith has brought us here for a reason. This is a new beginning for your new life."

"I wish I had your kind of faith." Sam was her past. Was Doc her future? She already had experienced so many changes in such a short time. She smiled. This change would be her choice.

Despite the coolness, Laurel remained in the gazebo after her mom left. She was still hoping Doc would come by. She had almost given up hope when he finally arrived. She watched him approach. Even though she had been waiting for him, she refused to greet him. Instead, she took up the book that was beside her.

Doc gently took it from her and placed it on the bench. "Are you okay?"

"I'm fine," she said without conviction. She was nervous wondering how their conversation would go. She wasn't sure what to expect.

"I know Kit came to see you." Doc waited for a response. There was none. "Kit's a special person, Laurel. She's as real as they come, but there has always been a directness about Kit that can be very annoying."

"She said the same thing about you. The part about being a special person. I'm the one finding you annoying."

A faraway look darkened Doc's eyes before his feeling of uncertainty disappeared, "This is all new to me so I might as well be as direct as Kit. I don't want to hide my feelings from you. Until now, I didn't understand the kind of love I have for you because I have never felt like this before. I hope that doesn't scare you, but I need to be honest."

Laurel heard the change in his voice. If she was confused about his feelings she wasn't any more. He had made them very clear. "Maybe this isn't the right time. We haven't known each other that long." Laurel knew how she felt but was still confused. She held her breath waiting for Doc to respond.

"It may be too soon for you, but I think I've been waiting for you my whole life."

Now it was Laurel's turn to be honest, "There have been so many changes in my life and there are times I'm still vulnerable. I'm a work in progress."

"We all are," Doc said simply.

"I suppose we are. I've adjusted to the changes in my life. It's the new ones that scare me and the new feelings I'm having to deal with."

"You're just having to work harder. The changes you've been dealing with recently have been traumatic and life changing. I would like to be part of the changes moving forward."

Happiness welled up inside Laurel and she gave him an easy smile. She wanted to give them a chance. Doc made her come alive and sparked something in her she thought had died with Sam and Gracie.

Doc's voice was husky, "I know you've been hurt in more ways than one but don't shut me out. As hard as it has been for you, I think it's time to move forward. It will be easier with a friend. I want to be part of your life, Laurel. I won't push you, but there are times when we have to trust and take chances. I ask you with humility and hope that you give us a chance."

Laurel studied him for a moment, taking in his sincerity. "I would like that. I've accepted what happened. I am ready to move forward and get on with my life." Her reference to her past was with acceptance.

Doc waited a moment before quietly asking, "Do you believe in fate? Fate has a way of bringing certain people into your life, especially when you need them most."

Laurel laughed, "My mom would say it's God's plan."

Doc took her hand, "Call it what you will. Either way, this is our time. I won't use the cliché of one day at a time. Let's just see what tomorrow brings."

Laurel felt better immediately and didn't bother to wonder why. She had always been strong, and that quality had returned. She could hear her mom's words in her ear, 'Our hopes for the future are based on our faith. God will not fail you.' Laurel realized she was willing to take a chance. "My life keeps changing but now it's in a good way. You make me want to look to the future. I don't want to move forward alone. I need a friend. We are friends, aren't we?" The whole day had been confusing, so she needed to be sure. When Doc nodded she knew she was willing to take a chance.

Doc smiled at her gently, "I hope in time I will be more than that. Here's to new beginnings." He knew it would require patience for him, trust for her. They looked at each other and smiled. They were both willing to see where their future took them.

CHAPTER TWENTY-THREE

Rio was taking his evening meals with the family. Tonight, Rio was providing the steaks and was in charge of barbequing. Kit had made both a potato salad and a marinated salad with the vegetables from Lola's garden. This year's produce had been abundant, and they had already frozen and canned enough to get them through the winter. Kenzie had become quite the little homemaker and loved baking, so she had made a zucchini cake for dessert. It always amazed them how much zucchini grew every year. They were always giving some away.

"Here, make yourself useful and take a beer out to Rio. Maybe you can help him with something."

Benny grabbed the beer and headed outside. He spent as much time as he could with his soon-to-be dad who was adopting all of them. Sweet little Benny was back. Finn, who had just pulled into the yard, called out, "Benny, can you grab a beer for me, too. A cold one will taste pretty good."

Kit had heard the exchange. They sounded like a family.

After supper, Rio stayed after everyone else disappeared. It was nice to have some time to themselves. It didn't happen often. "Your kids have grown up so much since I got here. I'm so happy to become part of this family."

"You already are."

"I mean legally. Thank you for allowing me the honor." The adoption of the kids was meaningful to all of them, especially Finn. For a young foster child who nobody wanted, he was about to be adopted for a second time. The irony of life.

"I'm looking forward to our wedding and becoming your wife." Everyone was hoping the fine weather would continue until after the wedding.

"Well, wifey-to be, why don't you grab a blanket, and I'll get us each a coffee and we can go outside and cuddle under the stars." Kit nodded, she loved the quiet of the country.

When Kit joined him, she snuggled into Rio's arms and sighed with happiness. Their deep love allowed them to sit in companiable silence as the night settled over the land. The sky darkened as the sun disappeared behind the mountains.

Rio released a contented sigh. He knew he had found his home. Of course there would be adjustments, but he already felt like part of the family. Rio looked over at Kit and had the distinct impression she was thinking of Trace. Rio sat back knowing Trace would always be a part of Kit. He had come to accept that.

A moment later Kit turned and smiled at him, "Finn wants a tattoo. He has ever since you showed up here."

"Are you going to let him get one?"

"He's of age so I can't stop him, but if he asked me my opinion I wouldn't object. I would want him to get one that's meaningful to him, something like, I love Mom." They both laughed at her ridiculous comment.

"Would you get a tattoo?"

Kit gave Rio one of her sassy grins, "I don't need a tattoo. I already wear your brand on my heart."

The look in Rio's eyes brought back the memory of his kisses. Before she could make her own move, his mouth was already on hers. "I love kissing you."

"You're as bad as a teenager, Rio Ortiz."

*****

The days were flying by, Thanksgiving was next weekend. When Kit and Rio became engaged they both agreed they wanted to get married at Lola Grande. This week they were busy transforming the Quonset that was being decorated for the ceremony. The wedding ceremony would highlight the Mexican culture and traditions, while honoring both cultures. They had invited only a few close friends, wanting their wedding to be small and intimate.

As soon as the engagement was announced, Lola had informed Kit that traditionally the bride's dress was sewn by family members. As a gift to Kit, Anna and Lola wanted the honor of sewing her dress. Lola didn't tell Kit they would also incorporate elements of good luck, prosperity, and fertility. As per wedding superstition, Lola and Anna would also add colored ribbons into the dress: a yellow ribbon to bring the blessing of food, a blue ribbon to bring wealth and prosperity, and a red ribbon to allow for a passionate marriage.

Today, Anna brought Kit's wedding dress, having finished the final details since the last fitting. Both women teared up when Kit stepped into her dress, a full-length, long-sleeved lace dress that was fitted at the waist and flared out. The colored ribbons had been braided together and worn as a belt with the rest of the ribbons hanging loose at the back. It was beautiful and Kit looked stunning. "It's perfect."

All three women were emotional. Lola cleared her throat, "I'll go put tea on while you change, and we can finish discussing the last-minute details."

Kit enjoyed working with both women. Today's main topic was the reception. They had already planned a specific menu that would include a variety of traditional Mexican food. The men were in charge of beverages and coolers. Lola was making the wedding cake. She had already asked Kenzie to help her bake it and they would decorate it together, so Kenzie felt like she was part of the wedding plans. They had spent hours looking online for decorating ideas that were a little more Mexican. By the time the ladies left Kit knew everything was under control.

Minutes later, Rio walked in. "I saw Anna was here today. How are the wedding plans coming?"

"Everything is under control. What about your plans? How are they coming?"

Rio couldn't resist teasing her, "What plans? All I have to do is show up." His mood suddenly changed, his expression much more serious, "Do you want me to cut my hair?"

Kit was shocked, "Do you want to cut your hair?" When Rio didn't answer she knew he didn't want to, but he would if she said yes. "I remember the first time I saw your hair unbraided. You had just moved to Lola Grande and were living in your camper van and you showered at the arena. You were walking back from the arena after your shower and your hair flowed like molten lava down your back. You were also bare-chested. Even then I thought you were one fine looking man, but I love you for who you are, not for how you look. That's a bonus." Kit smiled up at him lovingly, "I know we'll have a wonderful life together."

"I'm sure it will continue to be challenging. I better head back to my place. I need to finalize my plans for the wedding, or I might get married and divorced on the same day." Kit and Rio were going to spend their first night together at Rio's place and he wanted to make it look romantic in honor of the occasion. They wanted to start their new life together alone. He would then move into the main house as her husband and dad to her children and Finn would move into Rio's place. Lots of changes ahead for all of them.

*****

Kit woke early and rolled over. It was her wedding day. It would be nice to have a man in her house again. She giggled to herself. And in her bed. She knew it wouldn't be long before there would be a beehive of activity taking place. Kit grabbed a coffee and her sweater and stepped outside. She sat on the steps of the front porch pensively staring out at the horizon and scanned the familiar landscape. The view was as breath-taking as always. The Rocky Mountains, a spectacular backdrop to the west, were white capped at the higher peaks due to an earlier snowfall. Frost had come early with the arrival of fall. The morning dew on the lawn was slowly disappearing where the morning sun reached it. This morning the air was chilly but would warm by mid-afternoon. The forecast was for clear skies and above average temperature. Kit appreciated that it was a perfect day for a wedding.

It was like everything around her was paused before the day unfolded, a moment frozen in time. A reflective look clouded her eyes. Trace no longer occupied her thoughts as often, but every once in a while he would be there. She allowed her thoughts to drift when she felt the gentle breeze caress her cheeks. She believed it was Trace saying it was okay to move forward with Rio. Kit refused to get caught up in the past. Today was a day of celebration. She was marrying a wonderful man who loved her children. Of course, there would continue to be challenges ahead but she would have Rio at her side. Kit headed back inside. Lola would be down soon, and Anna was coming over early. When the time came, both ladies were going to help Kit get dressed. Everyone was busy finalizing last-minute details, but Kit was sure they were under the direction of Lola. Riley had become a one-day Marriage Commissioner so he would perform their civil ceremony.

Time had ticked away, guests were arriving and gathering in the Quonset. Other than family the only other guests were the Walkers, the Ortiz family and Doc Walker and Laurel. Doc and Laurel had basically been a couple since the Calhoun barbecue. Today was a special occasion for all of them.

Kit knew everything for the wedding had been done. It was time to check the kids. It was a proud mother moment when she kissed each one on the cheek and sent them over to the Quonset to join the others. It was time to get ready. Kit's eyes glowed when Lola and Anna walked into her room to help her with her dress. Lola had reverted to traditional Mexican attire. She looked regal, as did Anna. For them, it was a privilege to have this occasion to honor their heritage. As soon as Kit was ready they left to join the others. Kit said she would be there in a few minutes.

Kit opened her dresser drawer and took out a velvet box. Inside were her grandmother's pearls she had worn when she married Trace. She would have liked to wear them today, but she would respect the Mexican beliefs. Wearing pearls on your wedding day was frowned upon. They are said to represent the tears you'd shed during your marriage. Kit ran her fingers over the treasured pearls and closed the lid and put them back in her dresser drawer. She was ready.

Rio was standing on his own when Benny passed by on his way to join Lola. Finn and Kenzie were already seated. "Looking pretty spiffy, Dad," he teased. In just a few minutes Rio would have another family. Today was just a formality. He felt like they were already his family. He would do his best to be a good dad and husband.

BJ had offered to walk Kit down the aisle like he had when she married Trace, but she decided today she would walk down the aisle alone. She loved her dad dearly, but this wedding was about her and Rio. Once the

"I do's" were exchange their lives would take on a whole new meaning, not just as husband and wife but as a family.

As Kit looked at those gathered to celebrate this special day, she was more moved than she expected to be. The expression on her children's faces was pure joy. A feeling of contentment encircled Kit. She took a moment to acknowledge her family and dear friends who were gathered in a circle before coming to rest on Rio. Rio was standing alone waiting for her to reach his side. Kit's eyes sparkled with joy. Rio's eyes were serious as she walked toward him with love in her eyes. Kit and Rio moved to the center of the circle where a podium had been placed. Everyone in the circle held hands as the couple shared their vows. Despite being a little nervous, Riley was honored to officiate the ceremony. He handed Rio the coins that rested inside the ornate gold box during the ceremony.

Rio turned to Kit, his dark eyes full of emotion. "My life completely changed when I came to Lola Grande. The feelings between us took me as much by surprise as they did you. Neither of us were looking for love. You have given me your hand. I give you my love. You are my wife; you are my life. I swear before God and everyone here to love you faithfully for the rest of my life. I promise you'll never doubt my love. I have watched you triumph over tragedy and embrace changes you had no control over. Your strength and courage have been passed down to your children. You have raised them to be independent and they will face life head-on just like their mother." Rio handed the coins to Kit. "This is my gift to you, and it signifies my commitment to supporting you and your children. Family centers you, home and family are the foundation of everything." No words could adequately convey the love and commitment he wanted to give Kit and her family.

Rio had spoken with such love that Kit had to fight back her tears. She hadn't realized the depth of feelings he had for all of them. Kit took a moment before replying, "Today brings us new love, new family, new hopes, and dreams. I accept your gift along with your love. Love is the most important gift we will ever have. I am open to receiving it, giving it, and sharing it. I couldn't be happier to be spending the rest of my life with you. Here's to the next chapter of our lives as we move forward on this journey." Kit and Rio exchanged beautiful hand-carved white gold bands, and Riley pronounced Rio and Kit husband and wife. Everyone cheered.

After sharing their vows, Kit expressed their personal thanks. "Today is a day of two people coming together and pledging their love to each other. Rio and I are celebrating our union together as husband and wife with the people we love most in our lives. We are literally surrounded by our loved ones, and we will treasure the memories made today. Rio and I have vowed to make the most of every day, no looking back with regret, only moving forward with hope. Our lives have been blessed because of you. People come into our lives every day and they affect our lives in special ways." Her eyes came to rest on Doc and Laurel who were still holding hands. Kit hoped Laurel would experience this again one day. She looked at Doc and smiled. Kit became emotional, "Be grateful for all the little things every day because you don't know what tomorrow will bring. I said I would never get married again." She giggled, "In fact, I said it twice and here I am standing beside my new husband. It goes to show, never say never. None of us know what life has in store for us. We experience joy and sorrow, loss of loved ones, the birth of new lives. Everything in our lives has brought each one of us to this day. Life can be rewarding in so many ways because we can always triumph over tragedy."

EPILOGUE

The gift of life is today with the hope of tomorrow.
No one knows what the future holds.
Sometimes a person has to dig deep to find inner strength,
especially when life doesn't work out as expected.
Things happen. That's life and you keep on living.
You deal with challenges, embrace change,
and continue to triumph over tragedy.
Faith is a powerful force.
Hope and faith go hand in hand.
Amen

ABOUT THE AUTHOR

Linda Rakos was born and raised in Alberta
and now resides in High River
with her husband. Linda is a wife, a mother of two sons, and a blessed
grandmother to two wonderful grandsons.
Happily retired, she devotes her
time to her family and her writing. While writing her first novel, she
discovered how exciting it is to create characters, each one individual and
different. Meeting the challenge of describing
what she wants someone to see
with her words. To create emotions, strong
enough for someone to feel. Achieving
success with her first book, ignited her passion
that has taken her in a new
direction as she continues on this journey.

www.ingramcontent.com/pod-product-compliance
Lightning Source LLC
Jackson TN
JSHW022159300425
83504JS00001B/2